MARRYING THE REBELLIOUS MISS

Bronwyn Scott

Published in Great Britain 2017
by Mills & Boon, an imprint of HarperCollins*Publishers*
1 London Bridge Street, London, SE1 9GF

© 2017 Nikki Poppen

ISBN: 978-0-263-92586-9

Printed and bound in Spain
by CPI, Barcelona

Bronwyn Scott is a communications instructor at Pierce College in the United States, and is the proud mother of three wonderful children—one boy and two girls. When she's not teaching or writing she enjoys playing the piano, travelling—especially to Florence, Italy—and studying history and foreign languages. Readers can stay in touch on Bronwyn's website, bronwynnscott.com, or at her blog, bronwynswriting.blogspot.com. She loves to hear from readers.

Visit the Author Profile page
at millsandboon.co.uk for more titles.

For P.E.O. Chapter GC and Step By Step,
who support unwed and teen mothers.
Programs like this show how far we've come
from the days of foundling hospitals
so that babies can be raised in love.

Chapter One

Scotland—April 1822

The Day of Judgement had arrived, bringing Preston Worth with it. There was only one reason he was here. He had come for her. At last. Beatrice had known it the moment she'd seen him ride into the yard of the Maddox farmhouse. After months of anticipation and planning, the dreaded reckoning was here.

Beatrice closed her eyes, trying to find her calm centre, trying to fight the rising terror at the core of her, but to little effect. Months of knowing and planning were not the bulwarks of support she'd hoped they'd be. She fisted clammy hands in the folds of her skirt, desperate to find balance, desperate to hold back the swamping panic that swept her in stomach-clenching nausea, in the race of her heartbeat and the whir of her mind. From the window, she saw Preston swing off the horse and approach the house in purposeful strides. All coherent thought splintered into useless shards of what had once been whole logic.

She knew only two things in the precious seconds of freedom that remained. The first: she had to act now! Every panicked instinct she possessed screamed the same conclusion: grab the baby and run! Her freedom would end the moment he entered the farmhouse. The second was that her parents had out-done themselves this time. They'd sent her friend to be the horseman of her apocalypse. Therein lay the conundrum: she needn't fear her friend, the one-time hero of her youth, the saviour of her Seasons when no one else would sign her dance card. She need only fear his message. How did one fight someone who wasn't the enemy? But fight Preston she must. This was Armageddon, the end of her world as she preferred it, *if* she lost the battle that was to come.

She would not lose. She was Beatrice Pen-rose. She didn't know *how* to lose, even in the face of great adversity. She'd born a child out of wedlock and survived. What greater adversity for a young woman was there than that? There were low murmurs of voices at the door, Mistress Maddox and Preston exchanging greetings and introductions. Beatrice unclenched her fists and smoothed her skirts where her hands had wrinkled them. She drew a deep breath, giving panic one last shove. She could allow herself to tremble all she liked on the inside. She just couldn't show it, couldn't let Preston see how much his visit terrified her.

At the sound of boots at the parlour door, she squared her shoulders and lifted her chin with a final admonition: she was Beatrice Penrose, she would survive this, too. She had time for one last breath before the axe fell, his words chopping short her freedom. 'Hello, Beatrice. I've come to fetch you home.'

She turned from the window to meet her fate—no, not her fate, her future. Fate was something you accepted. The future was something you carved for yourself, something you alone decided. That meant taking charge of this conversation right now. The future was here, standing before her; tall and dark-haired with a sharp hazel gaze, Preston, the friend of her youth as she'd always known him and yet there was a difference about him today that transcended the dusty boots and windblown hair, something she couldn't put her finger on, not yet. Her mind was still too scattered. She desperately wished she could get her nerves under control.

Beatrice gestured to the chairs set before the cold fire. 'Please, come and sit. You should have sent word you were coming.' At least she'd found her voice even if it sounded reedy.

'And ruin the surprise?' Preston took the far chair. She took the seat closest to the cradle where her son slept oblivious. Her foot picked up the rocking rhythm it had abandoned a few minutes ago for the window, this time out of a need to quiet her nerves more than putting the babe to sleep. 'You must tell me all the news from Little Westbury. How are Evie and her new husband? He sounds like a paragon from her letters. I can't believe I missed her wedding.' She was talking too fast, rambling, and she couldn't stop. 'I want all the details and I'll want to hear about May and Liam, too. They must be married by now.' So much for hiding her nerves, but perhaps she could buy some time until she had her control back. At the moment, these questions were the shield behind which she could gather stronger resources.

Whether he recognised the delaying efforts for what they were or not, Preston obliged her. He was too much of a gentleman, too much of a friend, not to. She'd grown up with him. He'd filled the role of being an older brother to all of May's friends who had only sisters or, like her, no one, when they were younger. He politely regaled her with tales of Evie's wedding and the new house her prince had bought in the valley. He told her of Liam's coming knighthood ceremony and of May's elegant January wedding at St Martin-in-the-Fields. An hour ticked by and Bea began to hope that he might forget, that she'd succeeded in driving him off course. 'And May's dress? You haven't told me yet what she wore,' Beatrice pressed him when the conversation began to lag.

But Preston was finished. He had not forgotten. 'I won't say another word. There won't be anything left for Evie and May to tell you when you get home. They will be so glad to see you.'

His words brought the conversation full circle. The delaying action was over despite her efforts to steer it away from the one topic she didn't want to discuss.

Preston leaned back in his seat, arms crossed, his hazel gaze, so like his sister, May's, fixed on her with tenacity. The tension that had slipped to the background was front and centre once again. 'Bea, do you think I don't know what you are up to? You think to distract me with gossip and run out the clock.' She did not care for the suspicion of pity that shadowed his eyes. 'To what end is this game, Beatrice? I will only come again tomorrow and the next day, if I must.'

He spoke bluntly and in that bluntness she discovered the indefinable something about him that had eluded her earlier: reluctance. *If he must*. He found the job to which her parents had tasked him as distasteful as she did. Preston no more wanted to be here than she wanted him here. She could use that. It was the spark she needed to wage war in truth. If she could turn him into an ally, if she argued hard enough, he might be dissuaded. She could send him back to England with her decision to stay. Beatrice leaned forward in earnest, her nerves settling at last now that she had a glimpse of direction. 'I'm not going back.'

The announcement was met with silence.

It was apparently true—you *could* cut tension with a knife. She had misjudged the depth of his reluctance. Reluctant though he was, he meant to see this through. Her announcement was met with the faintest of smiles on his face, his hazel eyes contrite in silent apology, but his jaw was set in firm determination. Well, she could be determined, too, and it started with showing him she didn't belong in England any more. She belonged here.

Matthew William chose that moment to wake. His little arms stretched, making fists, his mouth puckering up. Bea reached for him, her own body responding to the waking needs of her son. There was no time like the present to show Preston this was where she belonged now, who she'd become. She was no longer the pampered daughter of wealthy gentry, but a sensible, grounded mother. The baby let out a squall and Bea tossed Preston a proud but apologetic smile for her son's noise. 'He's hungry. He always wakes up hungry.'

And hungry babies needed to be fed. Immediately and without qualms. Beatrice loosened the bodice of her dress and put the baby to her bare breast, an action that invoked no sense of embarrassment from her. How often had she nursed the babe these last months, regardless of who was around? She reached for a blanket to drape over her, but the action had already achieved the desired effect. Preston Worth, for all of his worldliness, shifted in his chair, no doubt uncomfortable with the maternal display. This was not the behaviour of a *ton*nish woman. Gentlewomen didn't nurse their own children. 'Have I shocked you? Would you like to go outside until I've finished?' Bea offered, but her sweetness didn't fool him.

Preston smiled back with a wolfish grin, making this a battle of faux congeniality. 'Is that a gauntlet you're throwing down? If so, you'll be disappointed to know I am more impressed than dismayed. You nurse that child as if it were the most natural thing in the world.'

'Because it is,' Beatrice shot back. There seemed little point in maintaining a polite veneer if he was going to call her out. 'I have nursed him for five months and I intend to keep doing it.'

'I dare say that will enliven the ladies' teas

in Little Westbury. Perhaps you will start a new fashion.' Preston was edgier, more sharptoned than she remembered. It was a reminder that they were not children any more. She had heard of Preston's life through May, of course. She knew he'd taken on an important position for the Home Office in charge of protecting the coast from sundry illegal traffic and arms dealers. But she had not spent time with him beyond an occasional mercy dance during the Season in London. Dancing, unfortunately, wasn't precisely the best venue for getting to know someone. She'd learned that the hard way. The father of her son had been an exceptional dancer and that had *not* been a fair recommendation of his ethics. It made her wonder now what she didn't know about Preston. He'd certainly ripped through her first line of defence with considerable boldness. He would find she could be bold as well.

She moved the baby to her other breast. 'I do apologise. My parents have imposed indecently on your time by sending you here. I trust they are the ones who sent you?'

Preston only needed to nod in acknowledgement. Of course her parents had sent him. There was no one else *to* send. Their

families had been friends for years, generations even, and the Penroses were sadly lack-
ing in male progeny, having been 'blessed'
with a single daughter. Preston was the closest the Penroses had to a son.

'I will not be going back with you. You can
take a message to my parents and convey my
wishes to stay.'

This was her next line of defence: refusal.

'I'll write a note immediately so as not to
delay your return. You can set out tomorrow.'
She put the baby to her shoulder and gently
rubbed his back, invoking a burp.

'Not without you,' Preston replied firmly.
Mistress Maddox came into the room and he
slid his gaze her way. 'Give the baby to the
goodwife and come outside with me.' The
steel in his tone caught Beatrice off guard.
She'd been focused on Preston as a friend,
she'd been heartened by the idea that he was
a reluctant messenger. It had lured her into a
false sense of security. She'd not been ready
for the harsh command. This was a man who
was used to giving orders and having them
obeyed. She was seeing perhaps a glimpse of
the man who commanded the coast of Britain, who protected a whole country. That man

would expect abject obedience, which if not given freely might possibly be forced.

So be it. Beatrice rose and handed the baby to Mistress Maddox. She let Preston usher her outside into the mild spring sunshine. She let him be the one to break the silence as they walked. He wanted this conversation, he could damn well start it.

'You are going back, Beatrice. Make no mistake.' There was the firm tone of command again. He was no longer just her friend, just the messenger, but a man used to taking charge.

'Even if you have to throw me over your shoulder and haul me off like a prize of war?' she said coldly. The gloves were off now, friends or not.

'Even if. But I hope it doesn't come to that. I have every hope you'll see reason before it gets that far.'

'Or that you will,' Bea replied drily. 'There is more reason to see than your own.'

They stopped at a stone wall defining the Maddox property. Preston leaned his elbows against it. The breeze blew his dark hair. For the first time since his arrival, she noted the weariness on his face. She could see the traces of it in the tiny lines around his eyes, the faint grooves at his mouth, all reminders that he'd been seriously wounded in October; had spent the winter recovering. Now, he'd made a long journey to find her. Whatever weariness he felt could be laid at her feet. Her parents had sent him on a fool's errand. She felt guilty over her part in it, but not guilty enough to grant him the thing he wished. She would not go with him just to appease the guilt.

'Tell me, Bea.' He sounded more like her friend. 'No more prevaricating. Why won't you go back?'

'Go back to what? Society will pillory me for this. There is no place for me. Why would I return to a place where there is only shame? There is no life for me there.'

'And there is a life for you here?' Preston questioned.

'Yes! No one looks at me with condemnation. My son is accepted. No one calls him a bastard.'

'Because you've spun them a lie. May has told me all about it. How long do you think your "husband" can stay at sea?'

'Until he dies. Merchants abroad for trade *do* die, you know. Mysterious illness, lightning-fast fevers. There's a hundred perils that might come up.' It sounded cold hearted even to her and she'd made the fiction up in the first place months ago when she'd arrived.

Preston gave a humourless laugh. 'You are a bloodthirsty creature, Beatrice. Your poor husband is expendable, then?'

'Yes,' Beatrice answered simply. She'd be a grieving widow. It was the best of both worlds. No one would shun her son and no one would expect her to remarry after having loved and lost her devoted husband. It would be good protection for them both. Her son would have the shield of a dead father and she would have the shelter of widowhood.

'Then what?' Preston pressed on, his voice low. 'You can't stay even if your fiction holds. Your parents will cut you off.' He paused with a sigh. 'Forgive me, Beatrice. It pains me to say such things, but they are the truth and it is the message I am charged to deliver. I am the polite option. You may return with me of your own accord, or be burned out, so to speak. There will be no more money to pay for your keep. How long can you infringe on the Maddoxes without it?'

Beatrice looked out over the fields, taking

a moment to gather her thoughts, to recover from this latest sally against her fortress. Hadn't she expected such a manoeuvre? 'I have prepared for such an eventuality.' It wasn't untrue. She and May had planned for it. They'd vowed together back in the autumn never to return to England, even if their allowances were cut, even if they lost the hospitality of her relative's cottage on loan. So much had changed since the autumn, though. Her plans had not been laid expecting the cottage to be lost to fire or May being forced to flee with Liam, leaving her alone. Could she manage their schemes on her own?

'I have some money set aside. I saved part of the allowance every month.' She forged on bravely, outlining her plans. 'I have found a small cottage to rent. I can grow herbs and bake bread to sell in the market. There is no school teacher here. I can tutor children, teach them to read in exchange for whatever I need.' The plans sounded meagre when she voiced them out loud, fanciful and desperate.

To his credit, he did not mock her. Preston gave a brief nod. 'Your efforts are commendable.' But she knew what he was thinking. They were her thoughts, too. Was she really willing to commit her financial well-being to the caprices of barter and trade? Not just hers, but her son's, too. What if it wasn't enough? But it had to be. The risk in going home was too great. It wasn't just the shame that kept her here. She could face the shame for herself. There were other fears, bigger fears.

'I won't let them take my son,' Beatrice said with quiet force. This was the real fear, the one that had plagued her since her pregnancy: that her parents would snatch the child away, placing it with a family somewhere in England where she'd never find him again. That fear rose now. Had Preston come with more in mind than simply retrieving her? 'I will not give him to you.'

Her family had chosen their messenger well, perhaps presuming on her friendship with him to let down her guard. They would find she was not so easily manipulated. Preston might be her old friend, but she would fight him, would make him the enemy if he thought to take the baby from her.

'Never, Bea. How could you think that?' The suggestion horrified him, breaking through the harshness. He was her friend once more. But they both knew how she dared to think it. It was what well-bred families did to erase the stain of scandal, to pretend the sin had never occurred. Preston reached for her hand and squeezed it, his grip strong and reassuring. 'I give you my word, Beatrice, I will not allow the two of you to be separated. I am your parents' messenger, Bea, not that it pleases me, but I am *your* friend. May and I have seen to it that your wishes are represented in this. We have made it clear that you expect to raise your son at Maidenstone.' He spoke as if her acquiescence was inevitable. Maybe it was.

Maidenstone. The family home. Oh, he didn't fight fair! Generations of Penroses had romped there, grown up there. There was no place like Maidenstone in the spring and the summer, the gardens full of wildflowers and roses. The thought of Maidenstone made her heart ache with nostalgia. Images of her son growing up there were powerful lures indeed. To show him the trails she'd walked, the lake, all of it, would be a wonderful joy. The allure must have shown on her face.

'Maidenstone is his heritage, Bea. Would you deny your son what is his in exchange for raising him in near poverty? Life here will not be economically easy without your parents' support.' Preston was relentless in pointing out the realities of her situation. 'Winters will be hard. Even more so without the resources you had this year.' She knew that. She'd already lived through one winter without a home of her own. She redoubled her resolve. She had to hold firm. May and Preston meant well, but promises could be broken.

'He is a male Penrose, Bea. Surely you see how that changes everything.' Preston pressed his case more thoroughly now, moving from the philosophical considerations to more practical ones that unfortunately resonated with her logical side. 'It is his protection. You have given your parents a grandson. He can inherit the Penrose land, the wealth. Maidenstone could be his.'

'That is a fool's dream. Do you think I haven't thought of that?' She had, of course, when she lay awake late at night worrying over the future. 'It would be better for him to never know, to never suffer the disappointment of what might have been.' Beatrice spoke honestly. 'Society will call him a bastard. I would not wish that on him. Better for him to grow up here and learn a trade, find his own way in a world of his making than to hover on the fringes of a world that doesn't want him, always on the outside.'

Preston's response was quick and impatient. 'Not if he's recognised. Your father can choose to recognise him. It would even be better if your son's father recognised him. You could give your parents the name of the father. He could be found and brought to account.'

Bea stiffened at the mention of the father. Malvern Alton. A deserter of women. A man who cared only for himself and for his pleasure. He had not cared for her any more than he'd cared for the consequences of their actions. It had taken her a while to recognise and accept the bounder for what he was—a rake of the worst order. For months, she'd clung to the illusion that he'd loved her and the hope that he'd come back. But now that she saw him clearly, any mention of Malvern Alton had to be met with the strongest of defences. She wanted nothing of him in her life. He didn't know of her son and she wanted it to stay that way. He would be even less of a father than he'd been a lover. Not that the courts of England would agree with her. Nobly born fathers held influence if they exerted themselves to claim custody. If Alton wanted her son, he could force her hand. The very thought made her shiver. She struggled to keep her voice even. 'No. I will not force a man who does not want me into marriage any more than I would force myself into marriage simply to appease society's dictates.'

It wasn't just Malvern she wouldn't marry. It was any of them—any man willing to take her and her son. Such a situation would be disastrous, it would sentence them all to a life of unhappiness. Another fear rose, threatening the calm she'd fought so hard to win. 'Don't you see, that too is a reason I can't go back. I will not go to London and seek a husband so that society can be appeased.' Marriage—that was the other thing well-bred families did to erase the stain. She'd not put it past her own family to do the same.

They'd barter her off to a man willing to overlook her sin and her son and she would pay for that every day. That sort of man would lord it over her and her son, making them feel grateful for even the merest of considerations from him. She met Preston's gaze, studying him for the truth. 'Are there plans for me to marry? Is that why you've come now?

To take me to London for the Season?' She could imagine nothing worse—a social hell to rival Dante's. No, that wasn't quite true. She could imagine one thing worse—coming face to face with Malvern Alton again, especially now that she had her son to protect. While she was in Scotland, there was little chance of that happening. Alton liked his luxuries. There were few luxuries here.

Preston lowered his voice and leaned his head close to hers in confidence, his gaze earnest. She could smell the scent of horse and sweat mingled with wind and sandalwood on him. 'There are currently no plans to marry you off to anyone.' Evening shadows were starting to fall, long and sure across the fields. They'd talked away the afternoon. Resistance, refusal and refutation were all exhausted and still there was no resolution.

'Come to Little Westbury, go home to Maidenstone. I won't pretend it will be easy, but you should try. For your son's sake. He should be raised among friends and we'll all be there, waiting for you,' Preston urged one last time. It was the third time he'd asked since this conversation had begun. Intuitively, she knew he would not ask again.

'I choose to stay,' Beatrice said firmly. Here, she was safe, not just from Alton, but from all danger, all men.

Preston bowed his head in a curt nod. 'Then you leave me no choice.' It was an ultimatum.

'That makes us even. You've left me with none either.' It was bravado at best. If she ran, where would she run to? To whom?

'I will come in the morning with the carriage in the hopes you will have reconsidered the nature of your exit.' The words left her cold. The idea that she had no choices left wasn't not the same as his. He was merely forced now to take action. But she was forced to the opposite—to take no action, to acquiesce. To surrender. For now. Perhaps it was not so much a surrender as a retreat. She was Beatrice Penrose. She would survive this.

Chapter Two

It could have been worse, Preston mused an hour down the road, the little village on the Firth firmly behind them. He could have actually had to bodily carry Beatrice out of the farmhouse. He'd more than half-expected to after their conversation the day before. He was glad he didn't have to. His shoulders were up to it, but his mind wasn't.

If it was up to him, he would have left her in Scotland. He knew all too well how it felt to be forced into an unwelcome destiny. Wasn't the very same fate waiting for him upon his return? Hadn't it already begun years ago when he'd been denied the chance to go to war for his country all because of his birth? He keenly felt the hypocrisy of being sent to retrieve Beatrice to resume a life she no longer wanted and force her to it if he must, when he, too, railed against such strictures. Would her rebellion be as futile as his had been thus far?

Preston studied her, her dark head bent slightly as she read, the baby quietly asleep in his basket on the floor. She was still the Beatrice he knew. There was still in her the girl he'd grown up with who romped the hills and valleys of Little Westbury with long strides, carrying a basket to collect herbs and plants during their hikes. But there was a difference to her now.

Motherhood had changed her, Scotland had changed her. Freedom had changed her. There was an air of serenity about her, moments of softness, and yet there was a fierceness to her that hadn't been there before. Beatrice had always been a strong personality, always the first to speak up against injustice, sometimes too rashly. He remembered the butcher in the village and the time Beatrice had caught the man cheating a poor woman out of fresh meat. That strength had permutated into something even fiercer than it had once been. Of course, she had something, someone, to protect now.

He'd seen that fierceness on display yesterday. She'd been formidable in her defence and he'd seen her point. Life in Little Westbury would be financially secure, but it would be difficult. She'd deduced correctly that her parents were eager to put the past year behind them, not necessarily by embracing it, but by erasing it.

Beatrice looked up from her reading and smiled tightly, acknowledging his gaze but nothing more as her eyes returned to her pages. She hadn't spoken to him since she'd set foot in the carriage. She was still mad. At him. He understood. She blamed him for this disruption in her life. But there was something else he more rightly deserved the blame for.

Preston felt the guilt return. It had plagued him since he'd ridden away yesterday. It wasn't his fault she had to come home. That decision lay firmly at the feet of her parents. However, it might possibly be his fault she was in the carriage under somewhat false pretences. He'd told the truth. He and May had advocated the baby be raised at Maidenstone and there were no plans to marry Beatrice off to anyone *specifically*. He knew the conclusion Beatrice had drawn from that last piece of information: she'd be allowed to stay in

Little Westbury, in seclusion. She wouldn't be forced to go to London and endure a Season. That was where he had not bothered to correct her assumptions.

There was always the chance she wouldn't mind. That was the balm his conscience had fallen asleep to last night. Once she got home, she might want to go to London. Evie and Dimitri would be there. May and Liam would be there. There was Liam's knighthood ceremony to look forward to. Surely, London's allures would be too appealing to resist. The baby stirred and he watched Beatrice's gaze go directly to the little bundle, her expression soft as she looked at her sleeping son.

No. Preston knew instinctively his hopes were futile. London had no allure that could compete with the contents of that basket. There was no question of the baby going to London. It was hard to catch husbands with babies clinging to one's skirts. The baby would have to stay behind and Beatrice would never forgive him for that.

The thought of earning Beatrice's enmity sat poorly with him. He'd argued against being sent on this mission from the start. He'd not wanted to do the Penroses' dirty work, but neither had he wanted someone less sensitive to Beatrice's preferences to come in his place. In the end, it was that which had persuaded him to accept, although he'd feared this duty would risk Beatrice's friendship. That, and the idea this trip was one last reprieve from the new responsibilities that waited for him. If it hadn't been for this journey, he'd already be at his grandmother's estate in Shoreham-by-the-Sea, picking up the reins of his inheritance, reins that tugged him in the direction of a landowning gentleman far sooner than he was ready to accept them. Becoming a landowning gentleman was much more bucolic than his current position as the head of coastal patrol. Having an estate that needed him would put an end to his patrol work and to any ambitions he held beyond that. He wasn't ready for bucolic and all it entailed. He pushed the thoughts away and focused on Beatrice.

'Are you truly not going to speak to me for an entire week?' Preston crossed his long legs, attempting to stretch a bit in the cramped space without kicking the baby's basket.

Beatrice gave him a cool glance. 'A week? That's quite optimistic. I intend to not speak to you far longer than that.'

Preston nudged the toe of her shoe, unable to resist the boyish response. 'You just did. Guess you'll have to start over.'

Beatrice put down her book in exasperation. 'You're acting like a thirteen-year-old.'

Preston grinned. 'It takes one to know one. I figured giving someone the silent treatment deserved an equal and appropriate response.' He managed to tease a smile from her with the remark. 'We both know you aren't going to hate me for ever.' At least he hoped not. 'Why don't you forgive me now and get it over with? This trip will be a lot more interesting with someone to talk to, especially if that someone is you.'

He gave her a boyish smile before he turned serious. 'If it's any consolation, I didn't want to do it, Bea. May told me how happy you were here. But if it wasn't me, it would have been someone else.' Preston shook his head, letting the gesture say what he could not put into words. 'I just couldn't let someone else come. That's not what a friend does, even when there's bad news to deliver.' Would she understand it was one of the hardest things he'd ever done? He who had faced gun runners and arms dealers in dark alleys, taken knives to the gut rather like she was taking the proverbial blade now.

Beatrice relented. He saw it in her eyes first, the dark depths softening as she began to see this journey from his perspective. She reached out a hand and squeezed his. 'Thank you for being the one. I doubt I could have borne it otherwise.' It was settled. They could be friends once more for a few weeks at least until he needed to beg her forgiveness again.

'Good.' Preston settled back against the squabs with satisfaction. 'Now that's out of the way, I can tell you about the latest letter from Jonathon and Claire.'

She tossed him a teasingly accusing glare. 'You were holding out on me yesterday.' Bea gave his knee a playful swat and just like that they were the people he remembered them to be.

'Ouch! A good negotiator always holds something back.' Preston feigned injury with a laugh. 'Do you want to hear or not?'

'Of course I want to hear.' Beatrice bent down to pick up her son, awakened by their banter. She put the baby to her breast with consummate ease, unbothered by the loudness of the baby's waking squall or the confines of the carriage that put them in such close proximity—a proximity, which to his mind, made the act of nursing seem more personal than it had yesterday.

Quite frankly, yesterday had been fairly intimate in his opinion. He had thought himself a worldly man, and maybe he was by masculine standards: well-travelled, well-educated. But this world of women was beyond his experience. Was there even etiquette for such a situation? He should look away, yet he could not bring himself to avert his eyes. Watching her with the child was new, fascinating, and it did queer things to his stomach, to his mind, filling it with reminders that while they were the same people they'd been growing up, they were different now, too, each having gone their own way for years. Beatrice was a woman now, the angular, thin girl turned into a lush woman made pretty by the contours of motherhood, a woman who knew the capabilities of a man's body. And he was a man now who had no small experience in that regard when it came to a woman's. It was an intriguing but uncomfortable lens through which to view an old friend.

* * *

Her eyes met his over the child's head. For a moment Preston thought she might scold him for his prurience, but while the act of watching her stirred him deeply, it was not prurient in the least, only beautiful, like a Raphael painting of the Madonna and Child. Beatrice arched her eyebrow in query. 'Well? Are you going to tell me your news or do I have to guess?'

He slanted her a teasing look. 'You haven't grown any more patient over the years, Bea. Jonathon wrote to say he and Claire are expecting a child in the autumn.' Preston cleared his throat. His voice had caught most unexpectedly at the last. He'd been excited for his friend when he'd read the news. He knew how important family was to Jonathon. It was a value the two of them shared.

'Oh!' Beatrice's face shone with pure happiness for her friend. 'They must be over the moon. They will be good parents. There is so much love between them and now there will be a child to lavish it on.' Preston did not miss the wistfulness in her tone. He'd felt that same wistfulness, too, when he'd first heard the news. Jonathon had moved on. Jonathon would have a family while he was still where he'd always been. Working for the government, conducting business for his family and their friends.

Preston's eyes went to the baby in the ensuing silence. Would he ever have what Jonathon had? What Liam had found? He felt a twinge of envy at the thought of his two best friends, Jonathon Lashley and Liam Casek, both happily married and both his own age, both with careers of their own. Jonathon was a diplomat in Vienna. Liam was about to be knighted and looking forward to establishing himself in Parliament as an MP. Both of them proved careers didn't exclude a family life with a woman he loved beside him. They proved a man could have both. And yet, Preston didn't. That hole had never felt quite as gaping as it did now.

'Would you like to hold him?' Beatrice offered, passing him the baby before he could refuse.

Preston took the bundle gently in his arms. 'He's so light. I guess I thought because babies look like a sack of potatoes, they felt like one, too.'

'He's sturdy enough. He won't break,' Beatrice assured him. 'You don't have to treat him as if he's glass.'

Preston adjusted his hold on the infant, starting to feel more confident. He looked down at the little face looking back at him and grinned. 'I think he smiled at me. I think he likes me.' It was such a small thing and yet it pleased him extraordinarily and ridiculously.

'Mistress Maddox told me babies often smile when they pass gas,' Beatrice said slyly, laughing and adding as consolation, 'but I'm sure he likes you.' She hesitated a moment before asking quietly. 'Are you jealous? Of Jonathon, I mean?'

'I shouldn't be. He's endured hardship over the last years. He deserves happiness,' Preston answered truthfully. Why should he be jealous? He could marry whenever he chose, within the Season since his inheritance had been established. It would be ideal and frankly preferred now that he had a home to look after. If he wasn't married already with an heir in the nursery next spring it was his own fault. His mother had ten willing debutantes to hand at any given time. Any girl would be glad to do her duty and marry him. Wasn't that part of the problem? Part of his resistance? He wanted a family, but not like that. Not with a girl like that. Bea was watching him with an odd look on her face as he rocked the baby and he couldn't help but ask her the same. 'Are you, Bea? Jealous?'

'Of Claire? No, of course not.' Bea shook her head hastily to dispel such an unworthy thought. No true friend would begrudge another friend happiness. 'I was just thinking about the child.' Two loving parents and the benefits of a well-born birth. By a random act of fate, the child was poised for success simply by the nature of its birth. Her throat thickened. All the love she possessed for her son couldn't compensate for what he'd never have. Watching Preston with him now drove it all home, the loss she tried not to think about. There would be no father to rock him, no father to run in the meadows with him, to teach him to fish and hunt and ride. No father to hug him, to help him through his first heartbreak, to usher him into manhood. Malvern could never be that man. It didn't matter, she told herself. She would be both mother and father to him. She would be enough.

Preston read her thoughts. 'He'll have uncles, Bea. He'll have Dimitri and Liam and me. He will not go wanting for male guidance.' Something moved in his hazel eyes. She feared she knew what it was and it was the last thing she wanted from anyone, but especially from him.

'I don't need pity,' Beatrice said firmly but quietly. She would not be made a charity case.

'I'm not offering it,' he replied with equal sincerity. 'Of all the people I've ever known, Beatrice, you are the least likely to need it.'

'As are you. You're handsome and well positioned. I know very well from having seen it first hand—the matchmaking mamas are angling hard for you. You could marry whenever you like.' Beatrice gave him a wry smile. She needed to direct the discussion away from herself. Their conversation yesterday had strayed in this direction, too, and she had no desire to head down that path again. If they stayed this course they'd end up talking about Alton, about why she wouldn't seek him out. They could talk about marriage, just not hers. 'Surely there's a pretty girl who has captured your heart?'

'Actually, no.' Preston was determined not to be distracted, though. 'Why won't you talk about him, Bea? Matthew's father? That's twice now. Don't think I don't notice how you veer away from the subject.'

Bea met his gaze with a strong stare. 'He is not worth talking about.' How did she explain talking about him seemed to make Alton more real? She let the silence linger, signalling the finality of that conversation.

Preston shifted in his seat, rearranging his limbs. 'So,' he drawled, fixing her with a mischievous stare in return, 'you think I'm handsome?'

'You know you are. It's empirically true.' Beatrice laughed, but the sound came out a little nervously, her mouth dry. Preston *was* handsome. He wore his dark hair brushed back off his forehead, revealing the lean, elegant bones of his face, the razor straightness of his nose, the firm line of his jaw, the sweep of enigmatic cheekbones that appeared stark and sharp when he was angry and gave way to a hint of friendly apples when he smiled. Perhaps, though, what gave his face its handsomeness were its two best features: his hazel eyes, intelligent and compassionate by turn, and the thin aristocratic structure of his mouth. It was a face that paired well with his body. His was not the bulkier, muscled body of a man like Liam Casek, but athletically trim. A fencer's body, lean and quick in its height.

Beatrice shifted, uncomfortable with the direction of her thoughts. It was something of a shock to think of Preston in those terms. She'd never catalogued Preston's physical assets in quite such a way—like a debutante or a matchmaking mama looking for a prime eligible *parti*. 'I'll take him now.' She reached for her son. She'd imposed on Preston long enough and holding the baby would give her something to do, something to think about besides Preston's physique.

Preston surprised her. 'No, if you don't mind, I'd like to hold him a while longer. You can rest, if you want. You must be tired with all the getting up every night. I think Matthew and I are getting on famously.'

She *was* tired. The nights were indeed difficult. Beatrice didn't need further urging. She leaned back against the squabs and closed her eyes, hoping the old adage was true—out of sight, out of mind. She'd very much like to dispel certain images of Preston Worth. Harbouring such fanciful notions was one sure way to destroy a friendship. It was probably why men and women were so often unsuccessful in their friendships with one another. It was more difficult than she'd expected to rid her mind of those images, but it was easy to rationalise why. They were in close quarters, there was the baby to look after. Jonathon and Claire's news had thrown the holes of their own individual lives into sharp relief. It was natural to reach out and grab at the person nearest to you. Even now, wasn't Preston doing the same thing? He wasn't the only one who could read minds. She knew very well what he was doing. He was sitting across from her, holding the baby and pretending at fatherhood.

Of course, Preston's situation wasn't nearly as dire as hers. He could change his circumstances. She could not. Should not. She had her rules now and the number one rule was that men were dangerous. Rule number two: passion was dangerous. But Preston didn't need to live by those rules. There was still time for him, all the time in the world. He could marry when he chose and he was young by male marriage standards. Many men didn't marry until their thirties and Preston was what? Twenty-eight? He was five years older than May and she. She remembered that his birthday was in early April. The realisation almost made her eyes fly open. His birthday was the tenth.

He would likely celebrate it on the road. Away from his family. That was her fault. He'd not wanted to make this journey.

I couldn't stand the thought of someone else coming for you.

He had sacrificed his comforts for her and she'd been shrewish with him. She would find a way to make it up to him.

Chapter Three

In terms of igniting dangerous fantasies about one's travelling partner, the day got markedly worse; everything seemed to feed those rather uncomfortable considerations. There was the picnic beside a quiet brook and a short walk through a meadow of wildflowers to stretch their legs later in the afternoon while Matthew dozed under the watchful eye of the driver, all of it accompanied by conversation, all of it seemingly meaningful to her, at least. It was a chance to get to know her friend again.

She learned about Preston's work along the coast. Thanks to high taxes, smuggling was always in season. Danger, too, but he seemed to take it all in his stride. In turn, he asked about her interests—science and herbs, things she hadn't devoted much time to since Matthew was born. She was starved for such conversation. It had been months since someone had paid attention to her as a singular entity in herself and it was intoxicating. The thoughtful conversation wove an intimacy all its own, a potency further enhanced by her earlier considerations—considerations that were becoming increasingly difficult to tamp down.

'I think this might be the most pleasant day I've had in a long time.' Beatrice let Preston hand her into the coach after their walk, suddenly conscious of his touch, of its warmth, its strength. 'Motherhood, I'm discovering, is a lonely occupation. I don't think I've talked to another soul about anything other than babies in for ever.' Not talking about them had been liberating.

Preston grinned and settled into his seat. 'I'm glad we stopped, then. I usually don't talk about my work much. I suspect most find it boring, or somewhat scandalous. It's one thing for a nobleman's son to have a position, to be an "officer" of sorts, but it's another thing to actually *do* the position.' Preston shook his head. 'I can't imagine just sitting around all day. Apparently, several of my colleagues can manage it just fine. I would go barmy.' He paused and turned more serious. 'It killed me not to be able to serve against Napoleon. I was envious of Jonathon and his brother. Jonathon was an heir, too. I thought surely if Jonathon's parents let him go, mine would as well.'

She hadn't known. Always a dutiful son, he'd hid his disappointment admirably. 'But you were posted to the coast instead?'

'And not even in a military capacity.' Preston gave a dry laugh. Beatrice could hear the lingering regret. She wanted to say something encouraging but not clichéd.

'Running Cabot Roan, the infamous arms dealer, to ground is a significant service not just to Britain, but to Europe. One that nearly cost you your life, as sure as any soldier,' she added pointedly.

'True enough.' He leaned back against the seat and pushed a hand through his dark hair. 'I'm sorry, Bea. I'm being peevish all of the sudden.' He was silent for a moment, but she felt the frenetic energy radiating from him, struggling to break free of containment. 'I do enjoy the work. That's the problem. My parents feel I should give it up now. I've spent my twenties serving the Crown, as many young men of noble families do, Bea, and now my parents believe it's time to move on to serve the Crown in a more traditional sense.' He chuckled. 'Of course, they disagree on which tradition that should be. Father would like to see me shift my career to more diplomacy. But Mother…' He held up his empty left fingers and waggled them indicating the lack of a ring.

Bea nodded her understanding. Of course his mother would want him to marry. Men of good birth were to oversee the land and those that worked it. Their service to England was to be gentlemen, protect the vast tracts of land that had been given into the care of their families generations ago and make sons to carry on the tradition. That was to be the purpose of his life just as her purpose in life had once been to marry such a man and produce that heir. It seemed both of them were determined to deviate from the path laid out for them.

'You're restless, that's all,' Beatrice said softly, realising that perhaps the conversation had been liberating for him as well. 'I feel it, too, sometimes.' In hindsight, she often thought it was that restlessness that had led her to the impetuous affair last winter. She could never regret Matthew, but she did regret giving in to the spontaneity and the desperation that had driven the decision to be with a man she knew very little about except that she found him exciting in an unpredictable sort of way.

She glanced at Preston, the words she wanted to say making her uncharacteristically shy. 'Do you suppose that makes me a bad mother? Wondering if there's more than nappies and nursing?' It was her guiltiest thought these days. Perhaps there wasn't anything more, perhaps this was why gentlemen preferred empty-headed debutantes. Those girls would never question the duality of motherhood.

Preston gave a friendly chuckle. 'No, hardly, Bea. You're a fabulous mother from what I've seen. I don't know how you handle it, how you *know* it all: when to feed him, to change him, how to burp him.'

Bea felt herself glow. 'I wasn't fishing for compliments.'

Preston gave her a wink, his good humour seemingly restored. 'I know.'

Bea gave him a considering look. 'I think

motherhood comes with a paradox: infinite love and finite limitations. Maybe being a gentleman's son does, too, in its own way: limited opportunities while providing for eternal perpetuity.' She'd always thought of men as having boundless freedom. Perhaps not.

'I think you've hit the nail on the head, exactly.' Preston reached for his book with a rueful half-smile before turning his attention to the pages and she did the same, allowing her thoughts, both old and new, to absorb her.

Even as she settled beneath the covers for the night, Matthew asleep in a makeshift crib beside her lonely bed, the thought was still with her that today had been a watershed; she was coming alive again, the rivers of her life diverging in different directions once more. She was not just a mother now, whose body was devoted solely to supporting another life, nor was she simply a girl with a past, but a woman with independent interests and needs. The sharpness of that realisation was a double-edged sword; those interests, those needs, carried her down dangerous streams, more passionate streams she'd promised herself not to navigate again for the sake of her son and herself. Hadn't she learned her lesson already?

She could not allow herself to give in to the reckless passions that had led her into Malvern Alton's arms, except perhaps in the middle of the night, alone in her bed where no one could see, no one would know. Bea slid her hands beneath the cotton of her nightgown, cupping her breasts, feeling the milky fullness of them and remembering that once, before they'd been a source of nourishment, they'd been a source of pleasure. It had been heady to feel a man's hands on her. She'd felt delightfully wicked and delightfully natural, a complete woman, able to give pleasure.

Her hands slid lower, over the softness of her belly, the roundness of her hips. What would a man think of her now? She'd been much thinner, much straighter in form before the baby. Perhaps too thin except for her breasts. That angularity was gone now. She had a fairly frank relationship with the mirror. She might not have got *her* figure back after the baby, but she'd got *a* figure back. She could see the difference in herself now compared to London's narrow-waisted debutantes.

Her hand slipped between her legs, to the one place that hadn't changed, her core quivering. There was pleasure here still, perhaps the only physical pleasure available to her under her rules. She had not done this for ages, not since Matthew had been born, and it felt good and right after today's realisations. She could be alive again. She was *entitled* to be alive again. She owed the knowledge of it to Preston.

But there, she had to be careful not to let her imagination get the better of her. This awakening wasn't about Preston. She wasn't pleasuring herself in her dark room because of her earlier fantasies. She was doing it in celebration of what he'd helped her realise. Nothing more.

That became her mantra in the early days of their journey. She and Preston were good friends and that made them good travelling companions. It was an ideal concept that explained the ease into which they could lapse with each other, the thoughts they could share with each other without fearing judgement, or the silence they could sit in. It explained the patterns that formed quickly and easily;

the days spent in conversation, the walks and roadside picnics as the miles passed, the evenings spent in a private dinner away from the general noise of the taprooms, the companionable stroll as he escorted her to her room and said goodnight before going to his own chamber next door. Often, he carried the baby upstairs for her.

It was the happiest and yet saddest part of the day, watching him talk softly to the baby, who clearly adored him. 'Pound on the wall if you need anything, Bea,' he'd say reassuringly. 'I'll be right there.' Sometimes he'd lean over and give Matthew a kiss on the forehead, his hand resting at her back, his body encompassing them in a little group as he said the words, 'Goodnight, little man, sleep tight.' Then he'd shut the door behind them, leaving her and Matthew alone until the morning and the sun shone again. Preston would make an excellent father. The instincts were all there: the caring, the gentleness, the devotion, the love. His children would be lucky. His wife would be lucky.

The fourth day was hard going. It managed to rain in the morning, turning the roads muddy. Progress was slow and there was no chance for outdoor breaks to stretch their legs. Matthew was feeling the confines of the carriage after three days of travel, having cried a large part of the day despite their best efforts to distract him. Even Preston's unflagging patience was reaching its limits. They put into an inn around five o'clock and Preston jumped down to see about rooms. She could hear the mud squishing around the impact of his boots when he landed and firmly shut the coach door behind him with an admonition, 'Stay inside, Bea.'

Peeking through the coach window, she saw the reason for it, unnecessary though the caution was. She had no desire to tramp around in the mud. Outside, the sight was dismal. The inn looked rougher and less well kept than the other places they'd stopped, the yard full of men in shabby clothes who apparently didn't care they were ankle deep in mud and the rain still falling.

This was not where they'd planned to stay tonight. Their destination was still several miles away, a journey that might take up to two hours in this slog, or might see them stranded along the road if a wheel got stuck, or a horse went lame in the dark, victim of a misstep. Matthew began to stir from his brief nap, another reason for not daring more miles on the road. The baby could go no further.

The inn door opened and she watched Preston come out, rain beating on the shoulders of his great coat, dripping in rivulets down his dark hair, turning him somewhat more primitive than the gentleman she was used to. A man called out to him, something she couldn't hear. Preston did not hesitate to silence him with a scowl and sharp words of his own. The man backed off. So it was *that* kind of crowd.

Preston climbed inside the coach, looking grim. 'Bad news, Bea. They've only the one room. There's a horse show in town and rooms everywhere are full. It's either this or driving on. I suppose we could try. There's a bit more daylight yet.' He didn't sound hopeful. Matthew was fully awake now, sitting on her lap and on the verge of another cranky bawl over being cooped up.

'Take the room. I am sure we can manage.' Beatrice smiled bravely. 'I think it's the only decision we can make. I know it's not ideal.'

Preston nodded and twisted at something

on his hand. His grandfather's gold ring with a square emerald in it, a very masculine ring, a gift to him on his eighteenth birthday. She'd been there the night the gift had been given, a sign of maturity, of coming of age, of being recognised as another Worth male in a lineage that spanned generations, a proud moment, a prized possession. He handed it to her. 'You should put it on, Bea.' He shrugged, his explanation modest although she'd already divined the reason for it. 'It will protect you.' From the bullies in the yard, from whatever clientele existed in the taproom.

Beatrice nodded silently and slipped the ring on. Preston's fingers were long and slender, a musician's hands, although she hadn't heard him play in years. As a result, the ring fit moderately well, only slightly loose. She curled her hand into a fist to ensure it didn't slide off. What a difference a ring could make. A wife was entitled to all sorts of protections and considerations denied a single woman. Wasn't that the reason she'd created her own fictitious husband in Scotland? Still, she was confident in her safety, ring or not. Preston would keep her safe. He always had. She had no reason to doubt his capabilities now.

Preston blew out a breath. 'All right, let's go. You carry Matthew and I'll carry you. I'll have a porter bring the bags.' He swung her up into his arms, the babe clutched against her chest, and made his way across the muddy inn yard.

The room was small, with barely enough space for a bed, a small table, a fireplace and a dressing screen in the corner. The smallness seemed to emphasise the reality that even between longstanding friends, masquerading as husband and wife carried with it a dangerous intimacy. It was the bed that did it, dominating the tiny space so that one could think of nothing else but bed and all that it implied.

Stay busy, Beatrice told herself. She set Matthew carefully in the bed's centre and set about starting a fire. Preston was downstairs, overseeing the bags, and he was wet. He'd want heat when he came up. She checked the cleanliness of the towels and the bedding, hanging one towel near the fire to warm for Preston. A maid popped her head in and Beatrice tried to order dinner, but was told the inn was too busy for special orders. Everyone who wanted to eat had to eat in the taproom.

Preston relayed the same information when he came up a few minutes later.

'The room is small.' Preston's eyes went briefly to the bed, perhaps drawing the same conclusions she had. Someone was going to end up in a chair or on the floor unless...unless they opted to share the bed. There would be no hiding in the dark if they did. But that was hours away yet.

'It's warm and clean, which is more than I expected. We'll manage.' She would rely on brisk efficiency to keep the fantasy at bay. 'Let's get you dry.'

Chapter Four

Spoken like a perfect wife. The errant thought came to him as he stood in the centre of her efficient whirlwind, letting Beatrice strip him out of his coat, his jacket, his waistcoat, laying them over the fireplace screen and picking up the heated towel. 'Here, dry off with this, it's warm. I am assuming a hot bath is out of the question if they can't be bothered to deliver dinner.' She let him mop his face and neck. His shirt was dry, protected from the damp by his other layers, fortunately for modesty's sake, but perhaps unfortunately for his other senses. He was rather enjoying being fussed over.

Beatrice passed him another towel, saying, 'For your hair', before pushing him down into the room's one chair and opening his travelling trunk. She pulled out clean clothes for him. 'Your clothes will be dry in the morning, but you'll need something for tonight.' She laid them out on the bed.

'Take care of yourself, Bea. I'll do.' Preston smiled at her efforts. Of course Beatrice would fuss over him. She took care of those in need whether it be a poor woman in a butcher shop or a hungry baby, or a soaking wet man. He didn't mind. When was the last time someone had done for him? When he was at home, his valet did it, but when he travelled for the Crown, he was on his own. His work often required stealth and one could *not* be stealthy with a valet in tow.

Beatrice was a caregiver, it came naturally to her, part of how she took charge. Look what she'd done for her friends this past year, inspiring them to take life into their own hands; his sister had told him about the Left Behind Girls Club where the motto was 'nothing will change until you do'. He'd seen evidence of it these last days, all the attention she selflessly lavished on her son. He supposed he'd always known that about Beatrice. She'd been the leader of the little group of girls since they were young. But to see it in action was another thing altogether, a reminder, too, that he might have grown up with Bea, but their adult lives had been spent separately. He might have known the girl she'd been, but he did not know entirely the woman she'd become. He'd like to know her, though. It was, in large part, what these past days in the coach had focused on. The journey was no longer merely a rescue or retrieval of an old friend, but a discovery. He had the sense she was doing the same with him, both of them exploring the same questions: who had they become in the absence of childhood and the presence of their own adversities?

Perhaps the more important question was: where did that discovery lead? They'd long since superseded the friendship of childhood in Little Westbury and they were fast becoming more than the sum of their friendship in London as new adults come to town. He knew it was due to the enforced proximity of the road. Once the road was gone and they were home, this sense of closeness would fade. It was how the road worked.

He watched her deftly change the baby into a fresh cloth, her face all smiles, her voice a gentle coo even when Matthew fussed and rolled, trying to thwart her efforts. Something inside him went soft. *Would* the closeness fade? He found himself trying on the old line of comfort: 'maybe this time it would be different'. Maybe he didn't want the closeness to fade.

Bea took a moment to play a game with Matthew, blowing on his belly before settling his clothes. The baby laughed, forgetting his own troubles, whatever they might be. Preston laughed, too, feeling some of the weariness of the day slip away when Bea looked over at him and smiled. It was not a special moment, the way milestone moments are, but he knew in his gut he would remember this moment for ever. His mind would keep a sharp picture of her at the bed, looking over at him with the laughing baby in her arms, as if this was his wife and his child. His family in truth. Then Matthew started to cry again and the moment was gone. Bea bounced him, trying to settle him down, undaunted.

Her patience was admirable, really. Preston knew she had to be as tired as he was after a long day in the coach and he wasn't the one who had to feed the wee little fiend. Matthew hadn't wanted to do anything today except scream and eat. He wasn't looking forward to taking the baby down to the taproom, but what choice did he have? 'Let me hold him while you get ready,' he offered.

She gave him a tired smile of thanks. Eating in public didn't appeal to her any more than it appealed to him, but perhaps for different reasons. 'Thank you. I will just be a minute.'

Preston kept a hand firmly and obviously at Beatrice's back as they navigated the taproom, letting everyone see that she was clearly with him, clearly under his protection. There was a knife in his boot if he needed it. He hoped he wouldn't. But not that hopeful. The room was just as bad as he'd anticipated, noisy with the excitement of tomorrow's horse sales and full of the odours that come with a room filled to capacity with wet, muddy men unaccustomed to washing.

The innkeeper caught sight of the baby in Bea's arms and ushered them to a quieter table in the corner, a small blessing. At least if there was a fight, he'd have a wall at his back, a far more preferable arrangement to being surrounded on all sides.

'We'll take wine if you have it,' Preston told the man, helping Beatrice to sit before taking his own seat that looked out across the crowded room. Most men were just in high spirits, but two tables worried him. The one near the door looked to be trouble in general, spoiling for a fight with anyone. It was only seven o'clock and they were already drunk. The table closer to them was a more immediate concern. That would be personal trouble. The big man had been eyeing Beatrice since they walked in despite his hand at her back, despite the baby on her lap and the bold gold ring on her finger. A man who didn't respect such signs was trouble indeed if he decided to do more than look.

The first part of the meal went better than expected. The rough inn had an excellent cook. The innkeeper had taken a look at Beatrice with the baby on her lap and had not hesitated to supply the table with the best his kitchen had to offer, perhaps as an apology for not being able to serve them privately. After a day filled with unmet expectations, the excellent meal was more than welcome. The rabbit stew was tasty and seasoned, the bread freshly baked, the wine a nice complement to the meal—so nice, in fact, Preston wondered if it was smuggled. He always wondered. Occupational hazard, he supposed. He and Beatrice were able to exchange a little conversation underneath the noise surrounding them. Baby Matthew was entranced by all the activity around him and was behaving. They were small blessings, like the moment upstairs, when just for a second, everything had been right.

After the day Bea had endured, he wished he could give her more, give her better. Maybe it was that desire to give her more than a rough night out that prompted his decision when the innkeeper had leaned close and whispered there was bread pudding available for dessert for his more discerning customers. Preston had seen Bea's eyes light up at the mention and he couldn't say no. He rationalised dinner had gone well enough so far, what would a few more minutes be?

He should have quit while he was ahead. They'd no more than taken two bites of the bread pudding when the big man a few tables over decided to make trouble. 'What about the rest of us? I want some dessert, too,' he bawled at the innkeeper. 'You've been sending the best to their table all night long.'

The innkeeper, well used to rough clientele and a burly man himself, was not daunted. 'Dessert's for patrons who pay their bill, Burke.'

But Burke wasn't done. Getting no satisfaction from the innkeeper, he turned his attention to Preston's table. 'Maybe I want something else for dessert.' His eyes passed over Beatrice. Preston readied his fists. There was a fight coming. It was nearly unavoidable. He'd give the man one chance to retreat.

'My *wife* doesn't care for your attentions,' Preston said firmly, drawing the man's gaze away from Bea.

'Your wife is pretty. I'm just wanting a little kiss, we don't get such pretty ladies in these parts.' The man was drunk, Preston could smell the alcohol on him, and the man was sizing him up, weighing Preston's leaner build against his own bulk and coming to certain, rather violent conclusions. Big men always did. Big men thought sheer strength counted for everything, they forgot about other elements like speed and height, and reach and athleticism, and that wasn't even counting what Preston did for a living. While most of the smugglers were unsophisticated sailors, there were arms dealers who'd been a good deal more dangerous. One drunk man in a tavern didn't worry him.

Preston rose, exposing his full height up close. 'Go back to your table before someone gets hurt. My wife doesn't want to kiss you.' He was aware that Matthew had begun to cry and the sound of the baby's distress angered Preston in measure equal to his desire to protect Beatrice from this scum. What sort of man made a baby cry? What sort of man came after another man's wife?

'Who do you suppose that someone would be?' Burke leered. 'Perhaps you should be the one sitting down if *you're* worried about getting hurt.' Burke reached for Beatrice. Preston swung.

'No!' Beatrice yelped and leapt back reflexively, clutching Matthew to her as Preston's fist smashed into the big man's jaw. The blow knocked the man sideways and Preston was on him, landing another hard blow before he could recover.

'Take your hands off of her, you bastard!' Preston's voice was a guttural roar, his fists landing hit after hit, but not without some retaliation. The bully regained his feet and struck back, a meaty fist burying into Preston's stomach. Preston doubled over from the force, but came charging back like a bull, taking Burke in the midsection and ramming him into a sturdy table, spilling plates and ale. It was all the provocation the rest of the taproom needed to join in.

Chaos was everywhere; tables tipped, chairs flew along with fists; tankards and plates became weapons and shields. Beatrice had never seen this much violence up close. She ought to be afraid, but she wasn't. She ought to find a way out, but she didn't. She felt quite safe in the corner. Preston stood between her and disaster and every other man in the taproom. Never mind there were forty of them to his one. Preston slammed Burke's head into the table and the big man fell unconscious to the floor.

'Bea!' he called over his shoulder. 'Stay behind me!' He grabbed her hand and pulled, tucking her in behind him, his body her shield. 'Come on!' They moved fast, ducking and darting through the melee, Preston's fists clearing a path towards the stairs, felling one man and then another without hesitation, his face a stoic mask of intensity, his eyes fixed on the next opponent and the next. At the stairs, he pushed her ahead of him, his hand at her back, urging haste. 'Go, go, go!' His eyes were fixed over his shoulder on the taproom.

Bea gained the landing before she was aware Preston had stayed behind at the base of the stairs. She looked back in time to see Preston swing at a tall, bulky man with thick arms who didn't go down. 'You knocked out my friend. I don't think I like that,' he growled, something glinting dangerously in his hand.

'Knife!' Beatrice screamed out of an instinctive need to warn Preston, never mind her voice was one of many, sucked up in the chaos of the taproom.

Preston bent to his boot and came up in a fluid motion, a blade flashing in his hand, already swiping at the man's arm, catching it. A trickle of red showed on the dirty shirt. Beatrice clutched the baby tighter, making him squall. The violence had suddenly become much more real now. Preston was fighting defensively, careful not to maim or worse beyond what was needed. She wasn't sure the other man was taking such ethical consideration with his punches. The bleeding scratch had the man angry. He wanted blood of his own.

'Bea, get in the room! Bar the door,' Preston yelled, not breaking his concentration. Blood or not, she didn't want to leave him. It was not in her nature to abandon a friend, but she had Matthew to think about and Preston, too. She would only be a distraction to him if she stayed. She took one last look at Preston holding the stairs, ensuring her safety, and ran for the room.

What if he didn't succeed? *Bar the door.* That was the reason for the command, wasn't it? Beatrice didn't allow for the thought until her back was pressed up against the door of their chamber, the heavy oak shutting out the sounds downstairs, the heavy bolt hopefully prepared to shut out intruders if need be. What if the man's knife got the better of Preston? What of other knives? What of other men who'd want to try him? He couldn't fight for ever.

Beatrice set the baby on the bed and glanced around the room for a makeshift weapon. A candlestick. No. It was heavy, but it would require her getting far closer to an attacker than she wanted in order to be effective. She wanted something longer. Her eyes lit on the fireplace. A poker. Perfect. Beatrice crossed the room and wrapped her hand firmly around the handle, testing the weight. It would even be better if it were hot. Bea put it in the fire, feeling inspired. Any unwanted soul coming through that door would regret it.

The only soul she was interested in seeing at the door was Preston. At first, she started at any little sound. Fifteen agonising minutes went by and then thirty. Still, no one came. The poker glowed hot at the hearth. On the bed, Matthew had fallen asleep, exhausted by the excitement and the long day.

Beatrice paced. Surely they weren't all still fighting? But it was almost worse to think of what it meant if the fighting was over. How would she explain to the Worths if something happened to him? She ran through a few experimental lines in her head.

I'm sorry, Preston was wounded in a tavern brawl. It was my fault because I wanted the bread pudding.

It sounded just as bad as she thought it would. It was all her fault, just as it was her fault he'd had to come to Scotland, had to be on the road for his birthday. Now, it was her fault he was embroiled in fisticuffs or worse.

Chapter Five

⁓⚬⚬⚬⚬⚬⚬⚬⚬⚬⚬⚬⚬⚬⚬⚬⚬⚬⚬⚬⚬⚬⚬⚬⚬⚬⚬⚬⚬⚬⚬⚬⚬⚬

There was a pounding on the door, at last. Beatrice snapped into action, snatching up the poker from the hearth. She took up her position beside the door as another pound came, this time followed with a voice. 'Bea, open up, it's me.' Relief made her clumsy. She dropped the poker, fumbled with the bar, dropping it, too, in her haste and excitement.

At first, relief at seeing him safe overwhelmed the details. Then, she saw them: the sleeve of his shirt ripped shoulder to wrist, the bruise along his jaw, the cuts on his cheek. 'You're hurt!' The words were entirely inadequate. Of course he was hurt. He'd just fought how many men on her behalf? She tugged him inside and struggled with the bar, lifting it into place. There was suddenly so much to do.

'Come, sit down. I'll heat some of the washing water.' She would have paid dearly for a kettle just now, to be back in her little cottage kitchen where she'd have all she needed to hand. She settled for wedging the ewer among the coals and the towels he'd used to dry off with earlier.

'Are you hurt anywhere else?' She worked his shirt off, desperate to see the damage beneath the slashed sleeve, hoping there was none. 'Are you cut?' She examined the arm, looking for signs of injury, but finding none.

'No, I was too fast for him.' Preston grinned and she could hear the cocky pride in his voice.

'Don't tell me you were downstairs enjoying all this while I was up here worried sick,' Bea scolded. 'I was imagining all sorts of horrid things befalling you.'

Preston chuckled, wincing from the effort. 'Oh, ouch!'

Bea gave him a stern look. 'Ribs?' She hoped not. That could be serious. She'd far rather treat a knife scratch. She ran her hands down his torso, feeling for any sign of a cracked or broken rib. The men down there had been big enough to deliver damage. He flinched where she pressed. 'I think they're just bruised. I can wrap them for you.' She was already running through possible make-shift bandages. She had a petticoat in her luggage she could sacrifice.

Preston shook his head. 'I'll be fine. I won't have you ripping up clothes on my account.'

'It's the least I can do.' Beatrice wrapped a towel about her hand and reached for the warmed ewer. She poured water into the basin and soaked a cloth. 'I saved some of the cold water for your face. That bruise will hurt, it needs cold, but your ribs will appreciate the heat.' She knelt and pressed the folded cloth to his ribs, realising too late what work and concern had obscured. She had stripped Preston Worth to the skin, had put her hands all over him and was now kneeling before him in what could be taken as a rather intimate position under other circumstances. Her body didn't seem to know the difference, although it should have.

It wasn't the first time she'd seen his bare chest. She'd seen him shirtless countless times before, during the long summers of their youth. But this chest was nothing like the chest he'd sported as a slender adolescent. This was the chest of a man blooded in battle.

Her finger traced the scar left by the wound this autumn. 'Roan?' She shuddered at the thought of how close the blade had come to doing permanent damage.

'Yes, but the stitches are all Liam's.' Preston laughed.

Bea grimaced, not sharing the humour. She ran her hands down his torso, feeling for further injury, the smooth expanse of muscle beneath her fingers as it tapered into narrowing planes and a lean waist—a waist she happened to be eye level with. She made the mistake of rocking back on her heels, which forced her to sit a little lower, putting her eye level with something far more intimate than his waistline; a man becoming aroused. Beatrice cleared her throat. 'Here, hold the compress in place.' She rose, suddenly needing to keep busy. She should *not* be staring at Preston's crotch. Preston shifted carefully in the chair, he, too, feeling the embarrassment of an awkward moment.

Bea rummaged through her luggage, talking too fast. 'I have some herbs that can help with swelling.'

Preston cocked a curious eyebrow. 'Do you, now?'

She flushed uncontrollably. Swelling was an unfortunate choice of words just now. 'Swelling, as in bruising,' Beatrice clarified, finding the packet she wanted.

'Of course.' Preston's response was far too benign to actually *be* harmless. 'What other kind of swelling could you have possibly meant?'

Beatrice chose to ignore the comment. 'This is calamine and elm powder.' She dumped a bit of the dried herbs into some warm water and stirred until it was pasty. 'I'm making you a poultice. I think we'll wrap your ribs after all. You'll be more comfortable.'

She wouldn't be, though. Getting the poultice on him would require close contact while she tied strips of cloth. She probably should have thought that one through a little better. Preston sniffed the air as she wound the strips about him. 'Calamine smells like mint,' she said before he could ask.

He lifted an arm to help her with the binding. 'And the lavender?' He breathed in again. 'I think that must be you. Lavender smells… peaceful.'

'Not like me at all, then.' Beatrice laughed. Peaceful wasn't a word she'd use to describe herself. She was outspoken, restless, some-times spontaneous, and as a result sometimes quick to impatience.

'You are more peaceful now than I remem-ber you, though,' Preston said as she tied off the last of the strips and stepped back to check her handiwork. 'I think motherhood becomes you.'

Most likely, he meant the remark empiri-cally, but the hour was late, the day trying and the evening more so. Such events tinged their small room with an undeniable intimacy as they looked at one another, perhaps seeing a little more of who they'd become: the mother, the gentleman warrior. Beatrice picked up her supplies, stifling a yawn.

'Get ready for bed, Bea. You're exhausted. I'll take the chair tonight,' Preston offered, saving her the awkwardness of bringing up the subject of sleeping arrangements.

'We should share the bed.' Beatrice disap-peared behind the dressing screen with her nightgown, suddenly self-conscious. 'With those ribs, you need to lie down.' Why was it she could nurse a baby in front of him, but was nervous about stepping out in her night-gown? The nightgown was quite a modest garment, loose and flowing, the cotton thick enough not to be revealing in the firelight, at least she hoped it wouldn't be.

He was going to protest. She could tell by the shifting of his body on the other side of the screen. He was thinking over the best way to argue. She couldn't have that. She was going to have to take charge and insist. Beatrice stepped from behind the screen and walked over to the bed, pulling back the covers with the same efficiency she'd relied on all night. 'Preston, don't be ridiculous about this. You're hurt and we've been friends for ages. We can surely survive a night together.'

She didn't worry they'd actually do anything. There would be no forgoing of common sense. That wasn't what she was concerned about. She was concerned her mind would never be the same—that she wouldn't be able to look at him the same way. All neutrality would be lost and she needed that neutrality to survive this week. What would happen without it?

Preston nodded, perhaps recognising his ribs needed the bed more than his gentleman's pride needed to be assuaged. 'I'll keep my trousers on, but I'm going to need help with my boots.'

'Of course.' She felt foolish all of the sudden. She'd forgotten about his boots. She knelt and helped him tug them off. Then she crawled into bed, trying to ignore the sounds of a man going through his bedtime rituals behind the screen. She had not realised intimacy came in so many varieties until this trip.

Preston lay down on the other side of the bed and turned down the light. The gesture swamped her with the sensation that this was what it must be like to sleep beside a husband every night, to feel the bed take his weight, to hear his body shift as he got comfortable. She didn't know.

'Bea, are you sure?' Preston asked from his side. 'I don't want you to think...'

She completed his thoughts. 'Think what? That you'd take advantage of me because I'm not a virgin? That you don't have to behave honourably because I've shared a bed with a man before? I don't think that, Preston. The man who fought for me downstairs is not a man I'd associate with those behaviours.' She paused and then plunged ahead softly. 'My lover never took me to bed, at least not in the literal sense.'

It seemed important that Preston knew that.

'We were never even naked together.'

She hadn't told May that in their long months at the cottage. She'd seldom spoken of her lover, but here in the dark with Preston the words were easy, perhaps because telling him these things didn't require a name and Preston wouldn't push for one.

'It was all furtive lovemaking in haylofts and barns,' she said. The kind of lovemaking done with skirts up and trousers down against a wall, clothing a mere yank or twitch away from being righted—just in case. It was just one more way Alton had failed her. She'd given him everything and he treated the gift, treated her, as something of negligible value, to be disposed of when he was finished.

Preston's hand found hers among the bedclothes. 'Did he force you, May?'

'Will you be disappointed if I say no?' Bea said quietly. Her parents had wanted it to be force. Rape was somehow a viable explanation for what had happened, whereas having consensual sex out of wedlock was not.

'No.' Preston sighed in the dark. 'I'm glad

you weren't forced. I wouldn't want you hurt or coerced. But I am sorry it wasn't a better experience.'

Should it have been? Better? The question was on the tip of her tongue, but she held it back, the question too leading to ask even in the dark. Still, the thought stayed with her as she drifted towards sleep. Admittedly, sex had not lived up to her preconceived ideas and she did have some, not only from the flowery allusions found in books, but from more scientific experiment. She could give herself some modicum of pleasure and that discovery had led her to believe sex would render an even larger pleasure when shared.

It hadn't. Instead, sex had been messy, sticky and quick. Thank goodness for the last bit because barn walls often had splinters, hay was prickly, and one's legs had a tendency to cramp up if they were wrapped around someone else's waist too long. But there had been none of the troubadours' pleasures or the scientists' hypotheses she'd come to expect.

Had she missed something? Or was it that the pleasure was for the man alone? Her lover had seemed quite pleased afterwards. Science was primarily written by men, after all. Perhaps they had simply not considered the woman. Perhaps lonely pleasure was all she should expect. But, what if she was wrong? What if Preston knew something she didn't? He'd certainly have more experience to draw from.

She twisted on to her side, contemplating Preston in the dark. The lucky man was already asleep. Preston was fast becoming a repository of secret talents. First, the dazzling display of boxing skills and knife work tonight and now this, the hint of sensual, forbidden knowledge. What sort of knowledge lay just six inches away? What did Preston know that she didn't? That particular speculation was scientific curiosity. It was a tempting concept, but not nearly as wicked as the next: what would it be like to test the hypothesis of pleasure with him? Would it be worth breaking her rules? Bea rolled on to her back and sighed. It was a hypothetical debate she held only with herself. Such an occasion would never present itself. Preston was a man of honour. Even if he did entertain such notions, he would never act on them. Still, it was a titillating thought to fall asleep on.

* * *

The baby woke him in the deadest part of night, somewhere around three and not for the first time. Beatrice had fed him a little over an hour ago. Surely the baby wasn't hungry again? Beside him, Preston felt Beatrice stir. She mumbled something incoherent in her half-sleep. That decided it. 'Hush, go back to sleep, I've got him,' Preston whispered, although his body protested at the movement *and* the idea of getting up. How did she do it night after night? They both didn't need to be awake. He would look after the baby until it became obvious he couldn't.

Preston swung stiffly out of bed, careful of his one side where his ribs hurt. He bent awkwardly to pick the baby up, found his way to the chair and settled in, Matthew cradled against his good side. 'Can't sleep, little man?' he asked softly. 'Me neither.' He'd dozed off and on, sleep eluding him in part because of the waking child, but also because his bruises made certain positions uncomfortable. He turned up the lamp enough to see Matthew's face in the dark, surprised to find the baby smiling up at him as if it were morning and not night. Suddenly, being sleepless was worth it to have these precious, quiet, smiling minutes alone. Perhaps that was how Bea did it, night after night of interrupted sleep, because these magic moments waited.

Preston smiled, too. 'Well, since we're up, we might as well have a story.'

He took a deep breath and began, choosing one of his favourite from childhood, an old French tale called *Drake's-tail*, about a little duck who believed one could never have too many friends. He told the tale from memory, his mind half-concentrating on the words while his thoughts wandered down dangerous paths to tread when late-night magic was at its peak.

The journey was coming to a close. Just a couple of days more remained. He was going to miss this; holding Matthew in the carriage, playing with him on the picnic blanket when they stopped, carrying him upstairs and kissing him goodnight in the evenings, watching him sleep.

He finished the tale. 'The people chose the little duck with the loudest quack to be their king and everyone lived happily ever after.' He looked down into Matthew's slack little face—the baby was asleep. His grandmother's estate was an hour's ride away, hardly an insurmountable distance, but it was *apart*—too far to be part of little rituals like this.

Even now, his throat felt a bit thick at the thought of not being there three mornings from now when Matthew would wake, happy and eager for the day, that adorable little smile on his face, that gurgling laugh on his cupid lips. How had that level of attachment happened so quickly? Somehow, this little fellow had grabbed hold of his heartstrings and wouldn't let go.

His gaze drifted towards the bed where Beatrice slept. It would be hard to let them *both* go. It wasn't only Matthew he felt some attachment to, but Beatrice as well. It was only natural. She'd been a friend long before this and it was concern for her as that friend that drew him to her now. She would face challenges at home, albeit different challenges than the ones she was anticipating. He wanted to protect her from that just as he'd wanted to protect her from the louts in the taproom.

Just the remembrance of that big oaf reaching for her, thinking he could lay hands on Beatrice tonight, was enough to start his blood in an angry simmer. He'd wanted to kill the brute, or at the very least cripple him. It had taken discipline to keep himself in check while still meting out the appropriate amount of justice. He'd defended Beatrice with his fists, his knife, as if she had been his wife and Matthew his family.

That was the sanitised version he told himself, but here in the dark, with her sleeping just across the tiny room, he knew it wasn't entirely honest. In the aftermath of the brawl, he saw his ferocity as a sign of how deeply ingrained he'd let the little fantasy become, a fantasy that had been unwittingly nurtured through long days in the carriage, afternoon walks and evening rituals. This was what it meant to be a family man, to glimpse what the private lives of Liam and Jonathon might be like, what *his* future could be like. When Matthew gurgled up at him with waving fists, there were moments he thought he could give up the coastal work if he had to choose between the life of a landed gentleman and the adventure of the coast.

Such realisations were hard to face. He was surprised and perhaps a little shocked the fantasy had got this far, this fast, perhaps helped along by the sight of Beatrice com-

ing around the dressing screen, her dark hair
down, her modest white cotton nightgown not
nearly as modest as it should be in the firelight, outlining the full swell of her breasts,
the lush curve of her hip, the hint of a dark
shadow at her thighs. It was enough to make
his blood heat.

But perhaps the nightgown was just carrying coals to Newcastle. He'd been on the
verge of arousal all night since she'd stripped
him out of his wet things, since Burke had
demanded a pummelling for looking in her
direction, since she'd laid hands on him,
bandaging his injuries. That state of arousal
raised the question: when had Beatrice become more than a friend? He wasn't making
headway here. Wasn't this where his conversation to himself had started? Where did it
end?

In answer to that question, another dangerous rootling began to set down; Bea, Matthew and him at Seacrest, his grandmother's
estate near Shoreham-by-the-Sea, the little
boy learning to toddle in the fields of wildflowers, learning to swim on the beach at
the base of the cliffs. There was another
image, too. This one was more unsettling—

him hugging the little boy tight, kissing Beatrice goodbye and riding off to apprehend an arms dealer or mercenary who'd far prefer gutting him than being hauled before the English justice system. How did a man balance the darkness and the light? How did he leave all he cherished behind to keep up the greater fight for good?

Preston adjusted the sleeping baby in his arms, letting his dreams catch up with his thoughts. His mind had picked out strong words, strong images. Cherished? Kissing Beatrice goodbye? Both implied an intense sense of intimacy, further proof his attachment wasn't to the baby alone. Where had that come from? He supposed he should have been more concerned about the issue of balancing work and family, but in his fantasy, his thoughts seemed to come back to this one instead, perhaps coaxed there by other images like the ones tonight: of Beatrice stripping him out of his clothes, laying hot towels on his wounds, of Beatrice kneeling before him to wrap his ribs, her eyes falling to the vee of his thighs, catching sight of the arousal he couldn't hide. Neither of them had been oblivious to the consequences of her closeness. Beatrice knew full well what a man's body was capable of and the signs.

Perhaps it was for the best this journey was nearly done. Enforced proximity and crisis were strong kindling indeed to fan the flames of attraction and they were beset with both. They'd be home the day after tomorrow, Beatrice and Matthew to Maidenstone, and he to his responsibilities at Seacrest, yet he'd prolong it if he could. One more day with Beatrice and her conversation, her herbs, and competent hands on him, one more day with baby Matthew in his arms... Beatrice and Matthew. A fallen woman and another man's child. Mad thoughts. Hardly what his parents envisioned for him when they thought of him marrying. Preston yawned, his body starting to relax. He'd do better to stay awake at this point. Dawn couldn't be far away, but he was going to lose the battle.

Chapter Six

Beatrice stretched, feeling luxuriously well rested and full. Full? Painfully full. The luxury of awakening under her own power faded quickly, sharply. Her eyes flew open, taking in the morning light. She'd slept through nearly the entire night since she'd fed Matthew. Memories of a whisper came to her. Preston! Her hand went to the other side of the bed, only to find it empty.

She sat up, her heart racing until her eyes found him across the tiny room, slumped in the ratty wing-backed chair, Matthew nestled against his chest. Both of them sound asleep. She could see their chests rising and falling together, sending her pulse fluttering again for different reasons.

She let her body slow, let her eyes drink their fill; Preston's bare and bandaged chest, his hair falling forward over his face, his jaw darkened with rough stubble, her infant son's tiny hand curled around Preston's finger, Preston's head resting against his. Beatrice shut her eyes, making a mental picture of the image, intuitively knowing this was an important moment as much as she knew it was an impossible moment. They were nearly home and that meant the fantasy had to stop. Now. Whatever playacting she'd indulged herself in this week had to end. It would be unhealthy otherwise.

The front of her nightgown dampened. She needed to feed Matthew whether he was awake or not. Bea padded towards her sleeping men and gently dislodged the baby. She settled with him on the bed, knowing physical relief as he began to nurse. She looked down at his little dark head, let the wonder of him sweep her. 'Very soon you'll meet your grandparents,' she whispered her conversation. She spent hours talking to him like this.

'Maidenstone is where I grew up and you'll grow up there, too.' It was hard to believe they'd be home, today if they pushed hard. They *should* push hard. She glanced across at Preston still sleeping, remembering. Today was his birthday. He should be home for it even if she wasn't ready to have this journey end. She couldn't hold him captive for her own selfish reasons. She'd stolen enough time from him. She returned her gaze to her son, continuing her conversation. 'You will love it at Maidenstone.' She suspected she said it more to persuade herself. Truth was, she'd never been so scared to go home in her life, so uncertain of what she'd find and what it would do to her.

She felt more than saw Preston's eyes on her. So, he was awake. And watching her, a thought that invoked a very different response from her than it first had. She'd originally attempted to shock him with her display of maternity, but now, there was something almost sensual about the idea of him watching her, a man not repulsed by a nursing mother as so many high-born gentlemen were. Something seductive, too, in the idea of *wanting* him to watch her. She lifted her eyes to meet his, acknowledging the electric undercurrent for just a fraction of a second. Any longer would be too dangerous. 'I'll change your bandages in just a moment.' Far better to talk about the routine and the tasks that needed performing.

A small smile tinged perhaps with rueful awareness flitted across Preston's mouth. 'Whenever you're ready will be fine.'

They were on the road by nine o'clock. They'd all slept late after the long, muddy day yesterday. But today the sun was out and the roads were passably dry. Travel was good in spite of their later-than-usual start. 'We'll be home by evening if the roads hold.' Bea dropped the window curtain and forced cheerfulness into her tone. The morning miles had sped by and there was no reason to stop for lunch at noon since they'd started late. Maybe if she thought more positively about getting home she'd start to *feel* more positive about it. It was nearly two o'clock. Another five hours would see them at Little Westbury, although they usually stopped for the evening around six o'clock.

'We don't need to rush,' Preston offered, taking a break from playing this little piggy with Matthew's toes. 'There's a nice inn between here and home. We could stop there tonight and then only have a couple of hours in the carriage tomorrow morning. We'd be home in time for luncheon. It would give you the afternoon to settle in.' He paused, having made his argument, before adding hastily, 'Unless you are eager to arrive tonight? Then by all means we can push on.'

Bea shook her head. 'No, it's not that at all. I was only thinking of you.' She hesitated, suddenly shy. 'I haven't forgotten it's your birthday, Preston. I thought you might like to be home with your family.'

'That's very kind, Bea. But I am in no hurry to get home for myself.' Their eyes met and held, an unspoken message passing between them. Neither of them were quite ready for the journey to be over, whatever their reasons. She didn't dare suppose the reasons were the same, because if they were... No. She couldn't even begin to travel down that path of thought any more than she could travel down the path her thoughts had taken last night. Preston was her friend and she'd already made one mistake with a lover. She could hardly afford to make another.

Bea sat back against the squabs, relaxing now that it was settled. She wouldn't face Maidenstone until tomorrow. There was peace in the procrastination. 'What are your plans when you get home? I don't believe you ever said.' That omission struck her as odd considering all the conversations they'd had over the week. 'Are you off on another mission for the government?' Preston operated on special assignment these days since his injury.

'No, not for a while. Cabot Roan comes to trial in June and I'll be needed in London, or at least close at hand.' Preston uncrossed and crossed his legs perhaps in latent restlessness at the thought of being at loose ends, a man of action consigned to merely waiting.

'Will you spend all your time in London, then?' Beatrice tried to probe without looking too needy. In theory, she'd known it was unlikely he'd spend the Season, the busiest part of the year for a man like himself, loitering in Little Westbury. In practice, the idea of him being that far away with no chance of running into him on the street or at a gathering was harder to tolerate.

Preston stretched out his legs, still restless. 'No, I just need to be near enough for a message to reach me. I'll probably split my time between Little Westbury and Seacrest.' She tried to remember who or what was at Seacrest that demanded his attention. For an awful moment, she feared it might be a 'who'. More specifically, it might be a 'she'.

Preston took pity on her. 'My grandmother passed earlier this winter, shortly after May's wedding. She was my mother's mother, if you recall. You would only have met her once or twice. She was fairly reclusive and very old. Even when we were little, I thought she was ancient. But she made old bones. She was ninety-five.' He drew in a deep breath. 'She left me Seacrest and, while it is in decent shape, you can imagine there's some natural negligence when an estate is run for decades by a woman over seventy.' Bea heard the underlying hint of pride when he mentioned the estate.

'I see. Congratulations,' she managed to say, her mind already five steps ahead considering the consequences. A man like Preston would be proud to have something to call his own, even more so to have something to *make* his own. Preston would be cognisant of the responsibility that went with such an estate, not just the running of the estate and overseeing its productivity, but the extenuating responsibility, too, for the land and its people. Both were expensive and time-consuming undertakings. A man with land and money needed a wife. The concept was as English as tea.

Preston would have to marry. Soon. She recalled their earlier conversation. He'd protested he was not ready to marry. But he would, personal preference aside, because family and duty and honour were everything to him. Beatrice reached across the small space of the carriage and squeezed his hand, wanting to reassure him as he'd reassured her countless times this week. She smiled. 'No wonder neither of us is in hurry to get home. Both of our lives are about to change.'

Preston chuckled, his hazel eyes crinkling at the corners. 'Seems like a perfect time, then, to stop for a late-afternoon picnic.'

Neither of them was hungry, but it felt good to be out of the carriage and to have the sun on their faces. Matthew certainly enjoyed the fresh air. Preston romped with him through a field of wildflowers, tossing him high and catching him while he laughed until they were both tired and Preston could no longer ignore the lingering soreness in his ribs. She scolded him for over-exertion as he lay down on the blanket and stretched out, hands behind his head, his jacket and waistcoat off, his shirt open at the throat showing the muscles in his neck.

'You'll be stiff tomorrow for all that.'

'I'll take my chances. I won't have an opportunity to toss the little man tomorrow.' Preston smiled, but there was sadness, too. 'I can't imagine your parents allowing such rough and tumble behaviour.'

'But you'll be able to sleep all night,' Bea tried to joke. There were a lot of things about coming home she couldn't imagine and some things she didn't want to imagine. How would she be treated by the people of Little Westbury, people she'd known all of her life? Would they turn their backs on her? Pretend she didn't exist? She was keenly aware that tomorrow everything would change for them and between them. Whatever this was that had sprung up on the road would go away. They would go back to being old childhood acquaintances joined in friendship through his sister, not these new adults they'd become on their own, together.

'Sleep is overrated,' Preston teased, but he yawned as he said it and his eyes closed, his body drowsy in the sun. Matthew was already asleep on the blanket beside him. Overrated or not, Preston joined him in a nap five minutes later.

Now was her chance. Beatrice rose from the blanket, careful not to disturb Preston or Matthew. She'd been thinking of a birthday gift for Preston all morning. There was no question of shopping for something without Preston wanting to come along and no guarantee of any shop being available or open when they arrived at the inn. Besides, she didn't think any shop-bought gift would adequately suit these circumstances.

At the coach, Beatrice opened her travelling bag and found a spare white cotton petticoat, a silk chemise and her sewing kit. Then she took a short walk through the wildflowers, finding the lavender she'd spied earlier when they were strolling with Matthew. Supplies gathered, she sat down at the blanket to work, cutting fabric and stitching seams while Preston slept, taking pride in the quality of her handiwork. The gift would be simple but neatly done and perhaps Preston would understand the purpose of it; she wasn't looking to give him a 'thing'. She was looking to give him a 'memory'. Something by which he could look back and remember this time on the road, this time out of time before his life changed. Maybe, if she was entirely honest, he would look back and remember her, too, and the way they were in this moment before the future happened.

Chapter Seven

The coach pulled to a stop in the inn yard of the White Horse and Preston drew a deep breath. The future was here—not at the White Horse precisely, but it was *here* in his mind; had been there, with him, all day. It was one of two thoughts that had managed to dominate his mind since the morning. When he wasn't thinking about Bea and Matthew and how much he'd miss them, he was thinking about the future, how today was his twenty-ninth birthday and the clock had started to run.

Preston jumped down and reached up to help Beatrice and the baby, noting with appreciation how much better kept this inn was. He'd known it would be, of course. He'd stayed here before. But there was still some relief in knowing they would be provided for tonight. 'They have the best venison stew,' Preston whispered to Bea. 'And they always have fresh vegetables.'

Bea laughed. 'But do they have any bread pudding?'

Preston smiled. 'Not if I have to fight anyone for it.' It wasn't just Matthew he was going to miss. He was going to miss the teasing banter, the conversation. He was going to miss *Beatrice*. The shock of it hit him rather hard. She'd always been his friend, someone he'd known. She'd always be somewhere in his life. But not like *this*. They'd become close this week, sharing with each other thoughts and feelings not everyone was entitled to know.

Bea squeezed his arm, as if she understood the thoughts running through his head, and maybe she did. Maybe she was thinking them, too. She leaned towards him as he ushered her through the door. 'Just get one room. I'll sleep better tonight knowing you're close. Besides, the place looks busy and I don't want to take up extra rooms when others may also be in need.'

'All right.' He didn't question the choice. He just accepted it. It was an easy choice to accept. It was what he wanted, too. He didn't want to waste a moment of the freedom that remained to him and he wanted to spend it with Beatrice.

They settled into their room quickly. There was little to unpack and they were used to the routine. Preston excused himself for a walk before dinner and to give Beatrice some privacy. But apparently she was just as eager for his company as he was for hers. She was already waiting for him downstairs when he came back from his walk.

She'd changed into a clean dress, a pretty green poplin with a simple white lace collar, very demure. She'd washed, too. He could smell the faint hint of rosewater on her skin and a dash of lavender rinse in her hair. Matthew was bouncy in her arms, reaching for him with pudgy arms as if he knew who he was.

Preston took him from Bea and Matthew laughed. 'He knows who I am,' Preston marvelled. 'It's hard to believe they know so much at such a young age.'

'He can tell emotions, too,' Bea said. 'He seems to pick up on whether I'm happy or sad. It affects him. I always try to be happy.'

A bottle of red wine was already at the table, waiting for them, and Preston grinned. 'Was this your doing?' He had a better idea now of what Bea had been up to while he was on his walk.

She smiled mysteriously. 'Maybe. Don't ask too many questions, it's your birthday, after all. We have to celebrate a little even if you are stuck on the road with me.'

'It's right where I want to be, Beatrice. You gave me the option to go home today and I chose this.' He poured a glass for each of them. He raised his. 'Here's to turning twenty-nine with a good friend in the middle of nowhere.' The last part wasn't quite true. They'd gone around London and were now somewhere between the city and West Sussex. Home was drawing near.

She clinked her glass against his, her eyes solemn. 'Me, too.' Was it just him, or did the air seem charged with an odd electricity tonight? There were a hundred reasons for it: the pressing weight of the burdens he'd find at home, the disappointment of losing Beatrice to the demands of real life, the knowledge that he was only one year away from thirty, the magical age of automatic male adulthood. The list was intense and endless. All those reasons aside, there was no denying that Bea's hair looked shinier, the obsidian depths of her eyes darker, the curve of her mouth, fuller, seductive even. She looked at him over the rim of her wineglass and he wondered—when had Beatrice Penrose become a beautiful woman, a tempting woman? Had that beauty always been there and he simply hadn't noticed?

Surely it must have been. One man knew, a man who had left her, a man who was not nearly good enough to be entitled to such knowledge. The thought roused a strong sense of jealousy and anger, two rather incongruent emotions considering their motivations. He was jealous that one man knew what he did not and angry at that same man for knowing and not appreciating. His rational mind understood those emotions made no sense. If the man who warranted his anger *had* appreciated Beatrice, Preston would not be sitting here now, drinking wine and contemplating thoughts that bordered on illicit.

There was berry pie for dessert with fresh cream, another of Beatrice's arrangements, and then it was time to head upstairs. Matthew was dozing, clearly ready for his bed. Today had been a much better travelling day for the infant than yesterday. When he said as much to Bea as she tucked the child in, she merely smiled. 'Babies need their schedules. Schedules give them security.'

Preston leaned against the stone fireplace, watching her as she sang a soft song to Matthew. It wasn't just babies. Grown men did, too. For a large part of his life, knowing what came next, what was expected, had provided him with security first as a child, and later as he grew, confidence. It was only now that he questioned what the schedule of his life held in store.

Beatrice moved away from the bed with a smile and a finger to her lips. 'He's asleep.' She stopped at her bag and rummaged through it for a moment before giving him her full attention. 'I have something for you.'

'For me? Why?'

She came to him with a laugh. 'It's your birthday, silly. It's customary to give a gift, a small token to commemorate the occasion.' She took his hand and pressed a fist-sized bag into it and curled his fingers around it. 'It's not much.'

Not much? No, quite the opposite. It was everything. Preston lifted the small sachet and inhaled. Lavender, the scent of her hair. The sachet was pretty, too, in its silk-and-cotton bag, tied at the neck with a soft blue ribbon. A suspicion rose. There'd been lavender at the picnic spot today and he'd had a very long nap. 'You made this?' He began to study the tiny stitches, taking in the details.

'Yes. I know it's simple…' She began to apologise, suddenly embarrassed.

He ran a thumb over the silk, thoughtfully. 'While I was sleeping?' He smiled.

'Yes. It was all I could think of.' He'd never seen Bea quite so flustered, a pink blush on her cheeks. Then she took a deep breath and she was Bea in control once more. Her chin went up just a fraction like it had that day in the farmhouse when he'd come for her. She was steeling herself for something. 'I wanted you to have something to remember our trip by.' It was a bold thing to say. He'd been thinking much the same thing all day, but she was the one who'd found the courage to say it. Of course she was. Beatrice Penrose had courage in spades.

'It's a beautiful gift, Bea.' An intimate gift.

He could see her now, sewing secretively by his side while he slept; lavender picked from the fields stuffed into a delicate bag made of cotton from a white petticoat, silk from a chemise and tied with its ribbon; his birthday gift all fashioned from a woman's undergarments, garments worn close to her skin.

A gift could not get any more personal, any more erotic, than that. Although he doubted she'd intended the eroticism. What would she think if he decided to take it that way? Whatever the reasons for it, neither of them was immune to the other; that attraction had been one of the many surprises this journey had held. Tonight, that attraction was running rampant.

The firelight played off her hair, her mouth curving up in a soft smile. These were magic moments, time out of time where nothing else existed but whatever existed between them. What happened in these moments stayed in these moments. If he did not do this now, he knew in his bones he would regret it for ever. Preston raised a hand to cup her cheek, to stroke the long column of her neck with his fingers, his voice husky. 'Beatrice, I have something for you, too.'

* * *

His mouth found hers before there was time to reason, to regret. There was only time to act. It seemed the most natural, intuitive action in the world to give over to the invitation of his mouth, to step into the embrace of his arms, to press her body against the hard planes of his, this body she'd already undressed, already touched. She let her hands twine about his neck, let her mouth open to him, let her tongue answer his in a slow exploration. She could taste the dinner's wine on his lips, could smell the lingering sandalwood of his *toilette*. She let her senses linger in the kiss, instinctively knowing the kiss in itself was complete. This was not a prelude to something else, something more. This was *it*. There was no rush to get through it because there was nothing to rush *to*. He would not lay her down on the bed and thrust into her in hurried anticipation of male completion.

She savoured the kiss, even as it left her hungry. Deep in her core, where instinct prevailed against logic, her body was craving the 'more' even as she knew there wouldn't, *couldn't* be any more—just as she knew there couldn't have been any less. In hindsight it was obvious to see this had been bound to happen. Hadn't her thoughts been toying with just such a thing all week from the first moment she'd started to view him as more than a childhood friend, but as a man in his own right?

She could feel him pull away, the kiss coming to an end and with it the intrusion of reality. She had kissed Preston Worth, her best friend's brother! What had she done? But he'd started it. What had *he* done? What had he been *thinking* to do it? Her eyes held his, her body refusing to step away from him entirely as she put the question to him. 'What was that?'

His hazel eyes burned a hot green undaunted by what they'd done, or lines they might have crossed. 'That was "thank you".' His voice was low, his hand still at the curve of her jaw.

'For what?' Bea's own voice was shaky. She was nowhere in as much control as he was. She was still reeling. When Preston Worth kissed a girl, she felt it to her toes. She was still feeling it, every part of her aware of him even now. His thumb stroked the high plane of her cheek. The fire behind them, crackled with a sudden burst as the logs shifted.

'For today. This is the best birthday I could have asked for.'

Bea gave a rueful smile, well aware of how far short this birthday celebration fell from the ones he was used to. 'There was no cake, no ball, no fancy gifts.' If the Worths were in London there would have been an expensive ball for two hundred of their closest friends. If they'd been in the country, there would have been a day full of games and contests, a fair-like atmosphere, and dancing on the lawn of the Worth estate at dark, perhaps even fire-works. Birthdays were no small thing if you were a Worth.

Preston shook his head. 'I didn't want all that. There's a lot of pressure that goes with such celebrations. You have to live up to ev-eryone's expectations, not just for the day but for the whole year.' He reached for her hand and brought it up between them so that the ring he'd given her caught the light. He chuck-led softly. 'Do you remember the year I got this? I never told anyone, but I was petrified when Grandfather gave me that ring.'

'It was the year you turned eighteen and went off to Oxford.' Beatrice smiled, remem-bering the occasion. 'Your parents ordered a chocolate ganache cake. It was the best thing I'd ever eaten. I had two pieces.' It had been one of the years the Worths had celebrated in the country since all the children were far too young for London. The Worths had let May and her friends attend the party that night. Bea had been thirteen. 'You might have been scared, but you were also proud.'

The words were tinged with the soft glow of memory. She could see him in her mind's eye as he was that night, leaner than the man who stood before her now. There had still been the look of stringy adolescence about him, but he'd had his height, even then.

'Bea, it's not just tonight I'm thankful for. It's the whole week.' He looked down at her hand with the ring on it and she had the sense he was gathering his words. She watched the space between his brows crease in concentration. 'I was sent to "rescue" you, to bring you home—your parents' words, not mine,' he added when she opened her mouth to protest the idea of a 'rescue'. 'But you were the one who did the rescuing, Bea. You listened to me go on about the coastal work, my grandmother's estate, my life in general.'

He made a sound somewhere between a

chuckle and a sigh. 'I don't know when I've ever talked so much about myself. I should probably apologise for it, but I find all I can do is thank you.' He squeezed her hand. 'If I don't tell you tonight, there will be no time tomorrow, no place for it. This week, Bea, with you, I got to be a man, just a man. A man who was entitled to his own thoughts and ideas, a man who didn't have to answer to society's expectations. I haven't been that man for a long time. Sometimes, I wonder if I ever was.'

'You are. You always have been,' Beatrice said the two words with conviction. She'd grown up with Preston, with the Worths. She knew exactly the wonders and worries of being a Worth. She'd lived them with May. The Worths loved their children, but they expected excellence from May and from Preston. It was a different sort of pressure than the pressure the rest of them grew up with. 'Ever since I've known you, you've always known what to do, what was right.' She gave him a teasing smile. 'Do you remember the summer we found the stray pup in the woods behind Evie's house?' She watched his face soften.

'Yes, you and May brought him to me. He was sickly, starving. He could barely walk.'

'We couldn't have been more than nine. We had no idea what to do for him, but you did. I remember, too, how mad your father was when he discovered you'd let the puppy sleep in your room. He demanded you give the dog away,' Bea said slowly. This wasn't a pleasant memory. May had told her how her father had yelled and yelled, and how Preston hadn't backed down because someone in want had needed a champion even though it meant taking on his own father—a man who could only be described as formidable with a capital F.

'Breese turned out to be the best hunting dog Father ever had.' Preston chuckled. 'Father retired him this autumn after the last Westbury Ride. Breese caught the fox, but his leg is acting up again. Father thought it best to end on a high note. Now, Breese gets to lay on the hearth rug in Father's office every day.' Anyone who knew Lord Worth knew how much affection he lavished on that dog *and* how much he liked to brag about his son saving that dog as a puppy.

'I don't think a weak person effects that kind of change, Preston,' Bea said. 'You've always been strong. Just because you've chosen to follow a path recommended by your family doesn't make you weak.'

Preston raised her hand, his voice a low rasp as his lips skimmed her knuckles. 'Thank you, Beatrice.'

'Don't.' She drew her hand away, half-fearful this would lead to another kiss.

A question flitted across his expression. 'Why?' He reached for her, but she stepped back with a shake of her head.

'We've already taken a great chance with the first kiss. With another one, we might ruin everything, change everything,' Beatrice cautioned, hoping he heard the unspoken message: that she'd liked this week, too, that it had meant something to have this time with him, but that time was over. Kissing Preston Worth was not something the real world would allow. She'd kept him from the real world long enough. If not for her, he'd be at Seacrest or in London getting on with his life.

Even if he were eligible for her consideration, there were her rules to consider. Men were dangerous, even well-meaning ones. Passions were dangerous when indulged in real time. 'Everything changes tomorrow, anyway,' Beatrice argued gently. Why invest in something that would end so quickly? Something they couldn't keep?

But Preston wanted to challenge those assumptions. 'Maybe not everything. Maybe we can keep this.'

'Maybe,' Beatrice acceded, not wanting to fight, but also not wanting to make false promises. She saw the hope and the reticence in his eyes, too. Despite his willingness to argue her conclusions, neither of them was convinced this fragile, undefined something-more-than-friendship they'd created would survive what waited for each of them in Little Westbury. In fact, Beatrice reflected, they were so sure it wouldn't, they were taking great care to say their goodbyes now while they still had the privacy in which to do so honestly.

Chapter Eight

⁓⁓⁓

It had been best to say goodbye last night, Beatrice reflected, staring out the nursery window at the empty front drive three storeys below. Preston's coach had driven away hours ago and the stilted, horribly formal goodbye he'd given her had been devoid of any of the emotion that had been present last night. There certainly hadn't been any more kisses. There had been, however, that brief moment in the carriage before he'd opened the door when he'd given her a reassuring smile with the words, 'You're home, Bea. It will be all right.' There had also been the furtive squeeze of his hand when he'd helped her down.

Despite Preston's acts of covert support, the whole episode of arriving had been awkward from start to finish. Her parents had been waiting at the steps to greet her; either because propriety demanded it and they didn't want the servants to gossip about giving their daughter a poor reception or because they were genuinely glad to see her. It was hard to know. She'd been an embarrassment to them when she'd left last summer. They'd been eager to have her far away before her pregnancy had begun to show.

To ease the awkwardness, there'd been Matthew to show off immediately. She'd had him in her arms so there'd be no shuttling him off, basket and all, to the nursery and pretending he didn't exist. It had gone better than expected. Her father had even smiled at his grandson and her mother had cooed, saying, 'He has dark hair like you, Bea. He reminds me so much of you when you were a baby.'

But Bea thought she knew what was going through her mother's mind: *Thank goodness he looks like her. It will cut down speculation on who the father is.*

She could already predict how her mother would want things to progress; pretend that the birth was some sort of immaculate conception, that a father had not been requisite. She might even manage to convince people.

It was amazing what society believed when it wanted to.

After Matthew had been properly adored, there'd been the required conversation over tea. Her father asked Preston how the journey had been, making mundane enquiries over the roads and the inns and the general state of travel. When the clock chimed two, precisely a half-hour after their arrival, Preston rose and made his very proper goodbyes. He shook hands with her father, gave her and her mother a short bow and was gone.

Truly gone, a fact emphasised by the fading sound of carriage wheels on gravel, and it nearly undid her. Her throat felt thick. Beatrice drew a shaky breath and hugged her son. She was home at Maidenstone, surrounded by servants and family, people she'd known her entire life, and she'd never felt more alone.

Lord, she missed Preston. Bea reached for another stack of cloth nappies and began to fold them. It helped that her hands had something to do. Matthew was sleeping, worn out from the afternoon, but she wasn't ready to leave him. Her old room was waiting for her the next floor down. That would have to be addressed. She couldn't be that far from her son. Either she would need to move up here or he would have to move down there.

The nursery door opened softly and her mother slipped inside, glancing around for Matthew. 'Is he asleep?' she whispered delicately.

'Yes, he's in the crib in the other room.' Bea nodded towards the antechamber where the little beds were. There was a crib and her old bed in there. It was too small for her now, but perhaps a larger one could be brought up.

'Wonderful.' Her mother smiled hesitantly. She'd been good with Matthew downstairs, wanting to hold the baby and exclaim over him. It made Beatrice hopeful that perhaps their relationship could be repaired. Her mother had struggled with her pregnancy, torn between concern for her daughter and the social consequences this event would have for all of them, while dealing with her own sense of betrayal—that her daughter had done something without her permission or approval or even awareness until it had been too late.

Her mother glanced at the pile of clothing on the table. 'You don't need to do the laundry, Beatrice. There's a maid for that and I dare say she'd love to have something to do. She's been sitting around twiddling her thumbs all afternoon.' It was a reprimand, a reminder that she wasn't in Scotland any more. She was a lady of good breeding and that came with expectations.

'I don't mind. I like taking care of Matthew myself,' Beatrice argued gently. She didn't want to pick a fight with her mother so soon. No doubt, there would be plenty of opportunity later for quarrelling, and over much more significant issues than folding nappies.

'Well, you're home now. I am sure you'll get used to everything again. After all, nothing has changed.' Her mother smiled determinedly as if saying the words was all it took to make the statement true. That was one remark Beatrice could not let pass.

'Nothing, Mother?' Bea pressed the issue in soft tones. Her mother's powers of denial bordered on astonishing. Bea wondered how long the denial would last when Matthew squalled in the middle of the night, or when she had to admit to all of Little Westbury her daughter had brought a baby home, but no husband.

Her mother offered another tremulous smile and Bea felt guilty for pushing the issue. Bringing her home was going to be difficult for all of them, not only internally as a family; they'd all have to learn to live with each other as adults. She had a baby. They couldn't pretend she was a child any more. It would also be hard socially. Her scandal would taint her mother and father as well.

'We wanted you and the baby with us.' That was all her mother said, uncomfortable with shows of emotion. It would be the closest she'd come to saying, 'I love you.' Her parents had that in common with the Worths. Neither were great demonstrators of affection and yet the affection for their children was there.

Her mother waited expectantly. Beatrice knew what her mother wanted to hear: that she was glad to be home, that she'd missed them, and she had, but Bea couldn't say the words yet. She missed Scotland because Scotland was easier. Scotland was known. She knew what to expect of life there. Preston was right, though, Scotland was only easier because her acceptance was enabled by a lie. Here at Maidenstone, she'd have to live with the truth. When Bea said nothing, her mother forged on to another, more dangerous topic.

'You'll probably need new dresses. The draper has pretty prints in for summer.' Her mother's eye roved discreetly over her figure. 'You've recovered well, darling. With the right styling it will hardly look like you've had a child.' Bea did not like the sound of that.

'Perhaps Evie could alter some of the gowns I already have. I don't need anything fancy for summer in Little Westbury,' Bea countered. She doubted she'd be going out much anyway. No one would be in a hurry to entertain a fallen woman.

'If she's not too busy. She and Dimitri are going up to London in a few weeks for Liam Casek's ceremony.' Her mother smiled as she pointed out, 'Evie's a married woman now—she has a home and a husband to take care of. All of you girls have grown up,' she said, referring to the families of her friends. 'First Claire and Jonathon, Evie and her prince, May and her Irishman. There's only Preston left and he'll be sure to marry soon now that he has Seacrest.' She slanted Bea a coy look. 'He's ripe for the plucking. He's watched his friends marry and he seemed quite taken with the baby today. You can always tell when a man is ready to settle down. It was the same with your father.'

Bea would have been positively horrified at her mother's insinuations if she didn't know better. For once, her mother was wrong. She knew something her mother didn't. 'I think Preston is rather wedded to his job for the government just now.' Bea put a stack of nappies on a shelf, feeling very smug.

Her mother persisted, undaunted. 'Well, he will have to rethink that dedication now that he has the estate to consider. It needs a strong hand *and* a wife if it's to be run properly. You'll see. He'll marry within the year.'

Bea doubted it. 'Yes, we'll see,' she offered neutrally, glad her back was turned so that her mother couldn't see her expression. The thought of Preston marrying raised complex emotions. She suspected those emotions would not have been raised a week ago. She would lose her friend when he married. Thankfully, it wasn't something she had to contemplate. Preston wasn't ready yet to resign himself to the quiet country life. That was some small consolation. She could have him as her friend just a while longer. But that day would come. Once he married, he'd be beyond her reach. No decent husband carried on a close friendship with an unmarried female friend and most certainly not with an unwed mother.

She ignored the other subtle implication underlying her mother's comments: that *she* might set her cap at Preston while he was 'vulnerable'. Perhaps even use Matthew as bait. Such a thing was unthinkable. Preston was an ambitious man and, as such, he could not settle for a ruined wife and another man's child the way a quiet, older, retired country gentleman might be persuaded to do.

She would absolutely not encourage Preston to stray from his ambitions. Yet one more reason she should be glad there'd been no further kisses. If there had, Preston might feel obliged to do the honourable thing, especially if gently pushed in that direction by her parents or his.

From the other room, Matthew began to wake. She went to him and lifted him from the crib, a suspicion taking seed. *Had* her parents sent Preston after her on purpose? Had they hoped something might come of their time on the road? Had they hoped he might offer for her out of respect for their families' long-standing relationship and pity for her 'desperate' situation?

A sick feeling formed in her stomach. She thought of the kiss last night. Attraction had been there beneath the surface, for her. She'd assumed it had been there for him as well, although neither of them had admitted it. Now she wondered if she'd misread him. Had it been planned? Had her parents actually asked him for his protection, put the circumstances to him in blunt terms?

Would you consider marrying our daughter and making her decent?

Beatrice cringed. She hoped that wasn't the case. Preston would be too much a friend and a gentleman to tell her. But surely the Preston she'd come to know this past week would not allow himself to be forced into an arrangement he didn't want. He was far too determined to bend to another's dictates. If he was thinking of defying his father in order to stay with his government work, he would certainly not bend to hers on the matter of marriage.

Bea sat in a rocker and undid her bodice. If her parents had expected anything, they would have been disappointed today. Preston had left this afternoon without a word in that vein, proving that he was very much his own man. He would decide for himself. She wanted him to be free, to be happy. So why was she unexpectedly sad that he was? She had no claim on him. Preston was free to choose the direction his life took next.

Chapter Nine

'You are the talk of London, Preston, my boy.' His father beamed at him from across the polished mahogany desk of the estate office. 'Your name came up several times when the posting to Greece was discussed. What do you think about that?'

What Preston thought was that he'd been home precisely seven hours and already he was wishing to be back on the road.

'What I wouldn't give to be a few decades younger,' his father went on with a chuckle. 'Are you not pleased? Isn't this the sort of opportunity you're looking for? A chance to travel and avoid your mother's matchmaking attempts a little longer?'

Was it? Preston had to wonder, not only at the answer to that question, but also why he was so reticent to give one. It certainly gave him a chance to travel, to represent his country's interests and to serve as he'd not been able to in the military. The Foreign Office wanted to appoint him as a special envoy to the newly formed Greek state in order to better assess the situation with the Ottomans. But now? 'Things' had changed in the last two weeks, although he was hard pressed to put that change into words.

'There's Grandmother's estate to see to,' Preston put forward. 'It needs attention if it's to be viable. Grandmother was not interested in the modern inventions.' It was a tangible aspect of that change, one perhaps his father could empathise with.

His father considered this for a moment. 'Your sense of responsibility does you credit. No one needs an answer right now and no one expects you to leave before September. You can give the office your answer when you go up to London after you've had a few weeks to think it over. You'll have most of the summer at Seacrest to arrange for a competent estate manager and get your plans underway.' His father winked. 'Who knows who you might meet abroad? Perhaps the pretty daughter of a diplomat.'

Preston nodded and smiled, giving the impression of enjoying the idea. In truth, he wasn't sure he wanted to go abroad, after all. This posting would keep him away for a couple of years, depending on what he found in Greece. His thoughts flashed to Bea and Matthew, how tiny Matthew had looked in her arms this afternoon at the Penroses'. The baby would be a precocious three-year-old, walking, talking, running, when Preston saw him next, and the little boy would have no memory of the man who'd held him for hours in a carriage, who'd rocked him to sleep and tossed him in the air. He didn't like how that felt.

'I have promises to keep here,' Preston began, trying to find words for his new feelings, feelings he hadn't quite sorted through yet on his own. Those promises started with Beatrice and Matthew. He'd told her the boy would grow up with uncles and here he was faced with breaking that promise hours upon his return. Dimitri and Liam would be here, of course. But that wasn't enough. They weren't him. With an intensity that surprised him,

Preston realised he wanted to be the favourite 'uncle'.

His father rose from behind the desk and went to the decanter, pouring both of them a brandy. 'A belated birthday drink, my son. You've earned it.' The family had celebrated quietly at dinner and Liam and May had come over. 'You did a great service to the Penroses these past weeks under difficult circumstances.'

He handed Preston a glass, his eyes serious. 'Now that their daughter is home, I think we've kept any promises that were required of us. I am sure it will feel good to get back to your regular life, Preston.' His father smiled as he said it, but Preston heard the warning hidden in the division of his father's language: 'their daughter', 'we've kept promises required of *us*'. His father had decided the Worths would distance themselves from the Penroses to some degree. If that distance did not include all the Worths, it certainly included him. Preston pushed for further clarification with a slight, enquiring raise of his brow and his father gave it.

'I would not want to give them false hope in a particular direction.' His father took a long swallow of his brandy, perhaps to give his implication time to make itself clear.

'The Penroses are our friends. Beatrice is *my* friend.' Preston mirrored his father, taking a long swallow to let *his* implications sink in.

'We *have* helped them.' His father's tone was terse. 'And we'll continue to help them. May will see to it that Beatrice will be surrounded by friends.' Ah, so that was how it would be. May would get that honour. May who was expendable and safe because she was married to a knight of the realm who supported lost causes and charity cases.

'There's only so much we can do, Preston,' his father warned with a cryptic look. 'The damage is done. Whatever the details, Beatrice Penrose has a child without a father. Her opportunities will be limited even with our help. Not just any man will want to take her on.'

Preston bristled at the classification. He didn't like hearing Beatrice dismissed in such terms. 'All the more reason to stay, I'd say.'

'All the more reason to *leave*, if I were you.' His father took a final swallow of brandy and put his glass down hard, the truth spilling out. 'You've a kind heart, Preston. You are a man who wants to serve others and that is admirable. I don't want the Penroses preying on that in their desperation to snare their daughter a husband and respectability.'

Preston almost choked on the last of his drink. 'I beg your pardon? You think I want to marry Beatrice Penrose?' Dear Lord, how did his father do it? Reading minds like a fortune teller? Had his feelings been that obvious? How could they have been when he wasn't even sure of those feelings himself? Certainly the idea had crossed his mind, but as a mental exercise only. And, in his opinion, quite a natural one after spending so much time together.

'I believe a part of you thinks you *should* marry her,' his father answered with a solemnness that said he wasn't joking. His father had thought long and hard about this avenue. 'You've been friends, known each other your entire lives. You get on well enough, our families have history together. It would likely be an amiable enough companionship as marriages went. You'd certainly make her respectable. No one would whisper about the boy's parentage if he were cloaked in the Worth honour and, at the risk of sounding cras but practical, Miss Penrose has already proven she has a passionate side. You could hedge your bets securely that other aspects of marriage would be enjoyable enough.' His father eyed him speculatively, perhaps wondering if anything untoward had indeed occurred on a journey that had taken the longer end of the standard travelling time.

Preston fixed his father with a hard stare. He tried not to disagree overtly with his father whenever possible, but *this* could not pass. 'You slander us both with such comments.' He used the steel tones he relied on when facing down armed smugglers.

'Don't blame me for being honest. A man must consider all things. For ever is a long time.'

'It is indeed, which is why I am in no hurry to marry anyone, Beatrice Penrose included.'

'Then you'll take the appointment to Greece?' his father pressed.

'I thought I didn't have to decide tonight?' Preston replied drily. He saw the appointment in a new light. His parents, who up until now had preferred he'd leave government service and retire to his estate, were now keen proponents of a new position that would take him deep into the Continent for possibly years. It was a very telling insight as to how concerned they were about the 'threat' posed by Beatrice Penrose.

His father clapped him on the shoulder, with forced bonhomie. 'Of course. *Nothing* has to be determined tonight. You've just returned home, after all.' But even the attempt at reconciliation carried a double meaning. Neither Greece *nor* Beatrice Penrose needed to be decided.

His father poured them another glass. 'You've spent seven days on the road with an attractive woman and a cute child in a very emotional situation. It's all still very close for you. Don't think I don't know. I remember how it was.' His father leaned back in his chair. 'The road makes for interesting companions. But the road also makes illusions, things that can't survive in the real world. I once spent two years of my life in the Caribbean with a fellow named Edgars, at least that's what he told me his name was. I don't know if it was true, don't know if it mattered. He had my back and I had his. We were running Grandfather's shipping business in Barbados, sailing cargo ships, avoiding pirates, outrunning storms to make deliveries. Heady times.' He raised his glass, toasting remembrances. Preston waited for the lesson. His father didn't tell stories, he told parables. There was always a lesson, always a reason. 'Edgars must have saved me a hundred times from a cutlass slash, or from being washed overboard or from any of the other thousand things that can go wrong in the Caribbean. Dangerous place. And I did the same for him at least as often. I thought with experiences like that, we'd be friends for ever. After all, a man who saves your life is not easily forgotten. I came home in 1791. Married your mother. The last letter I had from Edgars was in ninety-two. I haven't heard from him in thirty years.'

His father leaned forward. 'The point is, whatever you think you feel whether it's out of duty or emotion, *will* pass.'

Preston nodded neutrally, letting his thoughts make the dangerous comparison between this night and last night. He and Beatrice had talked of change, knowing it would come. But, oh, how quickly! And in ways unexpected. Three weeks ago, he'd been looking for a reason to leave, to seek out adventure. His parents had been the ones wanting him to stay. His grandmother's inheritance had been an albatross about his neck, limiting his opportunities. Now, he welcomed it because of the excuse it provided him. He had a reason to stay that went far beyond his grandmother's estate and his father's warning of disapproval.

His father was wrong on all accounts. Beatrice wasn't looking to snare him. Beatrice needed him as a friend, all kissing aside. He'd promised her he wouldn't desert her. He'd keep that promise starting tomorrow.

Malvern Alton had broken another promise. It wasn't the first and certainly wasn't going to be the last promise he'd break. But it might be the most dangerous. He was in a whorehouse and he couldn't pay. Malvern Alton slid his gaze carefully around the room, taking in the woman behind the desk and the two beefy bouncers standing on either side of her. The message was clear: woe betide the man who came between a whore and her money, especially when that whore was Madam Rose at London's prestigious House of Flowers. Malvern Alton held his hands out to his sides in a placating gesture of surrender, his gaze split between the brothel madam and the two thickset men who bracketed her, one of them thumping a blackjack against his palm with authority. His bill was due and he hadn't the blunt to pay it—not just this bill, but his other bills as well: the tailor, the club, the boxing salon and who knew what else. Collectors were starting to show up at his door. He wasn't worried. He would survive this, of course. He always did. He was lucky that way. He'd just prefer to survive with his teeth intact.

Alton offered Madam Rose a charming smile, showing every straight, pearly-white tooth in his dental treasury. 'Is this really necessary, my dear? How long have we known each other? More than a decade. I've been coming here since I was sixteen.' A darling dark-haired girl named Violet had been his first, a birthday gift from his uncles. 'You've always been paid—'

'By your father,' Madam Rose interrupted with the steely stare of a determined businesswoman. 'Your father has made it clear you've been cut off.'

'A temporary inconvenience soon to be rectified.' Malvern waved the news off as if it were nothing. 'Fathers and sons quarrel all the time.' It wasn't 'nothing', however, and Madam Rose seemed to know it, too. But it wasn't entirely a lie either. The situation *could* be rectified quickly enough if he'd accede to his father's wishes: marry a wealthy girl and receive the portion left to him by a distant great-aunt, a portion that he'd left unclaimed for six months out of an unwillingness to leg-shackle himself. He'd argued he didn't want to choose a bride until the Season when there'd be more selection. But now the Season was here and he was out of both time and money.

'Hopefully it will be rectified sooner rather than later.' Madam Rose made a gesture and the two men advanced from around the desk.

'I haven't any money tonight. Tomorrow.' Now, he was starting to panic. He didn't relish being beaten up and thrown out into the alley with nothing on but his shirt and trousers. The rest of his clothes—*expensive* clothes—were upstairs in Daisy's room, left behind when he'd been hauled down and called to account. If Madam Rose threw him out, he wouldn't get those clothes back.

'Turnabout is fair play. Pay up or take your punishment the way you meted out your pleasure tonight.' Madam Rose held firm. 'You hit one of my girls.'

Not hard enough, apparently. He'd like to hit the little bitch again. This was all Daisy's fault. If she hadn't screamed, none of this would have happened. Who would have thought there was something such as 'too rough' for a whore? That was their job, wasn't it? But Daisy had given herself airs when he'd brought out the riding crop and now he was standing in Madam Rose's office half-dressed and being forced to discuss money, of all things. It was disgusting, really. Madam Rose was showing her poor breeding by insisting on this degrading conversation. A gentleman never discussed money. It was a plebeian topic for the masses.

Alton spread his hands and opted for a smile he hoped was sincere. 'I *am* sorry about Daisy. I thought she understood our game.' It wasn't enough. The first punch took him in the stomach, knocking the wind from him as he doubled over.

Madam Rose raised a dyed dark eyebrow, unconcerned about the violence. 'I thought you understood *our* game. You play, you pay.' The second punch took him in the jaw, rattling his precious teeth. He couldn't afford to take a third.

'Please!' Alton gasped, finally desperate. 'You will be paid, you'll see. I am set to marry. A rich girl.' He gasped out the lie, word by painful word.

'Who?' Madam Rose made a gesture and the two thugs backed off. 'I need a name or my men need blood.'

Alton racked his brain, trying to think of a name she'd buy. It couldn't be anyone Madam Rose could actually research. That meant no one from London. He needed a girl from the country. Ah, the dark-haired virgin he'd fooled around with last winter on his repairing lease. What was her name?

He'd stalled too long. Madam Rose didn't believe him. The men were advancing again. 'Beatrice Penrose.' The words rushed out. He was fairly sure he had the name right. She'd talked and talked about science. He'd kissed her the first time to shut her up.

'Beatrice Penrose?' Madam Rose looked sceptical. 'When is the happy occasion? I hadn't heard.'

'June,' he blurted out.

She seemed to consider this before delivering her verdict. 'Very well, you have until June to settle your debt. I will expect payment plus fifteen per cent on your wedding day.' She gave him a cold smile. 'May I be the first to offer you felicitations?'

He tugged at his shirttails, trying to gather what dignity he had left; his jaw throbbed, his stomach hurt and he hadn't a pair of boots. 'I'll just gather my things,' he said.

Madam Rose shook her head. 'I think I'll keep them as collateral, Mr Alton. You can have them back in June.'

Great. Now he'd have to walk to his rooms barefoot and half-dressed. But he could stand a little humiliation if it meant his teeth were intact. Pride had its price after all—a price that would involve a short trip to Little Westbury in the near future to claim a bride.

Alton tried to concentrate on the money as he made the cold walk home in the dark. He'd marry the botany-spouting shrew and claim both fortunes: hers and his great-aunt's. He'd tuck her away in the country, maybe get a few whelps on her because he was definitely having sex with her. She had to earn her keep. After that, he'd not have to think much about her. It wasn't a bad trade. He'd make money on this marriage at the very least. In the final analysis, what did marriage mean for a man anyway? He was still free to be much as he'd always been except he'd have a dress bill to pay and a few more social obligations to attend. All in all, he supposed it could always be worse.

Despite the cold, he started to whistle a bawdy song—'Courting Leggy Peggy'. In a week he'd be in Little Westbury and this cold inconvenience would be over.

Chapter Ten

The loud, joyous sound of voices raised in singing as they travelled down the drive to Maidenstone brought Beatrice out front the next afternoon. She shielded her eyes against the sun with a hand and laughed in recognition. They were coming! Her friends were coming! And making a gay show of it, too. There was Evie dressed in a daffodil yellow aboard her chestnut mare riding beside Dimitri, the handsome dark-haired Russian prince who had swept her off her feet this autumn. In the rear in a bright blue riding habit was May alongside Liam on his prized horse, Charon.

Her gaze drifted over them all, gladness in her heart. They had come. They had not deserted her. It was one thing to stand by her when they had nothing to lose as wallflowers and when her secret was not yet known. It was another entirely to stand with her when there was a baby she couldn't hide and they had so much more to risk. They were married women of social status now. But it was at the head of the column where her gaze lingered. Preston rode there, dark head bare, head thrown back as he sang, his soul on display as he embraced the warm spring day.

Had it only been a day since he'd ridden away? It seemed an age. She'd missed him last night when she'd tucked Matthew into his crib for the first time and when she'd gone to her own bed, Matthew just a few feet away, the crib having been moved into her room. But Preston wasn't. The emptiness of the space in the bed beside her was missed as much as the nightly ritual of kissing Matthew on the forehead.

Her hand went to the small bump beneath her bodice where his ring hung on a chain about her neck. She'd meant to give it back yesterday, but there'd not been a chance. Now, having it near was like having him close and there was a certain, illogical reluctance to wanting to give it back. 'Preston! You've brought me company.' Bea sailed down the

curving front stairs to greet them, hands out-
stretched, throat suddenly choked with emotion as Preston swung off his horse and took
her hands. This was so much more than bringing company. It was bringing acceptance. It
was an unwritten rule of the *ton* that the best
way to protect a woman's reputation was
to cloak her in one's own. Her friends had
brought themselves today and their reputations. Everyone who heard them, who saw
them, would know they stood with her.

Preston squeezed her hands, smiling at her,
his eyes full of a thousand questions: *Are you
all right? How was last night? Were your parents good to you?* And, if she read it aright,
I missed you.

'Let me make introductions.' He gestured
to the tall man who'd helped Evie dismount.
'This is Dimitri Petrovich, formerly of Kuban.
I don't know if you met last summer.'

Dimitri Petrovich came forward and took
her hand, bending with consummate grace,
his deep brown eyes never leaving hers, and
brushed his lips over her knuckles. 'We met
once, briefly. You were shopping with Evie, if
I recall correctly.' He nodded to where Liam
Casek and May stood. 'You already know

Liam?' It was a neatly done segue to include the others. Bea thought it likely such social graces and inclusiveness came naturally to this confident prince.

Bea took the opening and moved towards Liam. 'Dear May and Liam, how good it is to see you.' She hugged May tight before turning to Liam. Between May and Liam, Matthew had been born safely in the little cottage in Scotland. She owed these two people more than any two people in the world. She moved to hug Liam, reaching up on her toes to do so. He was as tall as Preston. 'I hear you are to be knighted.'

Liam laughed. 'In a few weeks, in London.' He reached for May's hand and squeezed, making no mistake about where his affections lay. 'It *all* still feels like a dream.' No one looking at him could doubt he meant more than the impending knighthood felt like a dream. May Worth was the sum of his world, just as Evie was the sum of Dimitri's, no matter how attentive Dimitri's gaze was.

Bea's heart gave a happy-sad lurch. Her friends had found good men, perhaps, as they liked to think, empowered by her call to action. She was alone now. She'd helped them find happiness, but had not been able to claim that same happiness for herself. Preston came up behind her, the groom having gathered the horses. 'I don't suppose your cook has made any of those pink macaroons I like so much?'

Bea gave him a teasing smile. 'You know she always bakes them on Wednesdays. Is that why you came? For my macaroons?' She made a mock pout. 'I thought you might have come to see me.'

Preston grinned and something akin to the crackle of lightning sizzled between them, white, hot and jolting. Proof that the intimacy of the road had not been entirely quenched. 'Maybe I came for both. I've been telling Liam and Dimitri all about those macaroons. And you,' he added after a short, teasing hesitation. 'Shall we show everyone out to the back veranda?'

He took her arm, looping it through his, and she felt the comfort of his touch as well as the *frisson* of awareness, of attraction that had sprung up since that first day in Scotland.

It was hard not to notice what an easy trio of couples they made as they took tea in the sun, exchanging news and hearing about May's wedding. Bea found it too easy to engage in an extension of the fantasy that had formed during the journey home: this could be her life—her life and Preston's, the third couple in the group. This was what it would be like to enjoy the summers of their adulthood in Little Westbury, surrounded by their friends.

The nursemaid, Annie, brought Matthew down from his nap to show off and the sensation intensified. Preston took him first, Matthew giggling in recognition of his friend, before being passed off to the others who doted on him in turns. 'He's grown!' May exclaimed, eyes shining as she held the baby she'd delivered in November. 'Look, Liam, he's smiling at me.' The comment elicited a laugh and a quiet look between Bea and Preston.

'What?' May insisted, catching the glance.

'Nothing.' Bea smiled.

'No, it's something,' May protested. 'I saw that look.'

'It's just that babies sometimes smile when they pass gas,' Preston informed her.

'Are you saying Matthew looked at me and passed gas?' May's green eyes challenged her brother's in good-humoured sibling rivalry.

'Yes.' Preston grinned in response. 'That's

exactly what I'm saying. Now, give Liam the baby before you drop him like Grandmother's china, which I am sure you recall with shattering precision.'

May huffed and passed the baby over to Liam, giving her brother a stare. 'You are never going to let me forget that.'

'No.' Preston laughed and Bea's heart was full, wanting to catch every nuance of the moment; of being home, of sitting in the sun with her friends, of watching them with Matthew, all of them loving, none of them condemning. Maybe it had been the right choice to come home, after all.

'Thank you, everyone.' Beatrice meant it sincerely as she saw her guests to their horses later. Tea was over and Matthew was waiting to be fed. There was more she wanted to say as she hugged Evie and May goodbye, but her throat was thick again. She hoped they knew what was in her heart. It had been a glorious afternoon, a perfect way to complete her homecoming. Certainly, there were still hurdles to overcome. She hadn't had to face the society of Little Westbury yet. But for now, this was enough, *more* than enough.

She said goodbye to Preston last. 'Thank you, most of all,' she said in quiet tones just for him, 'for arranging this.'

'It was nothing. Everyone was coming anyway.' He smiled and moved to mount.

Bea put a hand on his arm. 'Wait, I forgot to give you your ring back yesterday.'

He shook his head and swung up before she could argue. 'Keep it for now. I'll get it when I come over tomorrow.'

'You're coming tomorrow?' She laughed up at him, a part of her already excited at the prospect of seeing him again and he hadn't even left yet. 'Why? We won't have the macaroons tomorrow,' she teased.

Preston leaned over his saddle, green eyes sparking. 'Precisely. I want to prove I didn't come for the macaroons alone.' He straightened and twisted to look behind him at the column of riders. 'All right, everyone, the hunting song again on three!' He kicked his horse into motion and they were gone, singing as they'd come, loud and merry, before she could ask the question he provoked: if he hadn't come for the macaroons, what had he come for?

Certain answers posed themselves naturally: for friendship? For honour? For *her* honour? Other more complicated answers rose: had he come for all of these or something more? That was the kiss talking, the kiss responding to the lightning sizzle between them. Such a response was dangerous. It was precisely the reason she had rules. Not just for her own protection, but for others' too. She couldn't let anyone guess at the fantasy in her mind; not her mother, who would do heaven knew what with that knowledge, not Preston, who might feel obligated to act on it. She could have his friendship, but nothing more, no matter what attraction lay between them.

Preston was as good as his word. He came the next day and the one after and the one after that until a week of visits had piled up between them, a week of afternoon walks with or without Matthew, depending on naps, a week of teas in the extraordinary sunshine as spring arrived at last after a very late start. Most of all, a week of talks. Perhaps because of her status as a non-debutante, or his status as an old family friend, they were allowed to be on their own, always with an open door or within sight of the house, but there was privacy to talk, to carry on the conversations they'd begun on the road. She craved those visits, craved catching sight of him coming down the drive on his horse. That worried her. Having rules was one thing. Enforcing them on a stubborn mind that wanted to pursue another course of action was another entirely.

She was coming to depend on him, his presence, and it couldn't last for all sorts of reasons. Some of those were practical; he would go away some day soon. London called and there was his estate to manage. Some of those reasons were less practical, and *all* of them could be traced back to that imprudent kiss. It had given her irrational hope and illogical possibilities which had fuelled the question: what did these visits mean? If they meant something, anything at all, could she continue to risk them without jeopardising her rules and something more?

She very much feared if she *did* allow them to continue, she might convince herself she was falling for Preston Worth—a most dangerous conclusion indeed. It would ruin their friendship and that was just the beginning. It might even ruin the longstanding friendship between their families. She was not for him.

She was not for anyone. She'd made that decision months ago. But it was hard to stick to that decision now that she knew him; the thoughts of him, the touch of him. How did one set aside ambrosia after only one taste?

Even now as they walked the perimeter of the gardens, she caught herself watching him in a conversation, her eyes going to the sensual, thin line of his mouth, remembering the press of those lips on hers, the feel of his tongue in her mouth, to say nothing of the habit she'd acquired of undressing him with her gaze, her mind remembering the smooth planes of his torso, all that lean muscle and strength marred incongruently by the one scar that had nearly killed him. Her mind remembered far too often how his body had responded to her touch, how it had quickened. And hers, too.

'You're a million miles from here, Bea.' Preston was staring at her. They'd stopped walking and she had the distinct impression he'd been silent a long while.

'I'm sorry.' She'd been caught out. She might as well brazen it out. 'I was just wondering what we were doing.'

'Walking?' Preston hazarded.

She didn't let him play obtuse. 'The visits,' she prompted.

'You need me.' Preston's answer was blunt without a hint of arrogance.

Bea laughed. He sounded very much as he had when they were growing up, always there to play the hero when one of the girls needed rescuing. 'Like I did when I was eleven and locked myself in the attic during hide and seek and couldn't get out?' The memory hung in the air, almost tangible, each of them recalling how Preston had picked the lock instead of going to her father for help, which would have resulted in all of them getting into trouble for rough play in the house.

She gave him a soft, sad smile. 'I'm not eleven any more, Preston. I can fight some of my battles without you. You've done enough and I am grateful for that. Besides, I think your work here is through. I'm having tea with the ladies tomorrow.' She tried to infuse the announcement with brightness. A successful tea would officially mark her acceptance into society, perhaps a chance to send Preston off. If the ladies took to her, he wouldn't need to play nursemaid, a bittersweet thought. She would miss him, but it would be for the best. Proximity bred all nature of perils.

'Nervous?' Preston raised an eyebrow in query. 'Don't be, they'll love you as they always have. I am sure of it.'

'But how could it possibly be all right?' She wanted to argue, to air all of her concerns. She had violated one of society's most important beliefs in chastity before marriage and she'd been caught.

Preston shook his head. 'Don't overthink things, Bea.' He looked down at his feet and then past her shoulder, pushing a hand through his hair. She had the fleeting impression that something about the tea or about what she'd said had made him edgy. Then the impression was gone, replaced by a boyishly conspiratorial smile as he leaned close to her, teasing. 'Shall I call tomorrow afterwards and we can talk it all through? You can tell me everything and we can toast your success.'

Bea gave a soft laugh, trying to imagine this very masculine man gossiping with a flowery teacup in hand. But no matter how incongruous the image might be, he would do that. She knew it. Because he was loyal and true, perhaps too loyal for his own good. 'You've bought me enough respectability. Tomorrow is proof of that, I think. You won't need to play nursemaid any more.'

'Is that what I'm doing?' Preston's response was a swift growl.

Beatrice stopped walking and looked down at her hands. 'I know what you've been doing, Preston. You and the others have been cloaking me in your own respectability. I'm grateful, but I'll have to stand on my own feet, and I'm sure you have better things to do with your time.'

His mind registered disbelief. She was dismissing him, trying to give him his *congé*. 'Maybe I don't want to stop.' The words fell heavy between them. Now they were getting to the heart of these visits, to the heart of what lingered beneath the surface of who they were becoming—not just one friend looking out for another in a difficult time—but something more they hadn't dared to define yet. Preston was certain 'helpful friends' didn't want to push one another up against trees and silence their protests with kisses. Yet that was all he wanted to do to stop her mouth, to stop her worries; press his mouth against hers, his body against hers. It had been a week since he'd kissed her in the inn room and his body was starving for another taste. As was hers.

He'd felt the current between them when he'd come with May and the others. He'd caught Bea's unguarded gaze on more than one occasion this week when they'd walked alone, yet here she was, trying to warn him off. 'You *should* want to stop,' Bea continued. 'There is such a thing as too much respectability. If you continue to visit, people will start to think your esteem means something more than perhaps what you intend.'

It was difficult for her to meet his eyes as she said the last, perhaps the idea too intimate. Preston gave a wry grin, forcing her to own her thoughts. 'Why is that? What do I intend?'

Her gaze came up, her eyes flashing at his relentless pursuit of the awkward truth. 'People may consider your attentions as a sign of courtship and that absolutely cannot be allowed. It would be a devastating rumour.'

'Would it? For whom?' Preston raised an eyebrow.

'It certainly would be for you. You don't want to marry. You said as much in the carriage. Even if you were looking for a wife, it shouldn't be me. You have ambitions that go beyond yoking yourself to a fallen woman and her illegitimate child.'

'*Shouldn't be you?*' Preston echoed, his anger starting to rise. He hated hearing Beatrice talk about herself like that. He said the next words without thinking. 'You sound like my father.'

'Your father is a smart man,' Beatrice said quietly but Preston didn't miss the hurt in her eyes, hurt put there by his words.

'My father isn't always right. He doesn't always know what is best.' They were far from the house. It was unlikely anyone would see them at this distance. He put a finger to her lips, watching the pulse flicker at her neck. 'Tell me the truth, Bea. Do you think about the kiss?' Her eyes drifted away, betraying her answer without words.

He nodded. 'I thought so. I do, too. I wonder...'

'No, Preston. You of all people *can't* wonder.' Bea was adamant. She tried to step away, to back up, but he'd planned his manoeuvre carefully and her back came up against the hard bark of a tree.

He advanced until he could feel the heat of her body through her clothes as his lips hovered over hers, his words coming low and fast as he staked his claim, his knuckles skimming the soft curve of her jaw. 'I want to kiss you again, Bea. I want to feel the way I felt in that inn room, the way I felt on the road with you: alive, happy, centred. And I think you want that, too, even if we don't know where that leads. If you tell me I'm wrong, I'll stop.' Maybe. He hoped he could. He hoped she wouldn't ask. Up close, he could see the signs of desire restrained, her eyes dark with the battle she waged. She didn't want to refuse, but she felt she had to, felt she had to protect him…and, Preston realised, herself. Of course, she needed to protect herself. Why hadn't he seen that in her protestations?

He murmured reassurances. 'You needn't be afraid of me, Bea.' He was not the cad who'd left her with a child. He despised the idea that she might measure all men by the one who'd ruined her.

In the end, the kiss was her decision. She opened her mouth and licked her lips as she reached up on tiptoes and whispered, 'Don't stop, Preston.' She let his mouth cover hers, let herself give over to the kiss, let her mouth open, her tongue roam, her body curve into his. He understood in her mind this was allowed because it had to be the last time. For her to think of it any other way was to court madness.

Dark madness. Even as he bent his head to claim her lips, he knew this was insanity. He knew she was right—they should not risk this heady, unexplored passion and the questions it unleashed. Where did this lead? Could it only be a stolen kiss up against a tree? If so, the chasm between him and the wayward cad would not be nearly as large as he liked. Would Bea let it be more? Let *him* be more? Would he? Admittedly, they both had a lot at stake, but did they have to decide today? There was already one kiss that hung like an omen between them, a portent of future possibility. What was one more?

Chapter Eleven

Tea with the ladies was going splendidly, a good omen at her first social engagement since she'd been home and an important one. This was the last step in establishing her legitimate acceptance in the tight-knit community: tea with the local women gathered in her mother's drawing room making conversation with her, sipping out of her grandmother's china and *talking* about baby Matthew, who'd been brought down for a few minutes of requisite passing around and cooing.

It was going so well as to be almost unbelievable. It was that premise which caused Beatrice to stop and consider. Everything *was* too perfect. Something wasn't right. Coming home was supposed to be *hard*. She was supposed to be battling social censure of the worst sort, facing a life of exile. But that hadn't happened. The first full day back, her friends had called, followed by daily visits from Preston. She spent her mornings and afternoons in the garden and in the little potting shed that served as a place to prepare herbs. She felt positively cosseted by her surroundings, both physical and social. Of a certainty, she'd expected visits from her friends. But not this—not being surrounded by the society of Little Westbury and smiled at, talked to as if she hadn't committed, what to them, was a grievous sin.

If the scene in the drawing room wasn't so entirely juxtaposed from the anticipated reality, if a few of the ladies had shot her a disdainful look, if old Mrs Loveridge hadn't leaned forward and patted her knee with a look of confidentiality, her mother might have got away with it. Bea might even have allowed herself to buy into the fantasy. But Mrs Loveridge did lean forward and whisper, 'I know today is supposed to be a happy occasion and we aren't to remind you of anything sad, but I have to tell you I think you're bearing up wonderfully. You're so brave to move forward with your life without your husband.' She squeezed Bea's hand while Bea's mind tried to process the words. 'It's what he would have wanted for you and that must be a comfort even when it's hard to carry on. There's the baby to think of, too, and I'm sure that helps. What a sweet fellow he is.'

A cold knot of disappointed realisation tied itself in her stomach. 'Thank you for the kind words.' She managed a vague smile, for which she would likely be forgiven. After all, she'd lost a husband. She would be forgiven *anything*, apparently, as long as it happened within wedlock.

Beatrice began to understand what had happened, why acceptance had come so easily. The way had been paved for her through lies and silence. Her parents, who'd never had a blemish on their quiet name in their entire lives, had facilitated the lie. They were going to extend on the ruse she'd begun in Scotland. Only this wasn't the remote fishing villages of Scotland and there were problems with the deception here that hadn't presented themselves in Scotland, mainly that Malvern Alton was alive and loose somewhere in England.

'How did you ever think you'd pull this off?' Beatrice barely waited before the servants had put supper on the table and withdrawn. She'd waited long enough, through the rest of the tea which had become a farce, through a few hours of grappling with her own thoughts before she had enough calm to voice them.

Her parents exchanged looks. Her father set down his fork and gave her a stern look that had never boded well for her growing up, but to their credit, neither of them pretended ignorance as to what 'this' referred to. 'The concept worked well enough for you in Scotland. It seemed prudent, if you were to come home, that the storyline continue.'

'Prudent for whom? For you?' Beatrice had never spoken to her father so sharply. 'You've both done this to protect yourselves, not me. I was perfectly happy in Scotland.'

'You will not take that tone with me.' Her father's eyes darkened with barely contained anger. 'Listen. We did this for you and for our grandson. If you can't accept this for yourself, then at least accept it for him. What kind of life did you expect to have with a baby and no husband to explain it?'

Her mother placed a hand over her father's. It was one of the few times Bea had ever seen them show an ounce of affection in front of someone else. But throughout her life, she'd never once questioned that they were together, as they were together on this. 'Do you know what happens to most girls in your situation?'

'Yes,' Bea shot back. Of course she knew. It was what she feared. 'They have their babies taken away.'

Her mother was relentless. 'Not just taken away, Bea. Those children are *given* away. By their own mothers, who, in spite of their best intentions, can't work for a living *and* raise their child or afford to pay someone to the watch the child in their stead. To keep their child is to court death for the both of them, a slow, horrible death in poverty and starvation.'

Her mother leaned forward over the table, her voice dropping. 'I've worked in the foundling homes, Bea, with the other ladies who do charity in London. The homes are full. One cannot simply drop a child off on a doorstep. A woman must interview for the right to have her child taken in. She must explain her circumstances to the board of directors. She is judged in all ways.'

Bea had heard of such proceedings. They were whispered about when the ladies gossiped at their London teas, home from a virtuous morning spent in doing good works. The interviews were more like morality trials. The entire process was designed to degrade a woman from start to finish and the woman would do it, would do *anything*, to secure a last glimpse of hope for her child's future. It was a concept she'd always accepted in theory, but now that she had Matthew, she understood the concept far better.

She wanted to argue such a thing wouldn't happen to her. The women who went to these foundling homes were lower-class women with no education, working women or women in service. But to argue that seemed elitist. She had an advantage by birth, born to wealth and security. It was also hypocritical to assume desperation belonged only to the poor. What wouldn't *she* do for her child? Hadn't she already done desperate things for him? She'd come home, hadn't she? She'd fabricated a husband in Scotland to save him from her sin. Who was she to rail at her parents for having done the same?

Beatrice drew a deep breath. 'How will we

ever support this lie? It will have to stand for ever.'

'Once you marry, everyone will forget.' Her mother didn't even hesitate. How could she say such things without blinking an eye? It was said with such cold-bloodedness it might as well have been a fait accompli. The statement also rang alarms. If her mother said it without hesitation, was there a groom already picked out as well?

'Marry?' Beatrice tried to match her mother's coolness, but it was hard to stay calm when she remembered Preston's words. He'd assured her there was no one specific being brought forward as a potential husband. Had he known what her parents intended?

'It's the fastest route to respectability.'

'It's the fastest route to disaster!' Beatrice burst out. 'You want to drag someone else into the lie. An unwitting someone else, I might point out, since I don't think you have any intention of telling him my first husband never existed. Have you thought about what happens if the father of my child suddenly shows up?' That was the biggest gamble of all the little calculated gambles in this mad scheme of her parents. In Scotland, she'd had a false last name and anonymity. Here, she had neither. Malvern Alton could come at any time.

Her mother's smile was chilling. 'Do you think he'll come back? He hasn't in over a year. Of course, you could give us his name and we could get him back. It would be a joyous, miraculous event, to discover he didn't die at sea. Those kind of mistakes are made all the time; boats go down and survivors take a long while to be found. They wash up on shore with their memories fogged, which would explain why he didn't come back immediately.' Her mother's imagination was a frightening place. She had an answer for everything. Was this really happening?

'No!' Beatrice pushed back from the table and set down her napkin beside an untouched plate. 'I don't want him or any husband.'

'You will sit down!' her father's command came through gritted teeth. 'You will not stomp out of here and give the servants something more to talk about.'

This was awful. She wanted to stomp out, wanted to slam doors as she went, wanted to scream at the top of her lungs. But those women, those who gave vent to their emotions, lost their children and their sanity. It wasn't just the foundling homes a single mother had to fear. There were asylums, too. A woman with loose morals must be deranged indeed. Stomping out would only prove to her father that she was the child he still imagined her to be. An adult would sit back down.

Beatrice sat, but she didn't let it go. She fixed her parents with a hard stare. 'Why are you doing this to me? Why couldn't you let me stay in Scotland?'

Her mother's gaze softened and she reached a hand across the table to clasp hers. 'You're a mother now, Bea. Can't you guess? What kind of life did you expect us to have without you and our grandchild nearby? You are our only child. Beatrice, we did this because we love you.'

The words tore at her. She felt the stinging onset of tears, her earlier thought echoed: *what wouldn't a parent do for their child?* Only this time *she* was the child in that equation.

'Just because your intentions are honourable doesn't mean they'll work.'

Her father's jaw was set in determination, not unlike the set of Preston's face when he'd come for her. This was a determination born out of resolve to see something through no matter how distasteful. 'We have papers, darling, and I doubt anyone who questions us will want to go as far as to challenge the British legal system.'

The last shook her as nothing else had, driving home how committed they were to supporting the ruse. Her parents, the flawless Penroses, were willing to stake their reputations on this. She should not let them do this. Her father's eyes were steady on her as if he could read her very thoughts. 'What good is a blemish-free life if it cannot be used to protect a daughter?'

She didn't deserve this painless reckoning. She'd been wild in her wanting, reckless with her reputation, carelessly throwing it away for a chance at momentary pleasure—pleasure that had been elusive. She deserved to pay for that gamble. She'd been angry with her parents and her friend for dragging her home, when all they'd wanted to do was protect her. It was too much and it broke her.

Beatrice Penrose, who could survive anything, laid her head on the table and sobbed, overwhelmed at last by the events of the day—or was it the events of the last three days, the last week, the last fifteen months?

In the midst of her tears, all she wanted was Preston. She was sorely regretting not letting him come over after tea as he'd asked. It was an irrational wanting, of course. He was as much a culprit in all of this as her parents. He'd known all along what waited for her. She should be furious with him and yet all she wanted was the feel of his arms about her.

Preston had come armed with flowers, worried that he might need them as an apology offering. He swung down from his horse in the drive, feeling a trifle nervous as he carefully retrieved the bouquet of daisies from the holster on his saddle. It had been two days since he'd kissed Beatrice in the garden and tea with the ladies was long done. He couldn't stand the suspense—not the suspense of how tea had gone, he knew very well how that would go. That event had been engineered to near perfection. The real suspense was whether or not Bea had figured out the ruse and if she had, did she hate him for it now? Or did she hate him for the kiss? Where did he stand?

Preston gave his cravat a tug at the door before knocking. His nerves over a visit to an old friend was a sign of how far out of control things had become, things for which he had no answers. He was starting to think his father was right; maybe he needed some distance. Perhaps a trip to Seacrest wasn't a bad idea, after all. Not necessarily for his father's reasons, but for his own reasons. He needed to sort things out.

The butler admitted him and showed him to the back porch where Beatrice was at work with her herbs spread out on a table, surrounded by flowers that made his bouquet superfluous. The Penroses had one of the best flower gardens in West Sussex, as evidenced by the profusion of blooms in a varying array of pinks, whites, yellows and purples just beyond the veranda. She hardly needed a meagre bouquet of daisies.

Bea looked up from the work table where she was grinding something with a pestle. From the faint smell, he thought it might be sage. 'Preston, hello.' She came around the table, wiping her hands on her apron and taking the bouquet, but something was off. She must know about the deception.

'If you've come to see Matthew, he's asleep, I'm afraid.' Bea gave him a smile, putting the daisies in an empty jar on her work table.

'I came to see *you*,' Preston corrected. 'I wanted to make sure tea went fine and to tell you I was leaving for Seacrest this afternoon.'

I was wondering if you'd been able to forget about our kisses, to pretend they didn't happen, because I haven't. It haunts me. You haunt me. At night when I'm in bed. In the afternoon when I'm out riding. In the morning when I wake. It haunts me pretty much all the time. I have hopes being at Seacrest will appease them, but I doubt it.

He couldn't tell her that. Such boldness would ruin everything. Then, he wouldn't even be allowed to visit. At least now, visiting could be his own private purgatory.

'Tea went fine, as I assume you already know?' Beatrice met his gaze evenly, her stare hard. 'You did know, didn't you? About my parents' plans to protect me? Apparently, my Scottish ruse has followed me home. I have a husband who died at sea and now everyone knows.'

Bea's eyes flashed, sharp obsidian shards looking for a target to rip into. She took a step towards him, hands on hips as she made her charge. 'Why didn't you tell me what my parents intended?' That was the real crime, Preston divined immediately. He was her friend and he hadn't told her.

'Because you wouldn't have got in the carriage,' Preston shot back. He'd known this would happen, that it would be this bad when she found out and she only knew half of it.

'Is that your code these days, Preston Worth? Say anything to get what you want? What else did you lie to me about?' Her words called into question every precious moment of the journey. His own anger began to rise. He would not have her taint their journey with her doubts. What they had shared, what they *continued* to share, might be confusing, but it was all honest.

'Beatrice, be fair. You lied first. You made up the seafaring husband.' She could be mad, Preston reasoned, but she could not stand there and play the hypocritical judge, not when she started it.

'But it was *my* decision,' Beatrice answered. 'Now, I find I am caught in a web of others' making and not by my own choice.'

Those words shamed him. He might not have supported the lie, or created it, but he'd gone along with it. He'd fetched her home to be part of it without her knowledge. Others had decided they knew what was best for another and he'd allowed it when he knew very well he would not tolerate others doing the same for him. Wasn't that the source of quiet conflict between him and his father currently? His father thought he knew best. His father wanted to decide his life for him. And yet, he'd allowed it to be done to Beatrice.

Beatrice's voice broke at its edges, but her eyes remained hard. 'My own friends decided not to consult me in a matter that would define my future for ever. What has been done cannot be undone. It is too late for that. It makes me wonder what else has been planned that I don't know about.'

Preston made a rapid assessment. Telling her couldn't make up for what had already been done, but perhaps it could save what was left of her trust. His voice was low and he spoke rapidly. The Penroses might not forgive him this indiscretion. 'London. You are to go to London for Liam's knighthood ceremony and to have a bit of a Season with all of us there to help.'

The calm with which she took the news would be misleading to a man who didn't know her well. 'Ah, so there is a husband picked out for me, after all. That's two lies you've told, Preston. Who is it? Does he have a name?'

'No one, in particular. Just a chance to get out and meet people.' Although he was liking that idea less and less. An errant stab of jealousy took him unawares. What if she *did* meet someone, someone who was worthy of her and Matthew? Of course, he had no claim on her, as she'd demonstrated a few days ago when she'd argued she didn't need his nurse-maiding any longer.

'I'm not interested in meeting anyone.' She gave him a pointed look that said the world of men, him currently included, had been a disappointment to date. She gave him a cold smile tinged with triumph. 'Besides, it's not possible. The ruse has made it too risky. Going to London during the Season increases the chances of running into Matthew's father. Something none of us can afford now.' Fear tinged her voice along with smug condemnation. 'He will know the lie for what it is. If he ever finds us, he'll ruin us. Does no one understand that?'

She was frightened and angry. He wanted nothing more than to go to her and wrap her his arms, perhaps kiss away her fears because he'd heard what she really meant in those words—why hadn't *he* understood the risk? Why hadn't *he* stopped the lie before it had become dangerous?

He had failed her. The realisation hung between them as assuredly as if she'd slapped him. They stood in stunned silence, facing each other, letting its wake drag into awkwardness before Preston squared his shoulders and said most formally, 'Good day. I will show myself out.'

Chapter Twelve

The moment he was gone, she wanted him back. Beatrice braced her hands on the work table in an attempt to steady her temper and her thoughts in the aftermath of their confrontation. She'd accused him of failing her, perhaps the worst affront to one's honour for a man like Preston. He'd wanted to protect her. He'd done nothing more than what her parents had done, what Evie and May and their parents had done: allowed the rest of Little Westbury to believe she'd married a seafaring merchant and lost him to the sea. The general population of Little Westbury had no reason to think the story flawed and those who knew—the Milhams, the Worths and the Penroses—weren't going to tell them otherwise. For the sake of *her* honour.

It was a rather elaborate secret to keep indefinitely and it wasn't without a price. They all would pay for it in risk and in trust. Her friends were willing to pay that price for her. And what had she done? She'd run Preston off.

The basil leaves on the work table blurred. She blinked back tears, furiously. She was not going to cry over this. Why did it matter so damn much what Preston did anyway? *Because he could have told you*, came the whisper of her conscience, *if he was really your friend, he would have told you.* He'd had seven days in a carriage, for heaven's sake. There'd been countless opportunities to tell her and he'd *chosen* to pass them all up. He might not have lied, but he had deliberately omitted some key details to the truth.

Beatrice breathed deeply, letting the aroma of her herbs bring calm. She reached for her pestle and went back to work, grinding, grinding, grinding. He'd told her personal things about himself, about his reluctance to retire to the country, how much he loved serving the country. He'd held her baby, rocked him, played with him, he'd fought for her in a taproom against armed men with knives. He'd taken injury for her. He'd *kissed* her. Not once, but twice.

He'd done all of that for her, and with her, and yet he could not utter the simple truth: *your parents will march you off to London and, by the way, it will be easy to marry you off because you're now a widow in the eyes of Little Westbury and society.*

Beatrice dashed a hand across her eyes, smelling the scent of basil on her fingertips. She should not have let him kiss her. It was all the fault of that kiss. It made her believe they were more than friends, it made her feel dangerous things for a man, things she'd not stopped thinking about since she'd arrived home.

She'd been betrayed by a kiss. Again. As if the first time with Alton hadn't been a disaster. This time was proving to be no better. Once more, passion had led her astray, led her to believe there was deeper feeling where there was none, or at least not enough to suggest he ought to tell her what truly awaited her at home.

The door from the house opened on to the veranda. Beatrice swallowed hard, wanting to appear steady, to give nothing away. She wasn't in the mood for probing or for company, especially not her mother's, not after what she'd just learned.

Her mother looked around. 'Is Preston Worth here? I told Annie to bring Matthew down. I thought Preston would like to see him.'

'He just stopped on his way to Seacrest,' Beatrice said tersely.

'He didn't stay long.' Her mother's gaze fixed on her, sharp and unyielding in the quest for information, as if she knew her daughter was responsible for their guest's early departure.

Beatrice grabbed another handful of leaves and began to chop, the knife blade coming down in hard, quick movements. 'He just stopped by to see how the tea went. It hardly requires a very long stay.' She reached for the pestle and shot her mother an accusing glance. 'Especially when he already knew the outcome.' Time to grind.

'Are you still upset about the ruse? Or is it something else? I hope you don't blame Preston for it. In time, you'll see that it was the right choice.' Her mother took the chair across from her, signalling her intention to stay. 'You look rather upset for such a brief visit.'

Bea's temper rose in spite of her best attempts to contain it. 'If I'm angry, it's because Preston told me your plan to take me up to London.'

'It will be good for you. There's Liam's ceremony to attend and all of your friends will be there.' Her mother glossed over her obvious resistance.

'It's the last place I want to be and the city is a terrible place for a baby.' If her mother would disregard her wishes, perhaps an appeal to Matthew's well-being would get her to reconsider.

'Of course it is!' her mother exclaimed as Annie the nursemaid stepped outside with Matthew.

Bea took him and lifted him high in the air, blowing gently on his fat belly. He giggled. 'Then, I'm glad that's settled.' Bea settled into a wicker rocking chair, bouncing him on her lap.

Her mother was all matronly concern. 'You didn't think we'd *make* you take the baby along, did you? He'll stay here with the best of care. Annie can look after him.'

'Oh, yes, mum.' Annie made a little dipping curtsy. 'I'll look after him like he's my own.

He's the sweetest baby. You needn't worry about a thing. Just go and enjoy yourself.'

Beatrice stopped rocking, stopped bouncing Matthew. She gave her mother an incredulous stare. 'Leave him? Here? Without me? Absolutely not. I am his mother. I belong with him.'

'It's just for a few weeks. We're not staying long,' her mother coaxed.

'No. I can't possibly go without him for even a few days.' Did no one understand? Or did they choose to ignore the realities? The risks? Without the bouncing to distract him, Matthew began to fuss, wanting his afternoon feeding. Beatrice undid her bodice.

'Oh, Beatrice, are you going to do *that* out here?' Her mother voiced her disapproval as if it were a scold. 'Really, that should be limited to the nursery where no one else can see. A gardener could walk by.'

'Horses, cows, cats, pigs, goats, sheep— they don't relegate feeding to the nursery,' Beatrice snapped.

Her mother dismissed Annie with a quick flick of her hand, leaving them alone. 'They're animals, dear. *You* are a gently bred young woman who knows better and it's time you start acting like it.' She leaned forward, her voice a stern hiss. 'Your father and I have done everything we can for you, Beatrice. We sent you to Scotland to have the child in privacy. We arranged for you to come home and keep the child while still being received into society—no small feat. We have asked our friends to support our ruse. All so that you can meet a nice man and have a nice life for yourself and your son. I'd rather you go to London and meet those nice men for yourself and choose one of them of your own volition. Matthew deserves a father.' Her voice dropped in warning, 'If you choose not to follow our direction, Beatrice, then I will choose for you. Come hell or high water, Beatrice Elizabeth, you will have a husband on the hook by September. You owe us. *That* is the price of your redemption.'

She'd seen her mother mad before, just last spring, in fact, when she told her about the baby. But not even that rivalled the intensity her mother displayed now. 'I can't go to London,' Beatrice said evenly. 'Not without Matthew. He needs me for milk.'

'We'll hire a wet nurse. Emily Blaylock, one of your father's tenants, just had her second. She has plenty of milk and they could use the extra money. The sooner the better. Once your milk dries up, you'll have your figure back entirely. Nursing ruins one's bosom. Husbands don't want wives with sagging cow udders for breasts. She could start tomorrow, if you like.'

'No, I don't like.' Beatrice shifted Matthew to her other side, fighting the urge to clutch him tight, to protect him. What if this was a ploy to send her away and then steal the baby? The old fear surged, coupled with new fears, too, selfish fears. Matthew might be able to nurse as long as he liked, but not her. Didn't her mother understand this was her only chance to nurse a child? Of course not. Her mother expected her to marry, to have another child or *two*. Reflexively, she squeezed Matthew tight. She wasn't ready to give this up.

If her mother wouldn't consider her wishes, maybe she'd consider the sheer risk of such a trip. Beatrice played her trump card, the one that had routed Preston. 'Have you thought of the other reason I can't go to London? My "husband" isn't really dead.' She had no desire to meet Malvern Alton on the streets or at a ball.

It had taken her a while to allow herself to fully embrace what he'd done to her and what that said about his character. Not the sex part—that had been consensual. It was the leaving part, the responsibility part, that had illuminated his true colours. He was a selfish man, out only for his own pleasures. She wanted nothing more to do with him.

Her mother gave her a condescending look. 'Do you truly think he'll come for you now? He's had over a year to come looking for you and he's made no contact in any way.'

'But what if he saw me in London? What if he told people about our…affair? Or worse, what if someone told him I'd married and had a child?'

Her mother raised her brows and smiled. 'That would be wonderful. Then he'd have no reason to come after you further. He never knew you were pregnant. He'd never suspect the child was his or the father was fabricated.'

'*That* would be sailing far too close to the rocks,' Beatrice countered. 'He'd only have to do the maths to know it's a lie. I would've had to have married someone and conceived within a few weeks of his leaving.'

'He won't do the maths, Beatrice, because

he won't come. You're making this difficult because you don't want to go. But if you're really worried about him and whatever threats a potential reappearance might pose, you should marry quickly and put yourself beyond his reach for good. A ring changes everything.' Her mother stood up, finished with the conversation. 'All roads lead to London, Beatrice. You need to resign yourself to it. We leave in two weeks.'

Beatrice was livid, seething even. No! She was *not* going to London. She was not giving up her right to nurse her son for the sake of fashion and a husband she didn't want. She'd consented to her parents' ruse, but she would not consent to this.

She called for Annie to come and take Matthew before her foul mood could wear off on him. She needed an ally. She thought of Preston's ring upstairs, tucked in her dresser drawer, gold with the emerald in the centre. She'd forgotten to give it back. Maybe that could be her peace offering when he returned. She had a promise to claim, if need be. If anyone could fix this, talk sense into her parents, it would be Preston. Would he do it or had he finally taken her advice and his father's advice and washed his hands of her?

Preston couldn't sleep. By rights, sleep should have come easily. He'd ridden long and hard to reach Seacrest, hoping to clear his mind with the wind and fresh air. He'd like to blame it on the unfamiliar bedroom at Seacrest, but he knew better. He couldn't sleep on account of a woman. Nearly twelve hours ago, Beatrice had called him a liar and he was *still* thinking about it. A sharp tongue wasn't the best quality to appreciate in a woman, even if the woman in question was right: he should have told her all of it. He should have given her time to accustom herself to what waited at home. He had not.

He shifted on to his back, trying to find a comfortable position. What was she doing now? Was she lying in bed hating him? Perhaps *he* should hate *her*. She'd assaulted his honour after all he'd done. Certainly, her insult was proof that a man wasn't judged by all of his good deeds, but by his one error in judgement. Just as a woman was judged by one indiscretion instead of a lifetime of virtue.

Taking his father's advice and distancing

himself from her would certainly make all of this easier. Yet, all *he* could do was lie here in the dark of these unfamiliar rooms and think about her with her hair down, with her hands on him, her lips on him, and want her. It was *not* making him feel better. He was, in fact, in a fierce state of arousal, aching and hard. That state would have to be dealt with if he was going to get any sleep. He put a hand on himself and slid down his length with a groan, allowing himself to engage in the fantasy of it being Beatrice's hand on him. In a few minutes at least the physical agony would be over. The rest would have to wait until he returned.

Chapter Thirteen

Malvern Alton drew back the curtain of the coach and surveyed the view outside his window; Bucolic and neat. Two descriptions he despised, although the words described Little Westbury perfectly. There was a tidy row of half-timbered shop fronts mixed with an occasional red brick and, every so often, a white bow window jutting out on what passed as the town's High Street. A white-steepled church rose at the end of the street, presiding over all of it. Spreading out from the main street were other businesses: the livery, the market, the butcher's and the baker's.

As country villages went, Little Westbury was all very standard. Not much had changed in the year since he'd been here. He didn't expect it had. Small places never did.

Small people never did either. For reasons that eluded him, country folk preferred to stay in the country. He was counting on that with Beatrice. It had taken him longer than expected to wrap up his loose ends in London and make this sacrificial pilgrimage to claim his future wife. He was flat broke and there'd been the enormous effort of scraping money together for the special licence, then the detour to pick up his grandmother's ring. Too bad he couldn't sell that.

Not that he was worried about what awaited him. Beatrice had been so eager, so passionate after that first kiss. He would court her, pick up where they'd left off, bring a few little gifts—ribbons and chocolates always softened up the ladies—and be married by June. She would be all too glad to see him. Not every man wanted to listen to herbology.

He felt for the ring in his pocket. Not that he'd use it today, he just didn't like the idea of something so valuable lying in his luggage. He had it all planned out: he'd explain a family emergency had prevented him from returning last winter, that the family had thrown another girl at him when he was home in the hopes he'd marry. He could even pretend he'd written countless times, but that his father had intercepted those letters in the attempt to push this other girl at him. He would smile and be charming. They'd take long walks, he'd ask her about her stupid science and herbs. He'd listen to her prattle on about them until he couldn't stand it and then he'd take her. At least courting a girl in the country was cheaper than in the city. Long walks didn't cost nearly as much as seats at the theatre or sending bouquets of flowers.

Alton leaned his head out the window and gave directions to the inn. He'd clean up and change clothes before he headed out to Maidenstone and put his plan in motion. This was Beatrice Penrose's lucky day whether she knew or not. Her lover had returned and was prepared to married her. He did not expect refusal. Country girls were much simpler to please than haughty London girls. But even if she did think to refuse, he was prepared to throw himself on the mercy of her parents.

He chuckled at his delicate phrasing. It was blackmail. That was what it was. They'd sneaked around last year, both of them careful not to get caught. Her parents didn't know what their darling girl had been up to. If she refused him, he'd tell her parents. They would force the wedding for propriety's sake and he, being the gentleman he was, would encourage it.

'Miss, there's a gentleman to see you.'

Beatrice looked up from her reading with a smile she could barely contain. Relief swamped her. Preston must be home from Seacrest! It had been five days since their quarrel, a very *long* five days. 'Send him in, Thomas.' Bea set aside her book and her notes and rose, checking her appearance in the small oval mirror on the wall. At last, she and Preston could set their quarrel behind them. She wanted to be the first to apologise. She'd still been stinging from her parents' ploy to pass her off as a widow and she'd taken out her frustration on him. She'd behaved poorly with a friend who'd done everything for her.

'Beatrice, my love, you don't need a mirror. You know you've always looked beautiful to me.'

The words turned her blood to ice water. The voice froze her. She shifted her eyes very slowly to the left corner of the mirror to take in the room behind her, the *man* behind her.

This was the nightmare come to life, the fear that if she was in England Malvern Alton would find her. There was no mistaking it was him, with his strategically tousled raven-black hair and pale aquamarine eyes that hinted towards the mysterious, looks she'd once found attractive.

'Mr Alton,' she said stiffly, keeping her back to him, wanting every second available to master her fear before she faced him. Why was he here? What did he know?

'*Mr Alton*? What is this?' He gave a low chuckle, a sound she would have once found sensual and inviting. 'I thought we'd come further than that, Bea.' His hands were on her shoulders, his lips at her neck. 'A lot further.' His voice was a husky invitation at her ear.

Beatrice did turn then, out of his presuming grasp, away from him. 'You assume too much, Mr Alton.' She wanted him out of her house, away from her before he could see how much she had to hide. His very presence could unravel everything.

'Beatrice, I understand you're angry. You have every right to be. I disappeared without a word. You must think I'm a cad. You are *right* to think I'm a cad.' He dropped his voice, but not nearly low enough for her tastes. 'I ask you, what sort of man leaves the woman whose maidenhead he's taken?' She wished he wouldn't say such things out loud where people could hear. She wished he wouldn't say them at all. She could hear the insincerity, the forced pathos as he attempted to pour out a heart he didn't have.

'I've come to make amends, Beatrice, to explain what happened and to prove to you that while my body was absent, my heart was not. Will you listen to me?' His plea reeked of falsity. He might be impressed with his monologue, but she wasn't.

He sat on the drawing-room sofa beside her without being invited and launched into his explanation, sounding like an actor rehearsing a soliloquy. 'My great-aunt's health was failing. The family needed me...' His face worked hard in creating a facsimile of sincerity as he spun a tale of duty and family. She'd once loved how mobile that face was. She didn't dare believe that sincerity now. How naïve she'd been to believe in him. There was a time, too, she would have given anything to hear those words, a time when she hadn't accepted the reality of what he was: a true rake who had used her affections for his own pleasure and then left her. Even in the early months of her pregnancy she'd refused to hate him entirely and she'd held out hope he would return. But that had been a while ago.

Now, she didn't want him back, not even if he could be trusted with what had become the family secret. A true gentleman did not take the honour of a girl. Period. The running off was entirely secondary. What he had done should not have been done to start with. He knew the limits of propriety and he'd encouraged her to exceed them. Then he had disappeared. Perhaps for family reasons. Perhaps to save himself from the consequences of his actions.

'Beatrice, I swear to you, I thought of you every day, *longed* for you every day since. I want to start over. I want a second chance,' he begged prettily. It was interesting how handsome simply wasn't enough any more.

'Miss, I brought the little master down, I know how much Mister Worth enjoys…' Annie sailed into the room, Matthew in her arms, and stopped short, her gaze fixing on Malvern Alton as her brain registered this man wasn't Preston Worth.

Alton's mind was fast. 'The little master?' A charming smile broke out on his face, directed at Annie, but Beatrice was equally as quick. He was *not* getting his hands on her child.

'Bring him to me, Annie, and then you may leave us.' She wanted Matthew in her arms where she could protect him. She had to be strong, but it was hard to hide her fear when Alton's eyes were on her, watching, calculating, doing the kind of maths only a rake has need of doing when he wondered if a child was his.

'I knew there was something different about you, Bea.' His voice carried the inflections of a man thinking out loud, sorting through his thoughts. Very soon he would piece it all together. 'Is this your son? Or should I say "our son"?' He crossed the short distance between them and knelt before her on the floor beside her chair, so that she couldn't deny him the sight of Matthew. He peered into the blanket. The sight should have melted her, the handsome man on his knee, seeing his son for the first time. How many times had she melted when Preston had held Matthew? But this sight only drew fear.

She drew the baby away from him, filled with trepidation that if she let him hold the child, he would run out of the room with him. 'You'll have to excuse us. He'll be hungry soon and I must feed him.'

Alton looked at her with wide eyes, voice full of awe. 'I have a son?' He would have been magnificent on the stage. She didn't believe that sincerity for a minute.

'*I* have a son. You left me alone to bear him and whatever disgrace I might encounter. I have done so. There is nothing I need from you. You needn't concern yourself with us.' Beatrice rose, putting distance between them. She moved towards the bell pull. If he didn't leave of his own accord in the next minute, she would call Thomas.

'Nothing except a name, Beatrice,' he pressed, rising to his feet, still playing the surprised father, the adoring suitor. 'I will give you that. We can marry. Don't you see how serendipitous this is?'

'No. I've asked you to leave.'

His joyous façade cracked in the face of her steel. 'I have a son, an heir. We can't ignore our association.'

'The lady has asked you to leave.' There

was movement by the door. Beatrice's gaze drifted beyond Alton's shoulder, relief warring with horror as Preston Worth strode into the room, his face rigid with determination. She'd seen that look before. So had a few men who ended up on a taproom floor.

Alton turned, a smirk on his lips. 'I'm Malvern Alton—who might you be?'

Preston crossed his arms and answered the smirk with a nasty smile of his own. 'The man who will see that you comply with the lady's wishes.'

'The lady?' Alton gave a derisive chuckle and Bea felt herself go paler. 'Is that what you call her?' He shrugged. 'Well, I guess everyone has their own fantasies in the dark.'

Preston turned slightly to include the butler, who'd come up behind him. 'I believe our guest was leaving, Thomas.'

Faced with the prospect of leaving or engaging in a drawing-room brawl that was likely not going to help plead his case, Alton relented, but his gaze slid towards her once more as he left, his words menacing. 'I have come here with a decent offer, Bea. I deserve better than this cold reception of yours. We are not done discussing this. How dare you hide my child from me?' He shot a sly look at Preston. 'Sorry, old chap, I hope you knew.' He mastered a look of incredulity. 'Or did she tell you the boy was yours? It's so hard to know with these kind of women. They'll say anything.'

'If you didn't want a fight so badly, I'd give you one,' Preston growled, standing toe to toe with Alton in the doorway. Beatrice thought for a moment there'd be a fight anyway. But Preston understood implicitly he could not be the one to throw the first punch and Alton had no reason to start anything.

'The father of Beatrice's child is back,' Preston began, pacing in front of the drawing room window, an ignored snifter of brandy in one hand. He was too agitated to drink. The necessary players had been assembled in short order. He'd sent Liam and Dimitri notes to meet him here. He flexed his fist in his free hand, regretting the peaceful exodus he'd allowed Alton. 'I should have hit him.'

The other two exchanged grim looks. Everyone understood the impact of Preston's announcement. If the father was here, then he couldn't be dead. Dimitri drummed long fingers on the desktop. 'You say he wants to marry her, that he was overjoyed? *Is* marriage a possibility? We could always explain that he hadn't been lost at sea after all, that his return is a miracle. There could be a "second" wedding ceremony to celebrate his return or to overturn the death certificate and officially reunite them.' He gave a shrug of one shoulder. 'It shouldn't be that hard to do.'

'We'd have to tell him about the ruse, then, and he'd have to uphold it,' Liam reminded them. 'Do you think he's reliable? Can he be entrusted with our secret?'

'No, I do not think he's reliable!' Preston all but yelled. 'He slept with her and abandoned her over a year ago. He left her pregnant. And now he's back, wanting to pretend he's innocent, that he had no choice but to leave her. Does that sound like a reliable man to you? Remember, it's not just Beatrice's secret at risk now, but all of ours because we bought into perpetuating it. I don't trust him to be on our side.'

'All right,' Liam placated him. 'Easy, Preston. I think Dimitri was just pointing out we might have a quick solution on our hands without panicking.'

'We don't. Even if we could trust him, Beatrice doesn't want to marry him. I don't blame her. He's up to no good.' Preston took a hasty swallow of the brandy. How could his friends understand? They hadn't seen her afterwards, pale and shaking on the sofa, the baby clutched close.

'How do you know that?' Liam shot him a close look. 'How do we know he's not sincere? Perhaps he regrets what he did because he genuinely cares about her? Babies can change people.'

'Not him.' Preston's response was fierce. The sight of the man kneeling next to Bea and Matthew had hit him hard. For a moment he'd feared the scene he'd walked in on was one of reconciliation. Then the man had opened his crass mouth and Preston knew the truth. This man was here for his own selfish reasons.

He took another swallow. This one larger. 'He left her. He hadn't made any contact for over a year. If he had sincere regrets, he would have found a way to be with her, to reach her. I would not allow anything to separate me from the woman I loved, especially if there was a chance of a child.'

'She's not yours, Preston.' Dimitri's voice

cut through his chagrin with quiet reason. 'Sometimes, I think you forget that. You went and fetched her. Your responsibility is done.'

'She's alone and she needs protection.' Preston fixed Dimitri with a gaze of green steel. 'Have you asked yourself why he's come back now, after all this time? He wants something and he's willing to use her to get it.' Preston pushed a hand through his hair. He was doing that a lot lately. 'If we were in London, I could get information. But out here, no one knows him. There's no one to ask.'

'May and I leave tomorrow for town. We're going early to get settled in before the ceremony,' Liam offered. 'I can look into it.'

Preston nodded his thanks. There was no better man when it came to tracking down information. 'That leaves Dimitri and I to manage the situation here.'

'What are you expecting?' Dimitri poured another brandy.

'Blackmail first and, if that fails, all-out scandal,' Preston said. 'Alton has more to gain at the moment by keeping his knowledge quiet and using it to pressure Beatrice into marriage. Shaming her with scandal might force the issue in his favour, but it wouldn't do his reputation any good either. If there's a silver lining to this, it's that the scandal won't break immediately or perhaps at all. He will be weighing whether or not he can afford to go public. We have time to think through our position.'

'*If* blackmail fails? Do you think there's a chance it won't? That the Penroses will simply give him what he wants?' Liam interjected.

'I think it depends on what Alton is after. But, yes, I think blackmail might be appealing to the Penroses,' Preston explained. 'If he's just after money, the Penroses might see blackmail as a type of middle ground that keeps Beatrice from having to marry against her will and scandal from breaking.' Blackmail would let Bea keep her secret, but it would also be a slow, continuous hell that would bleed the Penrose coffers. Nothing would prevent Alton from raising the price to keep the secret. If Alton was smart, though, he'd want more than cash. He'd want Bea, her dowry and the kind of permanent access to the Penrose wealth that only came with marriage. That was the question: how smart was Alton? How desperate was he? What was he really after?

Preston sat at last, his head in his hands. It was starting to hurt from all the thinking. 'Regardless of what the Penroses believe they can do in the short term, we need something more permanent that will put Beatrice beyond Alton's reach.'

'Marriage is the only thing that will put a stop to this,' Dimitri said solemnly. 'Perhaps Beatrice should reconcile herself to that.'

Not to Alton, though, but to a man who would not fail her if given a second chance. Still, all such plans were premature until Alton made his next move.

Chapter Fourteen

Alton made them wait forty-eight hours before he made his next move. It came in the form of a carefully penned note in the post. Perhaps because he was too much of a coward to risk another face-to-face encounter with him? Preston mused and rightly so. He doubted the odds were much in Alton's favour of getting off without a fist to the jaw a second time. Or perhaps because blackmail was always a coward's resort. It was much harder to blackmail someone in person, especially when the person in question was a woman.

Whatever the bastard's reasons, Preston had been expecting such a move. As a result, everyone else of consequence was, too. The note was no surprise, although that made its content no less devastating: the key players assembled once more in the Penrose drawing room, *sans* May and Liam, who'd already left for London as planned and notably without the Worths. His father had expressed dismay over the turn of events, but had not volunteered his services. If Preston wished to pursue this, he was on his own.

They passed the note amongst themselves in silent contemplation: Beatrice was to consent to an immediate marriage, for which Alton had a special licence, or he would spread word the child was his, letting it be known that he'd offered for her and she had refused.

'I'll say one thing for this fellow,' Dimitri began, 'he's smart. He's covered himself admirably here, making himself out to be a hero, or at the very least a gentleman cognisant of his duty. He's able to uncloak the scandal without doing himself too much harm other than exposing the truth that he dallied where he shouldn't.' That had dismayed Preston, too. In his calculations, he'd counted on Alton not being able to expose Beatrice without also exposing himself.

'He's smart *and* desperate,' Preston put in, eyeing the group: Dimitri and Evie, Beatrice and her parents. Everyone was sombre, suitably horrified by the note's contents. He explained, 'Special licences are expensive. Why make the investment? Usually those who do are after the immediacy such a licence provides.' There were all sorts of reasons people needed to wed quickly. Very seldom was it because of love. One could wait for love and have the banns read.

'Perhaps he feels sure of himself,' Dimitri argued for the sake of presenting both sides. 'He didn't know about the child until yesterday, so that can't be it. That only leaves Beatrice's affections.' He glanced towards Bea. 'Maybe he felt secure in the knowledge that Beatrice would forgive him and take him back, especially if he was promising marriage as part of his absolution.'

'No,' Preston countered. 'If he was that sure of himself, waiting for the banns to be read would make more sense. Why would he pay for something he was certain he'd attain *without* spending the money?'

He paused, waiting for the idea to take root in the others' minds, his eyes on Beatrice, watching her reaction. Alton was a cagey-minded fellow. Dimitri wasn't wrong about that. The man had not sent his blackmail until today on purpose. He'd wanted to give Beatrice time to change her mind about her refusal, time perhaps to ponder the sight of him knelt beside her with his son and to translate such an image into an image of the family they could be together. Only when she hadn't begged for his attendance at Maidenstone the next day had he sent the note.

'What are you suggesting, then?' Beatrice asked from the sofa where she sat, her hand tightly squeezed in Evie's for support. She was pale and there were dark circles under her eyes from a sleepless night. Preston's heart went out to her. She would be feeling enormously guilty about all of this, seeing it as her fault. He knew. He felt much the same way. This was all his fault. He'd been the one to make her come home. Beatrice had wanted to stay in Scotland, had wanted to fade into anonymity and safety.

What had he brought her home to but the same lie she'd been living in Scotland, only with more risk of exposure? The lie hadn't even lasted a month. Now, they had the father of the child on their doorstep, demanding marriage, and Preston's instincts to defend were at full force. This blackguard had come after people under his protection.

'I am suggesting that Alton is a very dangerous man.' He knelt in front of her, taking her hands to soften the blow. 'He is after you, Beatrice, and all that you represent. He's not just after money. He would have said so in his note. If he was after money, he would have named a price. Instead he named marriage. That tells me he needs money, large sums. He wants a dowry and access to a family that has more and he needs it fast. Hence the special licence. We won't know more about why until we hear from Liam.'

'Well, she's not going to marry him,' Evie put in staunchly.

'Evie,' Bea said quietly, 'he'll tell everyone the truth and you will all be ruined, called out as liars along with me.' The room was silent. That was the sticking point. Although Alton couldn't know it, everyone had a stake in this. Everyone's reputation was on the line. If Alton knew, it would give him even more power.

'Will he tell?' Preston posed the question, a bold idea coming to mind. 'Maybe. But do we fear his telling? He thinks we will cower, afraid. I say, let's call his bluff. It will be Alton's word against ours.' The only way to counter the threats of a man like Alton was to go on the offensive with threats of one's own.

'Let him tell everyone the truth?' Bea's mother look aghast.

'It's his word against ours.' Preston's gaze landed on Penrose. 'You have papers, a death certificate and a wedding certificate, with another man's name on them. Those papers prove Malvern Alton couldn't be Matthew's father.'

'Those papers are forgeries, Preston,' Bea warned, concern for the others involved surging to the fore of her conscience. 'To blatantly flaunt them…'

Preston was not daunted. 'Is *exactly* what they were bought for,' he finished her sentence. 'Why have them if you aren't going to use them? The papers will show Alton as the liar, a trait probably in keeping with his overall character. I'm sure Liam will uncover something unsavoury about Alton in London and we can use it to go on the offensive with him. Blackmailers seldom like being the victims of their own plots.'

'Ah, a stalemate, like in chess.' Dimitri

smiled knowingly. 'Neither side can move. Very good.'

Only it wouldn't be enough, nothing more than a finger in the dyke. But it was a solution for now. He had a larger solution in mind, one that had kept him up late last night as he reviewed all of its angles, triggered by circumstances and by something Beatrice had said in the garden. But in order to move forward with phase two, he needed to clear the room and get Beatrice alone. He'd already made the mistake once of not consulting her in decisions that required her approval. 'Dimitri, perhaps you and Evie could help the Penroses write an appropriately worded refusal to Alton while I speak with Beatrice?' He was already moving towards her, extending his hand, signalling that he wanted her to step outside with him.

Her senses were on high alert as Preston escorted her to the garden. There was something more he wanted to talk about and he wanted privacy to do it. She was braced for it. Whatever 'it' was, it was going to be serious.

'I've proposed a bold plan to stalemate Alton. However, it won't be enough,' Preston began, and Bea nodded. She had thought about that inside. Once stalemated, what next? Stalemates couldn't last for ever. 'We need to think about Alton's responses.' Preston ticked the options off on his long fingers. 'First, he might choose to scare. He'll see that this is a game that is quickly getting over his head and it will turn in on him. Or...' Preston held up a second finger '...he'll escalate the game because he has no other choice. At this point, we don't know how desperate he is. If he can't get what he wants by manipulation, he may try to take it by force.'

She felt his eyes on her, an intense warrior's gaze. 'That means you, dear girl, are at risk. Your father's forgeries protect the rest of us, but they don't protect you. Those papers might prevent a scandal, but there is nothing currently in place that prevents Alton from marrying you.'

'You mean kidnapping, the risk of a forced elopement, becoming the victim of a marriage that could not be annulled.' Beatrice did not mince words. Those were frightening concepts indeed, to be compelled into marriage against her will. It was horrible to contemplate.

'I am afraid it must be considered. Alton

will do it if he's desperate enough and I think he is.' Preston took her hand, turning it over in his, his warm touch sending a comforting ripple up her arm as he delivered his verdict. 'As long as you're unmarried, you're fair game for the altar. I didn't want to discuss this inside in front of the others, not just yet.' He paused. 'Do you suppose Thomas has any champagne to hand for a toast?'

His question took her unawares. They were talking about kidnappings and now suddenly there was a need for toasting. 'What do we need champagne for?'

'I want to announce our engagement,' Preston said solemnly.

'Our engagement? Are we even courting?' Beatrice burst out in incredulous shock. 'What new mad scheme is this?' Had she even heard him right?

'I wanted to ask you first,' Preston went on in those same calm, even tones, proving it was no laughing matter. 'As for the point of this scheme, it should be obvious. It's the only way to keep you safe.'

Bea shook her head, pulling her hand free, and walked away from him, wishing she could walk away from her thoughts as easily, but they chased her down the garden path. This was exactly what she'd feared, trapping Preston in a marriage of obligation. Only, she'd not seen it coming about under these circumstances. She'd thought only of familial pressure, a marriage of convenience. But this certainly wasn't *that*. There was absolutely nothing convenient about it for him or for her. For him, it meant giving up his ambitions. Those in power would not offer plum positions to a man who married so far beneath himself *and* under scandalous circumstances. She would be the ruining of him.

As for herself, she didn't *want* to marry. She couldn't face the guilt that would come living with Preston's gracious sacrifice daily. Most of all, she didn't want to fall in love again, to be hurt again when Preston came to regret his impetuous offer. It would leave her in a one-way relationship where all the love was on her side. She'd been swept off her feet by Alton, only to realise he hadn't wanted her, hadn't cared for her, not even in the beginning. It would be far worse to go through that a second time with Preston, knowing he'd rather live in his own private hell than to admit it and hurt her, even if it meant hurting himself in the process.

Boots on the gravelled path signalled Preston had followed her. Would a simple refusal be enough? She turned to face him. 'I can't marry you.'

'I thought you might say that.' Preston's eyes glinted. 'Who said anything about marriage, Bea? I only wanted to announce our engagement.'

'Oh.' Guns spiked. She could feel a blush creep up her cheeks. Of course, he was smart enough to know he *couldn't* marry her. She shouldn't have worried. But she was still wary as she felt her way through the maze of his plan. That had been too easy. 'It's to be a temporary engagement, then?' She knit her brow. That would certainly solve her misgivings. 'But our families, and others, people will expect a wedding.'

'Yes, people will expect. Alton will expect. That is the whole point, why this has to be just between us. I don't want anyone else to know it's a fraud. Not Evie, not Dimitri, not even May.' That explained his desire for privacy. 'I think it will be enough. We can have our engagement formally announced at Liam's knighthood ball in London. The sooner we can have betrothal papers drawn up and signed, the better. They can stand as legal proof of our intention to wed. If Alton chooses to breach that agreement with a kidnapping attempt, I have grounds to sue him in court for a broken betrothal. I doubt he'll want to risk that.'

'London?' Her brain had stopped on that one detail. London was the one place she'd wanted to avoid, but it seemed her reasons for avoiding it were slipping away.

'London would be best. It's where Alton thinks his rumours can do the most damage. But how much damage can he do if we're there, dancing every night and looking entirely happy?'

There was too much merit to that to argue. If Preston Worth was dancing with her at London's fine entertainments, in the homes of the wealthy, she couldn't be a disgraced debutante. It was the kind of social syllogism society thrived on: Preston Worth was an honourable man. She was dancing with Preston Worth, therefore she was honourable, too.

'When I'm safe, we will cry off?' She needed that assurance, for his sake. This was a ploy that could get wildly out of hand, especially with the pressures of London.

'Yes. I will take the blame when the time comes, you needn't worry.' It seemed Preston had thought of everything. As usual.

She eyed the house in the distance, thinking of the people inside, people she didn't want to lie to. What would she say if Evie asked her about the engagement? She nodded towards the house. 'Do you think they'll believe us? The engagement is awfully coincidental.'

'It makes perfect sense. Weren't you saying the other day that my visits might be seen as representing certain intentions? That seems a good place to start. We can tell everyone I fell head over heels in love on our journey home from Scotland. It's the kind of story people adore and it's plausible.' Preston had an answer for everything. Many of them untrue, however, and that bothered her. Her protection had been built on nothing but lies.

'Your father will disapprove.'

Preston shrugged. 'Perhaps. For a while.' Until the engagement was broken, Bea thought. Still, she disliked the idea of becoming a source of tension for the Worths. 'Your parents will hate my parents over this. They'll think my father put you up to it.'

'We can hope not. This was our choice, no one else's. No one will question the engagement if we don't. We have to show everyone *we* want this and they will follow our lead.' Preston leaned close, his mouth at her ear, suggestive in its proximity, sending a tremor through her. 'Can we do that, Beatrice? Can we show them how much we want this?' It was a wicked dare if ever there was one. He nipped at her ear and her pulse started to race.

'What are you doing?' Bea breathed.

'Creating verisimilitude.' Preston laughed under his breath, his mouth at her jawline, sprinkling it with kisses. 'Everyone will think this is why we went outside, not to plot. A newly engaged woman should look a little… mussed… I think. Don't you?' He drew her against him then, his mouth claiming hers in a long, slow kiss designed to leave her breathless and it did, his kisses always did. They did more than leave her breathless. They left her wondering where the line between reality and pretence existed and how it was being erased, at least for her. How would she ever survive this with her rules intact?

Preston stepped back and grinned as he assessed his handiwork. 'There, now you look ready to do it for the audience.' Preston squeezed her hand, leading her back to the house with enviable confidence. She'd only thought stolen kisses were madness. She'd been entirely wrong. *This* was true madness; faking an engagement and running off to London to prove to everyone how real it was.

Chapter Fifteen

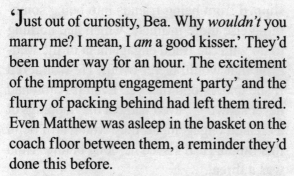

'Just out of curiosity, Bea. Why *wouldn't* you marry me? I mean, I *am* a good kisser.' They'd been under way for an hour. The excitement of the impromptu engagement 'party' and the flurry of packing behind had left them tired. Even Matthew was asleep in the basket on the coach floor between them, a reminder they'd done this before.

Beatrice gave him a wry smile. 'Probably for that very reason.'

'So, if I was a *lousy* kisser, you'd consider it?' Preston turned the thought around in his mind. 'Hmm. That seems backwards to me. I wouldn't want to marry someone who hadn't any skill in that direction and be stuck with them for ever.' Preston couldn't resist even when she shot him a scolding look. But he was starting to understand. It was the temptation that worried her.

'It hardly matters, since we aren't getting married,' she reminded him, making a point of picking up her book and opening it to end the conversation.

Well, he probably shouldn't have teased her. It was indeed a sensitive subject, one that brought home the reality that they'd somehow slipped from being friends into being something else more intimate, which had nothing to do with the fraud engagement or the wedding that would never occur. He wondered if she understood that yet. Even if Alton had never shown up, even without the trappings of a created engagement, they would still be in this limbo. He'd kissed her long before Alton was a threat.

Preston stretched his legs out, thinking about her conditions. She wouldn't marry him. She wanted the engagement to be temporary. She wanted to make sure they'd cry off. Not the best circumstances under which to begin life as an engaged couple. But he knew Beatrice well enough to know agreeing to them was the only way in which he'd get her to London and into safety.

In London they could combat Alton's rumours if he tried to spread any. They would dance at the balls and parties, carrying on like any happily engaged couple, making those rumours hard to believe. If it came to that. Preston remained hopeful that their refusal would stall Alton—that he'd have to think about what to do next. But why the hell wouldn't she marry him? He kept coming back to that as they jounced along.

A few answers came to mind. Duty or desire? Was she concerned he was acting out of duty only? Yet, how could she think that after their kisses? Surely they both recognised the desire. Or was it the desire she feared—not because she was frigid. Beatrice was anything but frigid. It was the loss of control. She'd made a mistake with Alton, let her desire lead her. Now, she was holding every man accountable for Alton's error. Damn him. Damn Alton for turning Beatrice Penrose, one of the bravest people he knew, into a coward.

Preston nudged her toe with his boot, making her look up. 'I know why you don't want to marry me.'

'Not you,' Bea corrected. 'Anyone. I don't want to marry anyone.'

Preston shrugged. 'Fine. Anyone. I know the answer to that, too.' He waited a moment as she set her book aside and fixed him with her full attention. 'You're scared.'

'Am not.'

'Are, too.' He couldn't stifle the little grin that toyed with his mouth.

'What exactly am I afraid of?' Bea was rigid in her challenge, a sure sign he was on to something.

'Intimacy. No, not physical intimacy, Bea.' He stalled her protest with a shake of his head. 'Emotional intimacy. You don't want to trust.'

'I don't want to trust another man again, is that it?' Bea's chin went up in her customary defiance. 'Then why I am here with you?'

'You don't want to trust *yourself.*' Preston met her eyes. 'You're afraid to trust yourself again. You're afraid of making another mistake. But you won't, Bea. Not with me.' He smiled once and picked up his own book.

Had he meant for her to find the line seductive? Because it was. Seductive as hell. Bea tried to focus on her book and couldn't. All she could do was stare at the pages and pretend. She was starting to understand why Eve

ate the apple. Bea would wager her allowance
the serpent hadn't slithered out and said, 'I'm
evil, eat my evil fruit.' Oh, no, the serpent had
most likely convinced Eve he was something
else entirely: a friend, a confidant who was
trusted for himself long before he started to
mouth statements that had Eve questioning
her conventional wisdom. It was one thing
when a rake said, 'You'll be safe with me.' No
one expected him to mean it. It was another
entirely when Preston Worth said it. She *did*
expect him to mean it. She wanted to believe
it. Therein lay the seduction.

She brought her eyes up briefly from her
pages to skim him, the strong jaw, the long,
straight nose, finally admitting what she'd
known for a while. She wanted Preston Worth.
All of him. In all ways. But to have him would
require breaking her rules. Both of them. And
then what? What happened after the having?
Was she brave enough to find out?

Those were the questions that occupied her
on the evening drive, cutting down the distance to London and expanding the distance
between them and Alton. 'To claim the high
ground,' Preston had explained to her parents.
'We will be in place before Alton can reach

us.' He'd also counselled Dimitri not to have their response to Alton delivered until tomorrow, knowing full well that a delayed answer kept Alton trapped in Little Westbury that much longer. But it was hard to think about Alton when Preston sat across from her, inviting a different direction of thought until they pulled in to an inn.

A night on the road. A night out of time where they were not accountable to anyone but themselves. The wicked thought came to her as she recognised the place; the same inn they'd stopped at just a few weeks ago on the way home. Preston handed her down from the coach as temptation whispered: could there be an exception to her rules? Did she dare find out what lay on the other side of having Preston? If she did dare, it would have to be tonight.

The innkeeper remembered them and was glad to see them, giving them the same room. The inn was full of memories, Bea thought nervously; the private parlour and the birthday dinner. The room and that first kiss, the acknowledgement of their attraction. Had it really been only three weeks ago? So much had changed. It seemed like an age. Or was it she who had changed?

They ate in their room due to the lateness of the hour, saying little, the conversation from the coach still lingering between them. 'Trust me,' he'd said. Did he have any idea what he was asking with those words?

Bea finished her stew and set down her spoon, picking up the conversation as if it had occurred a moment ago instead of three hours. 'It's more complicated than that. I made myself two promises, rules really, when I had Matthew.'

Preston nodded, setting down his own spoon. 'I'm listening.'

'Well, first, I promised myself I'd stay away from men. They've proven to be dangerous creatures where I'm concerned. Second, I promised myself I wouldn't seek out passion.' Would he laugh at her? Would he argue with her?

Preston did neither. 'Celibacy is a difficult life, I think. I'm not convinced our bodies are born to it although some of us aspire to it.' He paused and studied her, his intent gaze creating a warm flame at the core of her. 'How is that working out for you?'

Beatrice drew a breath. Time for some honesty. 'Fine until you came along.' She waited for him to gloat with masculine arrogance, to lord the confession over her. But Preston took it in his stride, only a flicker in his eyes betraying any emotion.

'And now?'

'Now, I wonder if it isn't time to break those rules and see what's on the other side of this thing between us.' A woman could not be any bolder than that. She waited, watching the flicker in Preston's eyes, wondering if he'd ever been so blatantly propositioned before.

'It is time.' His voice was husky as he rose from the table, offering her his hand, raising her up. His lips skimmed her knuckles as he breathed his vow. 'You can trust me, Bea. Let me show you that not every man is Malvern Alton.'

'That's not what I'm worried about,' Bea whispered, letting him draw her to him. 'I'm worried what you'll show me is that not every man is you.'

He silenced her with a kiss, long and hard, giving her no chance to question her resolve, only a chance to tremble, a chance for her body to take over and she let it. Tonight, it was time they both owned what lay between them for their own good. It might be the only time they could.

His hand rested over the flutter of her pulse at the base of her neck, his hazel eyes dark with desire as he reached for her hand and placed it over the pulse at the base of his neck. 'Do you feel that, Bea? Don't think for a moment you're the only one who is frightened by this.'

'What are you afraid of?' she breathed. It was hard to imagine Preston afraid of anything, least of all his feelings. He knew himself completely. Her other hand slipped between them, spreading flat against his trousers to press against the hard length of him.

He gave a sigh at the pressure of her hand on him. 'I could fall for you, Bea. But it's not enough to stop me from wanting you, from wanting to see what's on the other side.'

She kissed him then, pulling his head down to hers. 'Tonight, that makes two of us.' Just this once she could want him.

Chapter Sixteen

Just this once he could have her. It was a midnight promise he made himself, the kind easy to make in the heat of the moment and harder to keep in the hours that would follow. Preston breathed in the scent of her, inhaling the lavender of her hair, her skin, and exhaling a groan of desire.

They should have started here. He should have seduced her first and reasoned with her later. Giving Beatrice too much time to think was dangerous. But even as he thought it, his mind was already laughing at him. Did he really think Beatrice would have *allowed* a seduction for no reason? She was much too cautious, much too protective of her son and of their friendship to risk such a thing for pleasure alone. She was only permitting it now, perhaps, out of desperation. It wasn't the best recommendation, but he would build on that, change that.

His lips hovered just above hers, his words a hoarse confession of desire. 'I want you, Beatrice.' His mouth tasted her; the lingering tannins of the wine on her tongue. She gave a moan, low in her throat, a cry of encouragement and surrender, an acknowledgement that she didn't want to fight *them*. Her body leaned into his and he held her there, his hands resting low at her hips, his thumbs pressing evocatively against the curves of her.

His mouth slid to the column of her neck, to the vee of bare skin left unprotected by the gauzy fichu at her bodice. She smelled intoxicatingly like England in spring; all lavender and wildflowers, underlaid with the more sensual scent of a woman in arousal. *She* wanted him. The knowledge of it spurred him on, another groan welling in his throat as her mouth found his ear, her teeth nipping at his lobe with tiny bites that sent a shockwave through him as she cupped him in her hand. Desire had him hard in its clutches now, weeks of wanting coming to fruition.

He lifted her to the edge of the table, kneeling before her, running his hands up the smooth length of her legs; over calves, over thighs, pushing her skirts back until she was exposed to him, until his hands rested high at the juncture of her thighs, his thumbs bracketing the warm core of her, feathering the secret places of her womanhood with their touch, feeling the dampness of her for him. He groaned aloud, nearly undone at her readiness, despite all of his self-made promises that he would make this good for her, that he would exceed what had passed for lovemaking with that bastard Alton.

He brought his mouth to her, there in the warm vee of her legs, his breath gentle on her dark curls, at odds with his racing pulse as he breathed in the intimate scent of her, heard his name on her lips voiced in question, unsure of what he intended, felt her hands anchor in his hair as he licked, felt them tighten as he teased the nub within the folds with the tip of his tongue, tasting the sweet cream of her, heard her gasp with honest shock at first, then honest pleasure as her legs widened, giving him complete access, her breathing coming hard and fast, her body arching up to him, wanting the pleasure, searching for it.

And he gave it—oh, God, how he gave it.

Her pleasure was his pleasure, their breathing intermingled in a ragged rhythm, her gasps coming hard and fast now as conclusion neared. She bucked hard against him, a near-scream of release wrenched from her throat as she gave herself over to it, followed by sobs of panting disbelief as he knelt before her, his own breath coming hard, her hands rooted in his hair. He wouldn't have moved for the life of him, savouring this moment, this knowledge. She'd not known. She'd not known there could be pleasure such as this. Not until him…

He'd not understood until now how much it mattered to him that he be the first to show her pleasure. He rose slowly and stepped back, taking in the tousled look of her, wanting to capture this moment in his mind, this incredibly erotic, evocative moment: Beatrice on the table's edge, her hair falling down, her skirts pushed up, her legs spread, the candlelight and dinner behind her, her eyes blazing in comprehension, a comprehension *he'd* put there.

He found her eyes and held her gaze, his hand going deliberately to the bow of his cravat. He tugged, the linen falling away as he shrugged out of his coat. His fingers moved to the buttons of his waistcoat. Beatrice's tongue wet her lips, her eyes obsidian dark and glittering as understanding dawned. He folded his waistcoat and made a show of laying it aside before his shirt followed. This was not new territory for them. But what followed would be. 'Look at me, Bea.'

He rested his hands at the waistband of his trousers, watching her eyes follow the gesture to his hips. 'I want to stand before you naked, stripped to the bone for you in every way possible. When a man offers the protection of his body, a woman should see what she's getting.' Nakedness was the ultimate honesty, the ultimate intimacy. A man who could not come to a woman thus was no man at all, but a façade, reliant on tailors and illusions to support his image.

He flicked open the flies of his trousers, watching her watching him as the fullness of his nudity was revealed to her, watching her gaze drift to lean hips, to long thighs, to the ruddy proof of manhood his body offered. 'It's not a perfect body, Bea. A bullet wound or two and a knife scar have put paid to that. But it's mine and it's yours. If you'll have it.'

His throat was dry. The seconds stretched between them as he waited for her answer.

Bea's eyes held his, her hand pulling out the fichu at her bodice, in a gesture that mimicked his earlier one at his cravat. 'I suppose it's my turn, then.' She let the gauzy fabric drop as she slid from the table, her fingers working the fastenings of her gown. He thought those fingers trembled as she slid the gown from her shoulders and let it fall. The candlelight caught the shadow of her body beneath the thin linen of her undergarments and he went hard, harder than he'd thought possible. God, how he wanted her. The wanting had him sweating and his heart pounding.

She hitched hesitant, trembling fingers beneath the straps of her chemise as she considered the required action. In those brief moments she was the quintessential Beatrice Penrose, the brash girl he knew, moulded into the bold woman she'd become—a woman who understood even her bravery had consequences, but forged ahead anyway, knowing the actions outweighed the outcome.

Her voice was reminiscent of midnight whisky and fledgling confidence as she stepped towards him, pulling the chemise over her head, 'My body's not perfect. I've had a child. But it's mine and it's yours. If you'll have it.'

If he'd have her? Did she really think there was any chance he'd refuse? He let his eyes speak for him, lingering on her breasts with their dusky nipples, the curve of her hips, the soft plane of her stomach, the dark shadow at her thighs: a goddess's body, a lush, earthy body that gave life and nurtured it. To think childbirth had been unkind to her was an overstatement. It had been exceedingly kind to her. 'Beatrice, you're beautiful, a druid queen come to life. For me.'

Bea let Preston's words wash over her, let them wash away the self-consciousness that swamped her as she stood before him. She was acutely aware she could not claim to look as lovely out of her clothes as she did in them. Her breasts were too full, her hips streaked with red fingers where skin had stretched beyond the healing powers of witch hazel. Yet the gaze Preston lavished on her said he found her otherwise—*beautiful, a druid queen*. She wanted to believe that.

He reached for her, drawing her close with his hands, with his kiss, his mouth murmur-

ing hot words as their bodies met, bare skin
to bare skin, feeling the planes of one another without any hindrance between them.
She felt the heat of him, the strength and desire of him as his length pressed against her
stomach, hard and insistent, a reminder of
where all of this was headed: to bed. They
were naked body and soul now and far past
the point of no return.

His hands cupped the undersides of her
breasts, lifting them, letting the heaviness of
them fill his palms as his mouth murmured
promises of pleasure to come. *More* pleasure.
The interlude on the table proved her hypothesis true. There was indeed more and Preston
knew the secret to it. But that wasn't why she
was naked in his arms, letting him waltz her
to the big bed. This choice she made tonight
had nothing to do with curiosity satisfied and
hypotheses proven. This had to do with *them*
and only them. Hadn't they been wondering
and wanting for weeks now?

Preston swept her up and carried her the
last few feet, depositing her on the bed before following her down, his long body rising up over her, his arms bracketing her head,
his sweep of dark hair falling forward over

his face. She kissed him then, long and hard. But he was the master here and when he drew back, eyes open, she saw the intensity of his need for her. Reverence mixed with desire. He was burning. For her. If she hadn't been beyond reason the sight of Preston Worth in the throes of desire would have pushed her there.

She opened to him, relishing the feel of him settling between her legs, the caress of his open palm against her breast, the nudge of his phallus against her entrance and the way her body responded, slick and ready for him once again as he slid within. She arched, hungry for this, for him. Nothing mattered in these moments but joining him in the search for pleasure, a search that she was intuitively certain could not be reached by one person alone. She heard Preston groan in disbelieving awe as he thrust once more, his body starting the rhythmic slide and thrust of lovemaking, urging her to join him, to find him in it.

And she did. She wrapped her legs about him, holding him close, willing him to stay deep inside her. Her hips matched his, her body matched the rhythm he set, kept that pattern as the pace began to surge towards completion, she as eager as he to reach the glorious finish. His skin was slick against hers now from exertion, his muscles straining taut in an effort to keep his weight from her, an intuitive gentleman even at the height of pleasure, even with the rest of him unleashed and exposed in the very best of ways.

Preston's body tightened, gathering itself for a final effort above her and she gasped out loud with the pleasure and joy of it, of seeing him so entirely undone, that she had given him this. Oh, that was happiness indeed to know she was not alone in this chance. He was there with her as they fell, pushed over pleasure's brink together, and she clung to him as she shattered, suddenly born into an entirely new world where her rules were shattered and nothing could be the same again; Least of all her.

Comparisons were inevitable. Perhaps because she was a scientist at heart. Perhaps because she'd long suspected she'd been cheated in her earlier encounter with sex. Or perhaps, simply because she was human and comparison was the natural way of the mind when encountering the new and discarding the old. Even so, those comparisons were slow in coming and Beatrice was in no hurry to seek them out. This was new territory, new luxury, to lay in her lover's arms with no expectation of movement, no need to rush, no fear of discovery.

When they did come, they weren't entirely the comparisons one might expect. Lovemaking with Preston so far exceeded the rudimentary experience with Alton as to not even provide grounds for fair comparison. This had been entirely different, not only in the quality of the physical engagement—there'd been no awkward lifting and shifting of clothes, no furtive coupling—but in *feeling*. She'd not wanted this to end, she'd wanted to hover in the space between finish and fracture, where her body yearned for the pleasure that existed just beyond the finish, but wanting to hold off the fracturing that would come for as long as possible because she knew what waited for her on the other side of completion when she came down from pleasure's hill. It waited for her now, here in the dark, while Preston dozed beside her, one arm flung over her waist in sleepy possession.

A drowsy part of her mind pushed forward the question of what happened now. They'd indulged their passion and now they were on the other side of it. What next? Would Preston insist on being her husband now in truth? A lot of things might have changed tonight, her rules had been broken, but not that. No matter what they'd discovered in this room, she still had to give Preston up if it came to that. It was the right thing to do and she always did the right thing, even in the face of adversity.

Her hand drifted across her belly below Preston's arm, recalling the early days of her pregnancy when it had been possible to end it, encouraged even. She had not been able to bring herself to take the easy way out when it required taking a life even though her own life would likely be more difficult because of it. That same logic pushed to the fore now. She would not take Preston's life even if he insisted on it. He was meant for so much more.

He shifted beside her, moving his arm to prop himself up and look at her with eyes banked with latent desire. 'You should sleep.'

'Can't,' Bea confessed. 'There's too much to think about.' She felt his lips in her hair.

'Then don't think,' he whispered. 'Tonight's not for thinking. It's just for us.'

'And the morning?' Bea sighed, wishing she had his confidence.

'The morning will come whether we worry about it or not.' Preston rolled her beneath him, smiling down at her, his eyes flirting. 'Do you know what a good cure for sleeplessness is?'

She laughed up at him, setting aside her cares as she twined her arms loosely about his neck. 'I have an idea what that might be. Why don't you show me?' She paused. 'Wait. Why don't *I* show *you*? Roll over. I want you beneath me.'

Preston laughed, but she heard the hitch of desire in his voice and felt his body rise in anticipation as she straddled him. She smiled to herself, reaching a hand behind her to trail her nails up the sensitive flesh of his inner thigh, listening to him gasp an epithet as she cupped the sac between his legs. She loved holding him, loved what she could make him feel. Her own breath came faster. She drew her nails up his leg one more time, this time wrenching a desperate groan from him.

'You're killing me, Bea.'

She leaned forward and kissed his mouth. 'Just wait. It will be worth it.' She rose up then, levering herself over his straining phallus, let it tease them both at her entrance before she slid down its length, revelling in each inch as she took him. Oh, sweet heavens, this would be the death of them both. She'd never made love to a man before, never thought it would be this exquisite, this powerful to take the lead. Beneath her, Preston shook, his body bucked as she slid and rose, slid and rose again, her palms flat on his chest as the pleasure built.

His hands were at her hips, anchoring her as her body found the place where her own gratification resided. She ground her hips into his, releasing it, both of them swept away once more in pleasure's wave, this time at her behest, Preston bucking hard one last time beneath her. She laid her head on his chest, feeling his heart thumping hard against her ear as he filled her. Drowsiness crept up on her and still she was loath to move. Her last thought was that maybe Preston was right. The morning would take care of itself. If only they could stay like this.

Chapter Seventeen

If only they could have stayed. Preston was still wishing they were back in bed at the inn hours later as he pulled up in front of Liam's town house. He'd seen Bea and Matthew safely dropped off at Worth House on Bruton Street first. He would have liked to have helped Bea settle in, but time was of the essence and he was keen to see what Liam had learned. He'd stayed long enough to introduce Bea to the staff, accept their congratulations and to open the letter addressed to him from the Foreign Office.

He regretted the haste. Depending on what Liam had to say, other errands might be in order. If so, he wouldn't see Beatrice again until this evening. Bea would have a lot of time on her hands to think about last night, to think about this morning before they'd left the inn. To realise, as he had, that once was not going to be enough. He had no idea what sorts of conclusions she'd draw. But he had his. He'd make the engagement real if she'd let him. Only he couldn't say that to her. Bea would think he'd manipulated the whole arrangement to leave her no choice and that would make her stubborn. He had to be careful and let her come to him. Waiting would be hard.

Liam was being careful with his words. Preston had known his friend long enough to know when something difficult was on his mind. Preston watched him put a breakfast plate together at the sideboard with slow, deliberate selections. He was stalling. Preston cleared his throat. 'Time was; you'd simply pile a plate as high as it could go. You could fill a plate in ten seconds, if I recall rightly.'

Liam chuckled. 'That was a long time ago, before I had any manners. Things change. Time was, I could leave you for a few hours and be assured you wouldn't do anything outlandish either.'

Ah. So that was it. Preston unfolded his napkin and set it in his lap, waiting for Liam to take a seat.

'I hear congratulations are in order. You and Beatrice are engaged.'

'I thought you liked Beatrice.' Preston started in on his eggs, starving. He'd waited to eat with Liam. 'I thought the match would please you.'

'If done for the right reasons.' Liam buttered his toast with quiet ferocity.

'What better reasons can there be than to give Beatrice the protection of my name? The security of my wealth? To give Matthew a father?'

'In exchange for Greece?' Liam replied pointedly. 'The talk is all over Grillion's that you'll be offered the post. You can't have them both. There's no question of taking Bea and the baby with you. Greece is far too explosive right now.' Liam was going to break the toast in half if he buttered it any harder. 'Is she worth your ambitions? Because that's the price of this engagement if you haven't figured it out yet.' One could always count on Liam to be blunt.

'I had a letter waiting for me to that extent,' Preston said tersely. He'd not allowed himself time to consider the import of that letter and without the preparation to do so, Liam's bluntness called into question the darker places of his heart. Perhaps that was why he'd been eager to agree with Bea that the engagement be a sham. Maybe deep in his heart, he hadn't quite reconciled himself to what a real wedding meant. Maybe he was still playing at the fantasy of a family man.

The thoughts shamed him, as honest as they were, especially after last night. He had not taken Bea to bed without contemplation. There was no question of wanting Bea, of caring for her. He did. But marriage to Bea would commit him to a different lifestyle than the one he imagined for himself. He knew, deep inside, he had not yet reconciled those two pieces of himself.

Liam sensed his hesitation and pounced on his weakness. 'There's always the issue of love.' Liam gave up on the toast and fixed him with a blue stare. 'Love is also a good reason to get married. The only reason, really, and I haven't heard you mention it once when you catalogue the assets of this alliance.'

'Love? Really?' Preston was starting to get agitated. 'That's quite the hypocrisy coming from a man who wouldn't marry my sister because he felt he couldn't give her the very things I can offer Beatrice.' Preston returned Liam's stare. 'You once believed all you had to offer May was love and it wouldn't be enough.' Checkmate. Preston took a smug sip of coffee. Let him argue with that, although the whole idea of arguing over this at all was insane since it wasn't going to happen, even if last night had prompted some very different thoughts on the subject.

Liam chose not to make a direct response. 'I care for both of you very much. I would not want to see either of you committed to a match made out of desperation, even though I understand your motives for it.'

Time to switch conversational tracts. Preston had no desire to listen to Liam's marriage counselling. 'So, how bad is it? What have you learned about Alton?'

Liam obliged with a grim set to his jaw. 'Nothing good, I can you tell that much. I only had a twenty-four-hour head start on you, but I made the club rounds immediately. Malvern Alton has debt problems and everyone knows.'

Preston nodded. His instincts had been right. 'How bad?'

'Pretty bad. His father has cut him off in

order to pressure him into marriage. It seems there's an inheritance Alton has refused to claim because it requires he take a bride in order to access it. Without his allowance, Alton has run up debts at nearly every gaming hell and brothel in London. Even the ones he doesn't have vowels at won't extend him any credit at this point.'

Liam paused. Preston could see him gathering his thoughts. There was bad news coming. 'There are thugs after him. Madam Rose at House of Flowers has given him until June to pay his bill with interest. He beat a girl up last time he was there. I heard that from the famed madam herself after following a couple of leads and paying a few well-placed bribes. Madam Rose said he had plans to marry a wealthy bride. It was the only reason he's still walking. She was afraid if she damaged the goods she'd never get her money.'

Preston set aside his fork, his appetite gone at the mention of the beaten girl. 'Then he'll come for Beatrice.' Alton was dangerous in more ways than one. He didn't like thinking of what an angry Alton would do to Beatrice. 'We'd better be ready. I'll speak to the Penrose solicitor about getting the betrothal papers drawn up right away.' The sooner he had some paper to stand between Alton and Beatrice, the better.

Liam sighed and steepled his fingers on the tablecloth. 'I wish I had better news. I wish you didn't have to—'

Preston shook his head. 'Stop. I don't *have* to do anything. I *want* to do this. I am fond of Beatrice and the child. I don't want you or anyone thinking this is a sacrifice.' Especially since it was a sacrifice that would not come to pass. But in the meantime, this engagement had to look and feel real to everyone around them. 'I need a favour, Liam. I want to have our engagement announced at your celebration ball, after the knighting ceremony.'

Preston knew Liam would understand the need for pomp and precipitancy—the two of them had tracked criminals for too long. Malvern Alton was coming. It wasn't a question of if, it was a matter of when. But they still had some time. Two days by Preston's calculations. Dimitri wouldn't deliver the note until this afternoon. Even if he left right away, Alton wouldn't be in London until the day after tomorrow. They could have protection and emergency contingencies in place by then, although Beatrice wouldn't like the contingency when she learned about it.

Preston rose from the table and shook Liam's hand. 'I appreciate your help and your support.' He let Liam draw him into a strong embrace.

'If anyone can make her happy, I know it's you.' His friend clapped him on the back. He could, too. If Beatrice would let him.

Malvern Alton crumpled the short note in his hand. He was not happy. Once he arrived in Little Westbury his plan was supposed to take care of itself. Just the opposite had happened. Instead of being intimidated by his blackmail threat, Beatrice had left for London, the last place he would have thought she'd want to be, where her shame could be exposed to everyone. It was certainly the last place *he* wanted to be. Until he had money in his pocket to clear his debts, he didn't want to risk running into anyone he owed—all of whom who were in London, as it happened.

He began to pace the small room at the Little Westbury inn, frustration mounting. He might not have a choice. The simple plan had gone awry from the start. What had begun as an easy courtship of a wealthy country girl had derailed almost immediately. It was the baby's fault. Who would have guessed he'd got her pregnant? Who would have guessed she'd have *had* the baby *and* brought it home?

Still, he'd seen the immediate possibilities the moment the baby had entered the drawing room. He'd thought the baby would help his cause. She'd be eager to marry the father of her child. All of this assumed Beatrice Penrose was an ordinary woman, living by ordinary rules. He was starting to remember what he disliked about her so much. Beatrice was fiercely independent. She played by her own rules. She'd left him no choice but to lower himself to blackmail—she and that gentleman who was sniffing after her.

Blackmail should have been the end of it. The threat was fairly straightforward: marry me or I'll tell everyone the child is a bastard. But Beatrice hadn't scared. Her family hadn't scared. He'd bargained on her parents' fear, but they'd seen through the threat to the flaw beneath. The response they'd sent had said as much. He could not tell the world the child was his bastard without incriminating himself—what sort of man left a woman pregnant and unwed for over a year and then announced to the world what he'd done?

That assumed anyone would believe him. He unrumpled the paper in his hand and re-read the lines.

Our daughter married Baldwin Fielding last February. He died at sea and his child was born in November.

The enormity of the lie was nearly as incredulous as the idea that people would believe it. Then again, they didn't have to believe it. They only had to accept it and society would accept anything from those they championed.

The audacity of the Penroses was striking. They were simply choosing to ignore his presence. It was almost as if he were invisible. Who would believe him if he tried to expose the lie? How would he prove otherwise? Never had he imagined his threat would be faced head on. They were calling his bluff, daring him to go through with it. And he could not.

If his blackmail had no teeth, maybe it was time to rethink the nature of his strategy. Perhaps public exposure wasn't necessary to get what he wanted. That left force.

He would just take what he wanted. Possession was nine-tenths of the law, after all. Once he had Beatrice and that child in his hands, the Penroses would pay mightily to get them back, and while he had Beatrice in his power, she'd do anything for her child. Even marry him. Once the ransom was paid, the Penroses would find they'd got more than they bargained for, like a son-in-law. But in order for any of that to happen, he'd have to follow her to London. Carefully. London wasn't exactly safe for him at the moment.

Chapter Eighteen

Careful was the watchword of Beatrice's day. Her actions as she unpacked at the Worths', her words, even her thoughts were all very *carefully* chosen. She strolled the town-house halls with Matthew on her hip, trying to distract him from his teething. He'd been fussy since Preston had dropped them off and now he refused to go down for his nap. At least Matthew kept her from thinking too much. If she wasn't careful, her thoughts would run rampant. They would lead her to thinking about last night and what it *could* mean as opposed to what it *did* mean.

She'd come to a comfortable understanding of what it did mean: two people with a strong attraction to one another had satisfied their curiosity, their hunger. That the attraction ran deeper than the physical had only served to make the connection stronger and the realisation of that desire more powerful. She could live with that. She would have to live with that. It was all she could have, all she'd allowed herself to have. It was what her rules would tolerate and what her conscience would tolerate when it came to Preston. Preston had said she could trust him to give her pleasure and to keep her safe. He'd been true on both accounts. He'd taken precautions. There would be no child from their interlude and there had been pleasure aplenty.

Now, it was up to her to keep Preston safe. He'd promised her the engagement would end, that there would be no marriage. She didn't want him rethinking it after last night. The honour in him would push such a conclusion, especially if last night happened again, another reason why it could only be once.

Beatrice shifted Matthew to her other hip, finding a hard carrot in her pocket for him to chew on. If he didn't settle down soon, she'd have to opt for the whisky. Whisky on the gums worked like magic, but she didn't like the idea of giving drink to a baby. She shifted directions, heading towards the estate office where she knew the decanters were always filled, just in case.

It was a long walk and Matthew had calmed down with his carrot considerably by the time she arrived. Bea sat down in the chair behind the desk and began to bounce him, her eye drawn to the open letter on the desk's polished surface. She leaned forward, scanning the contents, reading twice to understand the stunning news: *the Foreign Office wanted Preston to go to Greece.*

She sat back, forgetting to bounce Matthew, stunned. How long had he known? He hadn't said anything in the carriage ride from Scotland, he'd only talked of Seacrest and how much he didn't want to go there. *Because he wanted to go elsewhere—to Greece. Because he'd been hoping for the appointment.* She understood better now why he'd not had a forthcoming assignment, but was expecting to linger around London due to the Roan trial. *Because of this.* Until she'd come along and ruined everything.

Well, that might be giving herself too much credit. She'd only thought she'd ruined everything. She'd thought, right up until a few minutes ago, Preston might actually push to marry her even though he'd promised her he'd end the engagement. Clearly, she was wrong. He needed the engagement to end as much as she did. Greece was waiting. His future was waiting and it wasn't with her. Maybe it wouldn't be so hard to keep Preston safe, after all. She should feel relief. She'd worried for nothing. He already had this planned out. She should feel better about that than she did. Right now, she felt unexplainably sick, because any explanation for the rolling sensation in her stomach defied logic.

'You've done what?' Beatrice fought to keep her voice down as she faced Preston in the Worth drawing room that night. The hour was late. Dinner was over, May and Liam had gone home and Preston's late-arriving parents had finally gone upstairs to bed, leaving them alone at last. She'd been expecting news of Alton, expecting them to perhaps talk about Greece. He was going to have to tell her some time. She'd not been expecting the first words out of his mouth to be, 'I've got a special licence.' According to the letter she'd seen upstairs, such an action made no sense.

'It's a necessary contingency, if you'd let

me explain.' Preston pushed a hand through his hair, his customary gesture of impatience. Bea begrudgingly took the licence from him.

'So, this is what you've spent the last seven hours doing since leaving Liam's?' He'd been waiting on the archbishop's office in the Doctors' Commons. She saw the reason for the wait. This was a true special licence that allowed him to marry her any day and any time of that day. 'It's a lot of trouble to go through for a wedding that won't happen.'

'The wait was worth it. While I was there, I learned an invaluable piece of news.' Preston's voice dropped, low to match hers. Neither of them wanted to be overheard. 'A week ago, Malvern Alton was there for a special licence as well.'

'Oh, dear Lord.' Bea sat down hard on the sofa, letting the shock settle. She didn't need to be a genius to know who Alton wanted the licence for.

'I don't need to explain the implications to you.'

'No. You don't need to explain.' Beatrice understood the danger to her had just escalated. With a special licence in hand, all Alton had to do was scoop her up and carry her away to some vicar willing to perform the ceremony. She'd not been eager to come to Worth House, but Preston had insisted it was safer than being alone at the Penrose town house. It seemed he'd been right. 'He is more desperate than we thought.'

'Quite desperate.' Preston sat down beside her. 'He has enormous debt, the kind of debt only a rich dowry will satisfy and he has to satisfy that debt by mid-June.'

Bea sat quietly, taking in Preston's news, letting her mind mull it over, looking for the silver lining. 'Then we only have to be engaged until June.' She tried for a smile. Surely Preston would be glad to know there was a 'deadline' to his engagement and it would leave him plenty of time to prepare for departure.

'Were you only looking for information at the Doctors' Commons? Why did *you* need the licence?' Bea queried, her eye drawn once again to the paper as he folded it up and put it in his pocket. Not of all her questions were answered.

'It's the emergency contingency.' Preston met her gaze. 'In case we can't cry off.'

It took Bea a moment to understand. 'In case we can't? What does that mean?'

'In case betrothal papers aren't enough to keep you safe. In case Alton is more desperate and potentially more deranged than we think.' Preston's face grew grim. 'I didn't want to tell you, but perhaps you should know. He beat a girl to near unconsciousness at the brothel because she refused to let him use a crop on her. If he's not deranged, at the very least he's a sick bastard.'

'But you don't want to marry me.' Bea began to mount her protest. 'I don't want to marry you.' Not quite true. She simply didn't want to ruin him.

Preston chuckled. 'You do know how to handle a man's ego, Bea. I don't think this is about want, or even about last night. I think this is about doing what it takes to keep you safe. He is coming for you and we may reach a point where the only protection you have against him is to put yourself beyond his reach with marriage. That way, if he did manage to force you, any marriage he had performed would be illegal.'

'We'll cross that bridge when we come to it. I don't think we're there yet. We've only just arrived and we haven't even made our engagement public.' Bea rose, wanting some distance from him, wanting to feel as if she had some control here. 'The Calvert ball is tomorrow night. We should attend if we want to be seen. It's the biggest gathering of the week. The Bristows' is the largest one next week. If Alton's on our heels, we can't start the charade too soon, it seems.'

All things considered, Bea thought the conversation was going moderately well. They hadn't talked about last night once. They had enough of a mess on their hands without bringing that into the mix, too.

What a perfect, hellish mess. Malvern Alton watched the parade of sleek carriages line up at the kerb in front of the Bristow town house from across the road, beautiful women in silks and jewels disembarking with the help of well-heeled gentlemen dressed in dark evening clothes. His eyes took in each of them, scanning the colourful crowd until he found what he was looking for. There she was! In the deep royal-blue gown with the whiter-than-snow lace wrap at her shoulders.

Beatrice Penrose stepped down from a luxurious black-lacquered town coach with the Latin words *semper luceat*—always shine—

painted on the door in scrolling letters above a regal coat of arms.

The effect of the blue and white was stunning even at a distance. Something expensive and sparkling in the dark depths of her hair caught the streetlight. Had she been that beautiful when he'd known her? He didn't think so. She'd always been daring, but even this was far bolder an act than he'd expected from her. She, an unwed mother with no decent reputation to her name, was literally waltzing all over London in fancy gowns, in the best of homes, while he; a legitimate son of a nobleman, was reduced to lurking in the shadows when it should have been he who was received. Stupid, stupid London. What would they think, what would they *do* if those silly matrons knew the whore Beatrice Penrose really was?

He raised the opera glasses to his eyes, watching her head tilt as she laughed up at her escort. Who had made her laugh? Made her face light up like that? Alton's magnified gaze shifted upwards to take in the man's face and locked on its target. Of course. The man from the Penrose drawing room that day in Little Westbury. Preston Worth. The little strumpet dared quite a lot to reach for a man like him.

Alton swallowed back his anger. He'd heard the rumours as soon as he'd arrived in town. They were what had prompted his stalking. Worth intended to marry her. It was floating discreetly around London, but he'd heard it in several places now. He hadn't believed it. It was ridiculous in the extreme that even someone of Beatrice's bold character would think to marry such a public figure after her behaviour. Unwed mothers lived in shame and deprivation, not much higher on the social scale than the whores. They weren't out angling for one of London's prime bachelors. Then again, Beatrice was a stranger to the notion of restraint.

That brought a twisted smile to his lips. He lowered the glasses, watching her and Worth join the crowd inside the mansion. He wouldn't mind tasting a piece of that boldness again, maybe in making her pay for her infidelity. A crop across that pale, luscious backside was definitely in order. The more he thought about it, the more he believed he was in the right. His demands were not unreasonable. He'd come back to her. He was willing to make an honest woman of her and the whelp so that he could claim his inheritance—an inheritance that would provide for her, would go to the little brat.

She should be on her hands and knees in gratitude. Instead, she was snubbing him for Preston Worth. Alton shifted his posture, rubbing himself, feeling his arousal take shape beneath his trousers. The bitch had been hot for him and what he had to offer once. He could make her feel that way again. Starting tonight.

There was something he needed from her and he couldn't leave without it. He'd get it, just as soon as he solved the problem of getting into a ball he'd not been invited to. Actually, it wasn't the getting-in part that was tricky. Folks crashed balls all the time. One only had to wait until the receiving line was through and there was no chance of being announced. The trick for him was getting out without being recognised. If word got back to Madam Rose he was out socialising, she'd be asking for more than the token of payment she was asking for now as a show of goodwill that he'd pay in June.

If he remembered correctly, there was a

gate behind the hedges in the garden just off the alley. He'd ask himself how it had come to this—covertly crashing parties he should be invited to—but he knew the answer. One stubborn woman was the cause of this. Slinking was certainly beneath him, but until he had Beatrice beneath him, it would have to do.

Chapter Nineteen

How had it come to this? This place where it was hard to remember it was a fantasy and nothing more? Beatrice took a breathless turn at the top of the ballroom, Preston's hand firm at her waist, flawlessly leading them through the crush of dancers, his hazel eyes looking down at her in a merry, sparkling dance of their own. Times like this made it hard to remember he was to leave for Greece, hard to remember she didn't want to marry him.

Every night reminded her of the possibilities. The dangerous 'what if' game would start. What if she and Preston were together *without* the pretence of an engagement? What if this was a real courtship? She'd never had one before and even this charade was intoxicating.

When they flew like this, when he escorted

her into an entertainment, his hand light but steady at her back in the receiving line, when he took her into supper after the midnight waltz, it was hard to remember the pretence existed at all. It was harder still to remember the pretence when they walked in a lantern-lit garden, or when Preston stole a kiss. In those moments, she was all too happy to surrender under the guise that the charade demanded it.

Yet always on the periphery, the guilt subtly hovered. She didn't deserve this. Her friends and her family had been so good in protecting her. Preston most of all. It was greedy of her to want more, to even *think* of taking away his dreams, dreams that had existed before her.

'Do you need some punch?' Preston asked, bringing them to a halt, the music ending. 'You look flushed. Would you rather have champagne?'

'Champagne.' She laughed. He knew all of her weaknesses. Aside from her girlfriends, did anyone know her so well? Would anyone know her so well ever again when this was over? 'I'll meet you in the garden. I hear the Bristows have a spectacular fountain imported from Italy.' She watched him go, broad shoulders parting the crowd with ease. A little trill of desire ran through her. She knew what those shoulders looked like bare. What *all* of him looked like bare. It was an image she'd not been able to expel. Would she ever be able to? When would she stop undressing him with her eyes every time they were together? Would she ever stop wishing it could be different; that there could be another time like the night in the inn? That she could be different? That she could be *better* for him?

In the garden, the cool air fanned her cheeks. She moved away from the crowds, letting her feet stroll aimlessly. She was being greedy again with her wants; wanting more than she could have. She should be thankful the ruse was going well. It had been a week and there'd been no sign of Alton. That was all to the good. It meant the engagement had taken, that London believed them madly in love and that Alton could not make society believe otherwise. It also meant Preston wouldn't have to use the special licence.

She should be glad. Because she knew, as Preston did not, he would come to hate her for trapping him in a marriage done only to avoid a crisis, a marriage that forced him to give up his dreams.

Bea had reached the hedges at the back of the property when she heard the whisper of her name. Once. Twice. She should have run. Instead, she stopped long enough to cock her head, long enough to think about the oddness of a bush whispering her name, long enough for a hand to whip out in the dark and grip her wrist, holding her fast.

'Hush, Beatrice, it's me.' A body materialised, stepping out of the hedges. Malvern Alton stood before her, brushing greenery off his dark evening clothes with his free hand.

'What are you doing here?' Beatrice hissed, tugging futilely at her arm, wanting it back.

'I wanted to see you.' He made a face. 'You're not the easiest person to see, Beatrice. The last time I tried, your self-appointed bodyguard threw me out of your home.'

'He's not my bodyguard.'

'What he is then, Beatrice? I hear rumour that he fancies himself your fiancé.' He was daring her to deny it, testing the truth of it. If he'd heard the rumours, then Dimitri and Liam had done their jobs well laying the gossip.

'We are to be married. It's not been announced officially.' Beatrice answered, pulling once more. 'He won't be pleased to find you here with me.'

'I suppose not.' He sounded almost boyish, like the charming man she'd been swept away by once. But she'd learned not to trust that charm. 'I don't mean to stay long, it's just that I'm in a deuced awful situation. I need some money.'

Beatrice stiffened. 'I haven't any.'

'Anything of value would do and I will scamper back through those hedges and be gone. Perhaps that sparkly piece in your hair? It would fetch a good price.' He sounded less boyish now. The threat plain. He would leave in exchange for something of worth that could be pawned for cash.

'And if I don't comply?'

'I don't think Mr Worth would like what he saw when he came out.' His eyes glinted. 'But you might, Bea. You used to like what I could do for you up against a wall. A fence is probably just as good. Have you tried Mr Worth out on a wall yet? Is he as able?'

She could feel the shame burning in her cheeks. What he had done to her and passed off as lovemaking was nowhere near what she and Preston had done together. His face was close to hers in a sneer that wiped all traces of boyish handsomeness away. Her wrist started to hurt. 'Don't be ashamed, Bea. You might as well screw the scion of the house of Worth. It's not like you're ever going to be a virgin again. He can never be first. Does that bother him, I wonder? That baby can never be his. That *will* bother him, I promise you. There's no man on this planet who wants to wake up and look someone else's bastard in the eye at breakfast every morning.'

Bea brought her free hand up ready to strike hard, but he was too fast. He had both her hands now, her back up hard against the fence, the rough brick snagging the delicate fabric of her gown. His body pressed to hers as his hips made a lewd gyration. Fear flashed through her. He wouldn't dare take her here would he? 'This is rape!' she ground out, shoving against him. But he was strong. She remembered that now, how she'd once revelled in that strength, the feel of his muscle beneath her hands.

He silenced her with a bruising kiss that punished her mouth, forced her head to the wall. 'Why don't you scream and we'll find out?' he leered in victory, knowing full well she couldn't scream. Screaming was what he wanted. He wanted everyone to come running into the dark corner of the garden and find them together—the nobleman's son and the well-born Penrose girl. They'd be married by the end of the week to silence the gossip. Exactly what he wanted. Exactly what Preston had feared. Only the darkness protected her from that discovery now.

'Preston will kill you.' Bea struggled wholeheartedly, but she was pinned to the wall by a body that outweighed her, her hands useless.

'Why don't you scream and find that out, too? Or, you can give me what I want—your hair piece.' He laughed cruelly. 'I didn't come for your body tonight, unless you insist. It's up to you.'

What choice did she have? She couldn't fight him and she didn't want Preston fighting him. Beatrice nodded her concession, felt him transfer her wrists into one hand, his other hand in her hair, tugging the elegant diamond-set piece free none so gently. 'You might want to go to the retiring room before you return to the ball and tidy your hair. You look like you might have been up to some mischief in the garden.' He grinned and stepped away. 'Until next time, Beatrice.' He made her a deep, mocking bow, his words leaving her shaking. 'I'll be watching you. And the estimable Mr Worth. It's hard to marry a dead man.'

Her body wanted to collapse on the ground, but her mind knew better. She could not give in to fear. Fear would require explanations. She certainly could not let Preston find her here. She was certain it was what Alton would want—Preston charging out into the darkness only to be taken unawares. She'd not missed Alton's threat that she was not the only one in danger. With Preston gone, there'd be no one to protect her and Alton was desperate enough to do it.

Beatrice pushed herself to action. She had to get to the retiring room and hide the damage; fixing her hair would be easy. Fixing the rest of her might be a little more difficult. If her hand didn't stop shaking, fixing her hair might be just as difficult.

Bea kept to the perimeter of the garden, groping her way in the dark to the servants' entrance near the kitchen. There was a back stair to follow up after that which put her into the upper hall near the ladies' room. The rest was easy and thankfully the retiring room was empty. Bea found a stool and sat down in front of the mirror. She looked up slowly, expecting to see a face that looked as ravaged as she felt.

Her hair was loose, messy, her skin pale, but that was all. After all that, shouldn't she look worse? She should be glad she didn't. She took a deep breath and began to work on her hair. She dropped the first pin and the second. She had to get herself under control. If not for her, then for Preston. She wasn't the only one who needed protecting.

'There you are!' May sailed into the room. 'We've been looking all over for you. Preston couldn't find you.' May paused, taking in her face in the mirror. 'Are you all right?'

'I'm fine.' Bea found a smile, somewhere. 'I just needed to fix my hair.'

'Where's your tiara?' May was far too astute.

'It fell out, in the garden maybe. It was too dark to find it.'

May picked up the hairbrush and some pins. 'Let me. Your hands are shaking, Bea. Now, you can either tell me what really happened, or I'll get Preston and you can tell him.'

That galvanised her. Bea gripped May's hand. 'Preston is not to know!'

May's hazel eyes went hard with knowledge. 'Alton was here, wasn't he? He threatened you?'

'Preston cannot know,' Beatrice repeated. 'You have to swear on the honour of the Left Behind Girls Club you will not tell him. I'm fine and it's over now.' The first was a weak truth. The last was an outright lie. Alton was stalking her, waiting to catch her alone again. The next time he might *take* more than a tiara, and there *would* be a next time. It had been one thing to hear Preston outline the evolution of a desperate man's actions. It was another to be the victim of those actions. These horrible things were happening to *her*. The only defence she had was to stay close to Preston, it would protect them both and if the price was the further fuelling of the magical fantasy, so be it. There were only a couple weeks left. She summoned her mantra. She was Beatrice Penrose. She would survive this, too.

Chapter Twenty

The note from May came in the morning, tucked inside a note from Liam, asking Preston to come over as soon as possible. Beatrice had cancelled yet another outing with she and Evie—the third one since the Bristow ball. It was confirmation something was off. The cancelled outings weren't the only sign. The usually independent Beatrice had become considerably more attached to him of late, never leaving his side at evening events and refusing to leave the Worth town house without him.

In and of themselves, these behaviours were nothing terribly troubling if this was a normal engagement. An affianced man was expected to dance attendance on his betrothed. But normal was not a term he'd use for his engagement with Beatrice, which meant there was some sorting to do. He chose to walk to Liam's, wanting the crisp morning air and the exercise to channel his thoughts.

Bea's behaviour was the opposite of what he'd expected at this point, particularly after her reaction to the special licence. As the supposed engagement ball neared, he'd anticipated a withdrawal from her, a protest of sorts that he must keep his word and break the engagement. But just the opposite had happened. Beatrice had drawn closer to him, a clear indicator that there was something more at play. The question was what? What motivated this closeness? Perhaps a growing emotional tie or something else?

Not that he minded more of Beatrice's company. He enjoyed the walks in the park with her, pushing Matthew in the pram, a task Beatrice insisted on performing even though there were maids aplenty willing to do it. He enjoyed the evenings of dancing and escorting her to musicales and academic lectures, although they posed enormous temptation. Enjoyed was far too tame of a word to apply. He *coveted* these moments even as they left him torn between Greece and Beatrice. These moments were a glimpse of what life would be like for them together.

Did she see it too? Did it tempt her as much as him? Could that be the reason she wanted to keep him close? They'd not discussed or repeated their night at the White Horse. The practicalities of doing so were far too complicated under his parents' roof and he *refused* to lower himself to Alton's level with furtive meetings and hasty couplings in ballroom alcoves, even if that choice left him aching at the end of the night.

The wanting worried him. What happened when he had to move on without Beatrice? Without Matthew? He'd have his answer too soon. Mid-June loomed on the calendar— Alton's deadline with the madam. Sometimes Preston thought the waiting was killing him as much as the wanting. The wanting wasn't eager for this to be over. Alton's presence kept Beatrice beside him. But the waiting was eager for resolution. When would Alton act?

His sources had caught wind of Alton's presence, although the rogue was keeping a low profile. He'd moved out of his rooms at the Albany and was at a cheap inn. To Preston's knowledge, Alton had made no contact with the Penrose family or with Bea. But the man had to act soon, he hadn't the funds or the time to wait much longer…

At Liam's town house, he was shown into the breakfast room. Liam had already assembled a plate and was dining alone without May, a sure sign it was to be breakfast as usual. That meant good food and bad news. 'Well?' Preston began without preamble, taking only toast and coffee to start.

'I have something to show you.' Liam was all seriousness. He reached beside his chair and put a box on the table, removing the lid.

Preston froze. Bea's tiara. The one she lost at the Bristow ball. 'Where did you find it?' Liam's grimness suggested this wasn't a simple case of the Bristow's gardeners having found it and sent it over.

'My man on the street heard rumour that Alton was in town and had paid part of his bill at Madam Rose's.'

'Part?' Preston lifted an eyebrow. 'This tiara is worth quite a bit. What sort of bill does he have at House of Flowers?'

'A big one. One big enough to need a dowry to clear along with his other debts.' Liam passed the tiara to him. Preston inspected the head piece, sensing more bad news was forth-coming. 'What else did you learn?'

'He told the madam the tiara was from his fiancée, Beatrice Penrose.'

Bad news indeed. Preston winced. He didn't want Beatrice's named bandied about in a brothel no matter how prestigious. It was another indication of the sort of man Alton was—a man who had no sense of respect for a decent woman's honour.

Liam gave him a conspiratorial grin. 'I might have spiked Alton's guns just a bit. I told Madam Rose Beatrice Penrose was en-gaged to you and that it would be announced in two nights.' His grin widened. 'You should have seen her! She went red and screamed for her two henchmen. Alton won't be able to pass off any more items there.' He paused and chuckled. 'Although I don't know why she was so mad. She's making good money on the tiara. She got Alton's payment and I paid her double to redeem it.'

Preston ran a thumb over a rounded edge of the tiara, feeling the smoothness of the tiny diamonds in their settings as he contemplated the news. 'You've flushed him out, then.' He'd been wishing for action on the way over, but now that it was imminent, there was a certain tension, too, not just over what was to come, but how things had got to this point. 'How do you suppose he got hold of the tiara to start with?' Beatrice had said nothing to him and apparently there'd been something to say. His mind kept going back to one singular idea: why hadn't she told him?

'There's really only three options, isn't there?' Liam knitted his brow. 'He stole it from Worth House, which seems preposterous, or it was given to him voluntarily by Beatrice or...' he paused before saying the last '...he took it from her by force.'

The last made the most sense although it was accompanied by an acute twinge of betrayal. 'At the Bristow ball, when I went to get champagne,' Preston said grimly. That evening had marked the onset of Bea's reticence to be in public without him. The bastard had taken it from her, had accosted her. Preston remembered the awful clenching of his stomach when he couldn't find her. But May had found her. May had come back and said everything was fine. Bea was just fixing her hair.

A little flare of anger surged. It took all

of his control not to send for May and call his blasted sister to account for her damnable loyalty to Beatrice. He'd bet his grandfather's ring his sister had known all along. 'Why didn't Beatrice tell me?'

Liam gave him a meaningful look over the rim of his coffee cup. 'For the same reason May took a bullet for me. Beatrice wants to protect you.'

'But I am supposed to be protecting her,' Preston argued. What protection did he need? He'd faced far worse men than Alton.

'Can't you guess, you poor sod?' Liam chuckled. 'She's in love with you, even if she won't admit it to herself.' That mitigated his anger, but not his disappointment. He might understand her reasons, but he didn't accept them...

'You should have told me.'

Beatrice eyed the box he'd placed on the low table between them with a healthy amount of scepticism. Whatever was bothering Preston today had something to do with what was in the box.

'Go on, open it,' Preston urged. They were alone together in the sitting room at the back of Worth House, a room she'd informally taken over where she could do her correspondence and play with Matthew. She lifted the lid, keeping her expression carefully neutral when she saw the tiara nestled inside. So, he knew. That's what had him bristling. Beatrice waited for Preston to speak.

He was out of his chair again, pacing. He seemed too big for the walls of the room today, the warrior within on display instead of the gentleman. 'Liam picked it up at a brothel. Alton used it to pay part of his debts. Alton told the madam he was marrying you.' He pushed a hand through his hair, a clear sign he was upset. 'Did you give it to him, Bea, or did he take it?' Ah. He was more upset about *how* Alton had come by the tiara.

She rose, too, no longer able to sit, her own emotions getting the better of her. She understood the difference. Giving implied some assent on her part. Taking indicated an act of force. Neither option created an answer that would appease him. 'I didn't exactly "give" it to him.' She still had trouble recalling those events in the dark without shaking. Preston would want details and that would hardly help quell the fury smouldering in his eyes. Details were not in his best interest.

She had to negotiate this cautiously, always aware Preston had a special licence in his pocket. 'If I tell you, you have to give me your word you won't hare off and do something foolish.' Her hand went unconsciously to his grandfather's ring beneath her bodice. She pulled it out on its chain and held it up between them. 'Swear it, on your grandfather's ring.'

He stepped towards her, near enough to close his hand around the ring, his words reluctant and intimate, his voice low, just for her. 'I swear not to do anything foolish, but that does not mean I will do nothing. How can I protect you, Bea, if I don't know what's happening?'

To his credit, he did listen quietly, the only tell-tale signs of his angst being the clench of his fists as she spoke and the hand that covered his mouth when she finished. For a long while after, he said nothing. She let him think. Let him feel. 'You were right to make me swear you a promise,' he said at last. 'I would like to do violence to him for what he did to you. When I think of you alone with him in the dark, forced to make unpalatable decisions, it makes me want blood.'

She gave him a wry smile. 'Perhaps you understand why I couldn't tell you. I don't want blood on my account, especially not yours, Preston. You've done enough.'

'Not nearly enough if he's threatening you at balls.' Preston's features were hard. 'He will come soon. By exposing the lie of his engagement to Madam Rose, we've flushed him out. He'll have to make his move and he can't wait longer than the engagement ball.'

Two days, then. Beatrice swallowed hard, understanding what Preston had left unspoken. When Alton came again it wouldn't be for tiaras or jewels. That pathway had been effectively closed to him in the move to the end game. But she knew more than Preston. 'He's not coming for me alone. He threatens you, too. If it was just me, I would perhaps have fought harder to keep the tiara.' Other realisations came to her, too. Liam and Dimitri would be at risk because they would defend her, ride after her if she was taken.

The guilt swamped her yet again as she thought of her friends in jeopardy. 'This is all my fault.' She met Preston's gaze, suddenly cognisant of her mistake. In her attempts to protect Preston from regret, she'd perhaps put him in greater danger.

Preston took her hands, his grip firm, his touch her rock with its strength. 'I can still put you beyond his reach, Bea. Say the word, I will marry you now, tomorrow, the day after.'

Bea shook her head. 'Don't you see? There's no good answer for me—none that I can live with. If I marry you, I put you in far greater jeopardy. Alton will seek to have you permanently eliminated.' Marriage firmly put Preston as an obstacle between Alton and her. 'You will not die for me, Preston Worth.'

To say the words seemed dramatic in the extreme, but that was what it had come down to, wasn't it? She'd become a pawn in a desperate man's game.

Bea drew a deep breath. There was no time like the present to talk about endings instead of beginnings. 'So, this might be over in two days or it might be over in two weeks. Perhaps we should be talking about how we want to end it.' Maybe if they created an ending, maybe if they knew how it would end, it would keep them, her particularly, from thinking about alternative endings where she got to keep the fantasy.

'Endings?' Preston raised an eyebrow. 'Are you that eager to get rid of me?' He tried to tease, but she heard the edge to his voice.

'How do we want to end the engagement?'

'Well, we don't want to end it too soon,' Preston began, and she rounded on him fiercely.

'You promised me this was all for show.'

'We want the show to be successful. If we cry off immediately, Alton will smell a rat.'

Bea pulled her trump card. 'You can't wait too long. You have Greece to prepare for.'

Preston gave her a sharp look. 'What do you know about Greece? Did my father say anything to you about it?'

'No,' Bea put in quickly, unwilling to be a further source of tension between the Worth males. 'I saw the letter the day I arrived.' The day he'd come back with the special licence.

'Nothing's decided.' Preston's jaw was tight.

'What is there to decide?' Beatrice's sense of alarm was on alert. 'You are perfect for it and it's something you want. You said as much in the carriage ride from Scotland.' The idea that there was room for indecision was significant.

Preston faced her, eyes dark, voice low with import. 'It is something I want. But maybe there's something I want more.'

'As long as that something isn't me.' She could be bold, too. He wasn't the only one in the room who could say audacious things.

'Why not?' Leave it to Preston to ask the hard question instead of dropping the conversation like a normal gentleman. Then again, if he'd been a normal gentleman, this topic would never have come up.

'Do I need to itemise what you already know? I am entirely unsuitable for you. In every way.'

'Not in bed.' Preston moved close to her, his hands at her arms, his voice a seductive caress. 'Not in ways that count, I think. You know me, Bea, like no one else except May and Liam. I would not trade that for worldly honour.'

He kissed her then, long and slow, sending trills of temptation through her body, every synapse of her remembering the feel of him, the possibility of *them*. He tipped her chin up to meet his gaze. 'I want you in my bed again,

Beatrice, but the next time is up to you. It's your decision.'

She swallowed and nodded. Her decision. She would come to him when this was settled. When she didn't put him at risk. When it didn't have to mean anything other than passion shared. After all, Preston might be risking a future with his thoughts, but she was risking her heart.

Alton had made his decision. He would have to risk it—making a public appearance in order to confront Preston Worth and to make his claims about Beatrice Penrose. Recent events had left him no choice. Madam Rose, furious over the lie about the tiara, had sent her men after him. He had a few bruises to prove it and he was lucky it wasn't worse. Worth's partner in proverbial crime, Liam Casek, had exposed the truth behind the tiara to the brothel owner and just like that, everything had come to a head.

He couldn't continue bleeding Beatrice for a few expensive baubles to keep himself afloat. He had to produce a bride by June. So did Preston Worth. Alton did wonder how much of the supposed engagement was a bluff.

Worth had done an admirable job squiring her about town and putting on a besotted show, but he'd have thought Worth would want a better sort of bride, especially knowing the truth as Worth certainly did. Worth might be a family friend to the Penroses, but he was also an ambitious man. Ambitious men had needs soiled brides couldn't always fulfil.

In Alton's estimation, it was bluff against bluff. His against Worth's and all of London to act as witnesses. Casek's celebration ball was turning out to be quite the event: celebration, charity ball and a potential engagement all rolled into one. A high-stakes evening for all involved. Himself included. Alton sat down at the rough table in his rented room to pen one last note, one last warning, to be delivered when it would be too late to do anything about it.

Chapter Twenty-One

It was too late to back out now, was the only thought going through Bea's head when she came down for luncheon. Worth House had become a whirlwind. One would have thought a real engagement was about to take place. There was activity everywhere and Mrs Worth and May were in the centre of it all.

May caught sight of her and called out from atop a ladder where she was fixing a swathe of royal-blue fabric. 'Oh, good, you're here! Evie wants to do a final fitting on your dress for the day after tomorrow.' She began to climb down.

'Evie's here?' Beatrice dodged to the right, barely avoiding a young man carrying a heavy urn full of flowers.

May laughed. 'We're all here. Liam and I

decided six streets were too far to keep driving back and forth with everything that needs doing. If you're looking for Matthew, he's with Preston in the ballroom.'

Whatever were they doing in there? Bea wove her way through the workers in partial panic. A bustling ballroom was no place for a baby. But the scene inside made her rethink that conclusion. Preston sat in the middle of the floor, shoes off, feet bare, shirtsleeves rolled up, no jacket in sight, with Matthew on an old quilt, spilling rose petals over the baby's head while Matthew laughed, his fat little hands reaching out randomly to grab the soft petals as they fell.

'Oh! Here they come again! It's raining.' Preston cupped the petals in his hands and let them fall over Matthew's head. Over and over until Beatrice couldn't tell who was laughing harder, he or Matthew.

The sight did funny things to her stomach, to her throat, to her eyes. If any man was ready to be a father, it was Preston. But was he truly ready to be her husband? A man who would be brought down by his wife's shame? A man who would devote his life to raising another's child? Preston spied her in the doorway and fixed her with that wide, genuine smile of his, and she felt a carefully guarded tear slip. She wanted to hold on to this moment, hold on to him, against all logic that said she shouldn't. She didn't deserve him.

Preston waved to her. 'Do you need him? I thought Evie wanted to do your dress.' He seemed reluctant to give Matthew up. 'I can keep him. We have to go check the kitchens.' He stood, scooping Matthew up. 'We might find something to chew on, maybe a cold carrot for those teeth. He has three of them, you know.' He sounded amazed.

Bea laughed. 'Yes, I know.' She counted them daily, ran her finger along his gums to feel for new ones pushing through. It was nice to think someone else celebrated those little things, too. That the person to do so was Preston Worth, was more than nice. She felt another tear slip. She hastily brushed it away, but Preston noticed.

'What is it, Bea?' He shifted Matthew to his other arm to give her his hand.

'You two. Together.' She shook her head. 'I'm sorry, it's silly. But recent events have been rather overwhelming.' He would think she meant their earlier conversation. The centre of a ballroom, surrounded by workers and commotion, wasn't the place to tell him that walking into the busyness of Worth House, of seeing him with Matthew in the middle of it all, was like coming home. She didn't dare give any man that much power, not even if that man was Preston Worth.

The feeling of homecoming persisted in May's big bedroom where the girls gathered for the fitting. Evie had outdone herself, having taken a dress from a trunk in the Worth attic and refashioned it. 'Oh, Evie, it's spectacular.' Bea reached out a hand to touch the rich, red-silk damask.

'Red for joy, red for love, red for boldness, for showing everyone this widow has thrown off her weeds.' She winked in conspiracy. 'Not to mention, it's just spectacular with your dark hair,' Evie said, showing off the sloped styling of the shoulders and the vee-necked bodice, all original. 'The lace is new and I tailored the skirt so it isn't quite so full, but more like the style now.' But it was still full enough, Beatrice noted, to sway against one's ankles and to bell out when one danced. She didn't mind, she liked the fuller skirts.

She let Evie help her into it, slipping it over her head and doing up the red ribbon laces at the back. She liked how the fuller skirts made her waist look a little trimmer, her hips a little less wide. When she said as much, Evie and May shushed her, insisting that she'd always looked fine. 'Quiet, Bea. Just look.' May's hands were at her shoulders and the three of them looked in the long mirror together, not at her or the dress perhaps as much as looking at themselves, the three of them together.

'We've come a long way since last year, Bea,' Evie said softly, squeezing her hand. It was hard to say who had come the furthest. Each of them had overcome significant obstacles, not just to catch a husband, but to find themselves again. 'I can't believe you and May are going to be sisters, real sisters.' Evie's happiness for her was transparent. 'It's the most perfect ending I could devise—you marrying Preston.' Evie gave a little sigh. She truly believed in the engagement. She'd poured that belief into the dress.

May hugged her shoulders, meeting her gaze in the mirror. 'It is a *real* engagement, isn't it, Bea? We'll truly be real sisters?'

Evie looked stunned and Bea wanted to kick May for voicing the doubt. 'Of course it is,' she said crossly. 'You don't think your brother is in the habit of making commitments he doesn't intend to keep.' Bea stepped away from the mirror and began picking at the laces she could reach. She had to be compelling and nothing was more compelling than the truth. 'Things changed on the trip home from Scotland. It was like we were seeing one another for the first time.'

May gave a misty smile. 'Good. It's really a romance. I just want the two people I love so much to be happy together. I know circumstances aren't ideal and I feared—'

Bea cut her off with a squeeze of her hand and a smile. Bea didn't want to hear what May feared: that behind the decorations, the flowers and the gaiety downstairs was a lie, the engagement a sham, the whirlwind romance around town a sham. All too soon, May would discover she was right in her concern. May would be hurt—hurt that there was no romance, hurt that Bea had not confided in her. Unless she chose to change the outcome. In those moments, something began to change in her. If she wanted happiness, she would have to claim it.

Preston's words came to her, *'There is something more I want,'* and the sight of him with Matthew in the ballroom. Bea recalled the motto of the Left Behind Girls Club: nothing changes until you do. She could continue to resist Preston's offer, could continue to be stubborn, and it would cost her, or she could change. She could make the sham into a reality by accepting that she deserved Preston, that she deserved love and passion, that Alton didn't define the full potential of that experience.

It was a rather big challenge she was requiring of herself. Those were not ideas she could easily accept. The idea that she needed to be alone had been her armour and her obstacle for a long time. She'd used it to keep people at bay, even her friends. It was time for a change, starting tonight with Preston. There'd been enough lies told for her protection. Love could only be built with truths.

The hallway clock chimed the last of midnight as Beatrice slipped into the room at the end of the hall: Preston's room. A *frisson* of excitement shot through her at the prospect of what awaited. She approached the bed, letting her dark wrapper fall to the floor, the cool air on her bare skin as she whispered his name. No response. Nothing, not even the rustling of bedclothes in the dark. Something was wrong. Bea reached out a hand, unromantically groping for a body. There was none. Beatrice threw back the covers, disappointed but not daunted. She'd come this far. She wasn't turning back. She could wait, and she would, right where Preston was sure to see her. In his bed.

There was something, *someone*, in his bed. Preston let his eyes adjust to the gloom. There was just enough light from the lamp beside the bed to make out the form—a lamp he'd not left burning. He felt a wicked smile play at his mouth as he took in the dark hair spread on his pillow. Beatrice. His body began to rouse at the thought. If he'd known she'd be here, he would have come up earlier. As it was, he'd selfishly kept Dimitri and Liam up way past their bedtimes, knowing his own sleep wouldn't come easy knowing that Beatrice slept down the hall from him. Part of him still wanted to hunt down Alton and make him pay for assaulting her. She was *his*, no matter what she thought to the contrary, and no one harmed what was his, not while he lived and breathed.

Preston undressed quietly, sliding beneath the blankets to wrap an arm around her and pull her warm body into the cradle of his. 'Bea, wake up.'

'Hmm…?' She sighed, her buttocks wiggling teasingly against his hips. Now, she really was going to have to wake up. How he loved this woman, her passion, her strength, even her stubbornness because that's what made her unique. He kissed the column of her neck, waking her with the slow lovemaking of his mouth, his hands on her body. He felt her stir, felt her become aware of him and where she was.

She rolled in his arms, turning to face him with a teasing scold. 'That's not fair, seducing a girl in her sleep…' her hand slid low between them, cupping his arousal '…especially, when I came here to seduce you.' Her voice had gone smoky, low and throaty in the interval.

'Made your decisions, have you?' He'd

thought it would take her longer. He was glad it hadn't, but he'd like to know what they were. What had brought her to his bed?

She stroked him in answer and he gave a growl, letting her flip him on to his back. Apparently verbal answers were going to have to wait. She slid down his body, breasts brushing his chest in the lightest of touches, her mouth at his navel, her breath feathering his skin until it rose for her. Her hands were at his thighs, parting them, her hands tangling in the dark thatch of him, while her mouth sought him, found him.

She looked up once, dark eyes flaring with desire, hair loose about her shoulders, a potent stare, from a potent locale. He was nearly lost then. Whoever argued fellatio made the woman into a sexual subordinate was patently wrong. He was entirely at her mercy, his pleasure at her pleasure. She bent to him, her tongue making one long, licking pass at his length. He wasn't going to last long at this rate, and, oh, how he wanted to last, wanted to enjoy every minute of this. He reached his hands overhead and gripped the headboard with all his remaining strength.

The headboard became his only ballast in

the wake of Beatrice's seduction, all that kept him anchored as her mouth teased the tender tip of him, her hands on his length, caressing, cupping, until he tightened, his release beyond his control, set into motion by the physics of his body. He could no more hold himself back than the moon the tides. The point of no return had been met and exceeded. Beatrice moaned, the act exciting her as much as it excited him. She had him in her hand as he bucked in climax, his heart pounding as release swept him. Had anything he'd ever singularly experienced been as powerful as what had just happened?

Beatrice wasn't done with him. She slid up his body, her nipples grazing his chest, her mouth finding his in a long kiss. He could taste the sex on her, his body answering the invitation. She was going slowly with him, teasing him, tempting him while he recovered. Which wasn't going to take long at this rate. Thank heavens, because she was talking to him now, her smoky voice as it whispered decadence at his ear in words he didn't think a lady knew, but probably should. It made sex so much more exciting. All he wanted was to roll her over and take her, hard and fast until she cried out, until she admitted she wanted this beyond the night. For ever. With him. Not because of fear, not because circumstance demanded she accept him. Not because Alton had pushed her to this, but because she wanted *him*. Only him.

She put a hand on him, testing his readiness, a wicked smile on her lovely mouth when she found him hard. He felt inordinately pleased with himself as she straddled him, her hand on his erect phallus. Beatrice brushed her hair over one shoulder, a beautiful, naked Godiva riding him astride. He put his hands at her hips, steadying her as she began to ride, a slow steady pace, one in which they might have some conversation before he lost himself body and mind.

'What decisions have you made, Bea? You wouldn't be here otherwise.' Perhaps in the dark, they could be honest with their words as well as their bodies.

'I deserve happiness and I deserve you for as long as I can have you. May helped me see that today. Nothing will change until I do. I've been the biggest creator of my own obstacles. I made a mistake with Alton and I continue to make myself pay for that.'

'I'll have to remember to thank her for it.' Preston strained forward, catching her lips in a kiss. He didn't fool himself that the rightness would last, but for now all was right with the world and he'd take it.

Chapter Twenty-Two

The rightness she'd felt in bed with Preston lasted well into the next day through a constant parade of workers in and out of the town house, through another night beside him and sneaking back to her own room at dawn, through the knighting ceremony in a stifling drawing room and the reception that followed. That well-being lasted, in fact, right up until the evening of the ball. She'd put on Evie's delectable red creation, fastened her pearls and done up her hair when the knock on her door came.

'Miss, you're wanted in the blue room right away,' a maid said with an urgency that worried Beatrice even as she repeated her new litany silently in her head: *she deserved happiness.*

It was hard to maintain that degree of optimism, however, with everyone assembled in the drawing room. The families had been together all day to celebrate Liam's title. But these were not the expressions of celebratory people. Her mother rose and took her hand. 'My dear, I'm afraid something's happened.' Bea's gaze went instantly to Preston, who stood at the fireplace already dressed for the evening in dark clothes. It wasn't her mother she wanted, it was Preston.

'It's Alton's latest salvo.' He waved a paper, his jaw set. 'He wants the engagement announcement cancelled.'

'Or?' Beatrice prompted. It seemed an odd request since there was no monetary gain.

'Or, he'll send information to the gossip rags about your previous marriage, calling it a fake to cover up for the illegitimacy of your child and alluding to the baby's real father.'

'He has no proof,' Bea argued.

'Gossip columns don't care about proof. Speculation is good enough for them, good enough to start a scandal,' Liam pointed out.

'The one thing we wanted to avoid,' her mother replied sharply.

'Why would he do this?' Beatrice was still stuck on motive.

'Petty revenge. There's no money involved, so one must speculate it's just the first of a series of moves he plans,' Liam hypothesised. 'And of course, if he could win our concession, it keeps you away from the altar. It gives him another chance at you, I suppose.'

Right. The forced-marriage gambit. She looked for confirmation from Preston, who nodded. 'I agree with Liam. Those are likely his motives. Whatever his reasons, though, we have to decide how we want to meet this latest threat. I say we call his bluff. It worked once. It will probably work again. The man's a coward at heart.'

'Risk those things being printed about Bea, about *us*?' Her mother found Preston's idea appalling.

'I don't think he'll send the information to the papers,' Preston replied firmly, fixing everyone in the room with a hard stare, taking in each by turn. 'Why would he? He gains nothing that will help him in settling his bills.' Liam was the first to nod, followed by Dimitri, the agreement of the two men helping to sway the others in the room.

Bea wished she felt as sure as Preston. She stood and waited for the others to leave the room before she voiced her doubts. Preston took her hands, kissing her lightly. 'Relax, Bea. This is nothing more than a spoiler's trick. He wants to ruin our big night because it's all he has left. He has tried blackmail and threats and nothing has thwarted us.'

'Do you think he'll come tonight?' That was perhaps her worst fear. She didn't want to be looking over her shoulder the entire evening.

'If he comes, he won't leave. He knows that. He won't show. It's not in him.' Preston raised her hand to his lips with an admonition. 'Tonight, we're going to dance and smile. We're going to celebrate our friend's good fortune and ours.' She felt his eyes on her, lingering and warm. 'You look stunning. Is this the dress Evie did? It's spectacular. I hope it's not too hard to get out of?' he teased wickedly.

'Not if there's two of us working at it.' Beatrice laughed, wanting the rightness back, wanting the surety that came with it, but no matter what assurances Preston gave her, she knew she wouldn't relax entirely until the papers came out the next day and there was no mention of her indiscretion.

Preston stole a kiss. 'Remember what you

said last night, Bea? You deserve happiness. I'm going to make sure you get it.'

Preston did his best, working hard to be his charming self, never leaving her side, and she managed to dance and smile her way through the night. It helped to remember the night wasn't only about her and Preston, but more importantly about Liam Casek. The ballroom at Worth House reflected that. It had been transformed by hundreds of white roses and impossible-to-imagine yards of royal-blue fabric and bunting. The immense crystal chandelier, pride of Worth House, hung blazing in the centre of the ceiling, presiding over it all, its dazzle only superseded by the dazzle of May's and Liam's smiles as they sailed past on the dance floor with eyes for each other alone.

'Maybe we should wait,' Beatrice whispered to Preston as her two friends swung past in a wild turn, May laughing up at her husband, heedless of their recklessness. 'This is their night.' She didn't want to call attention away from them.

Preston grinned, turning her sharply on the dance floor. 'No, we're committed now. I don't want Alton to think he has any grounds with us. Besides, May and Liam are counting on it. This, here…' he waved a hand to indicate the decorations '…is as much for them as it is for us.' The music ended, the evening approaching midnight. Preston winked. 'Stay close, Bea. This our moment. We'll be needed shortly.'

Bea caught sight of his father moving towards the dais, giving a discreet signal to his wife, May and Liam, her parents, and Evie and Dimitri, gathering allies. With the customary ease of those used to being obeyed, Albemarle Worth gestured to the musicians in the balcony above to ready a waltz and Beatrice felt her palms go sweaty. Her pulse started to speed as she looked at Preston, who was irritatingly cool.

'Aren't you nervous?' she whispered. The engagement suddenly seemed real. Too real.

'No.' He grinned down at her, his confidence infectious. 'Why should I be? I am about to be engaged to an incredible woman.' She wasn't sure if he was teasing or if he was serious and that troubled her. It wasn't part of the deal she'd made herself. Her happiness could be had up until it infringed on another's.

Understanding she could have Preston as long as she could did not preclude him taking the post in Greece. But she worried Preston didn't see it that way. Perhaps he thought there was room for negotiation when it came to the truth of their engagement.

Around them the crowd fell silent and Preston's father began, his voice devoid of any of the misgivings that had created tension between him and Preston. 'Tonight, we are gathered to celebrate the knighting of Sir Liam Casek, my son-in-law.' Albemarle Worth flashed a wide grin in Liam's direction and Beatrice's heart soared for him and for May. The two of them had fought hard for this moment. 'Sir Liam is a man I could not be more proud of if he were my own son.' There was a loud outbreak of applause. Liam was well liked. Preston's father continued when it died down, 'Speaking of my son, we have another announcement to celebrate tonight. I am proud to share, with all of our friends gathered here, the engagement of my son, Mr Preston Worth, to the lovely Beatrice Penrose. May the sorrows of her past year be replaced by years of happiness starting tonight.' It was neatly done, reaffirming her status as a widow in case anyone had forgotten, or in case anyone had the audacity to wonder.

There was an excited rush of exclamation that circulated through the ballroom, perhaps some gasps of disappointment, too. Preston was a prize and now he'd been claimed by a widow none the less, not a fresh-faced debutante. If anyone thought the match was anything other than a love match, Preston quickly dispelled that, sweeping her into his arms for a kiss that would be talked about in the papers tomorrow. 'There's more where that came from,' he whispered as they accepted congratulations.

They had to wait quite a while for that bit of 'more' Preston promised. The last guest departed at three and it was four before he could sneak into her room, taking great efforts to evade the staff who'd already begun the task of cleaning up. Still, Beatrice thought it a fine way to spend the early hours of the morning.

She lingered as long as she could in that afterglow, putting off the journey to the morning room as long as possible. She didn't want to see the papers, didn't want to see the look on others' faces when they saw the words of her shame in print. Fortunately, only Preston was present when she made her way down.

His hazel eyes met hers solemnly and she knew before the hot chocolate was served that Alton had done as promised. When they were alone, Preston handed her the papers. 'It's not as bad as you might think. It's been published, but it's hardly been a focal point. Everyone was far more interested in the Casek ball and our engagement.'

'A small victory, I suppose.' Bea tried to smile.

'There's more.' Preston set down his cup. 'My men report that Alton has checked out of the inn where he was staying. We don't know where he went. He obviously doesn't want to be found.'

'It means he's gearing up for phase two,' Bea said quietly. 'Will he go for me or for you?' Her promises of personal happiness seemed petty in light of more serious considerations. How could she ever have thought to keep them?

'For you, definitely,' Preston said without hesitation. 'I am only an indirect route to the altar. You are the direct route. He needs to marry you more than he needs to kill me. Besides, killing me is too risky. People would notice. He could hang for it. He knows his desperation isn't worth his life. It would be better for him to flee England than to take a shot at me.'

'Is that supposed to make me feel better?' Beatrice managed a sip of chocolate. 'Because, oddly enough it does. I want you safe.'

'I want the same for you, too, Beatrice,' Preston said with a sombreness that superseded the solemnity already in the room. He rose and came to her chair, kneeling down beside it and taking her hand. Her skin prickled, with awareness, alertness over where this was leading. 'Which is why, in light of many circumstances, I want the honour of making you my wife as soon as I possibly can.'

Bea felt her eyes go wide. 'You want to marry me to protect me.' All the flowery words in the world couldn't hide what motivated this proposal at its base. He was still making sacrifices for her and that could not be tolerated. 'When I said I wanted you for as long as I could have you, having you assumed I could do so without damaging you, Preston.' She tugged at her hand, but he held fast, perhaps guessing how much his touch affected her, persuaded her and how much he needed every weapon in his arsenal.

'Your parents—' she began, looking for new angles to the fight.

'My parents,' Preston interrupted, 'taught me to think for myself and to follow my own path. They will understand.'

'Preston, protection is a noble reason for your offer, but have you thought of what happens after Alton is dissuaded? He moves on to another unsuspecting girl and you and I are now committed to one another for ever. *For ever*, Preston.'

'We're friends,' Preston countered. 'Aren't we already committed for ever?'

'Not like that. If we were friends, you could still go to Greece,' Beatrice persisted. It should have been a winning argument, but Preston was full of surprises.

'I am not going to Greece. I decided this morning. My refusal has been sent,' Preston said evenly. 'What I want is here, if you'll have me. And if you don't, I'll just keep trying until you say yes.'

'Marriage ought to be about love.'

Preston nodded soberly. 'I agree. What makes you think this one isn't?'

She couldn't argue with that. If one looked back, one could see the markings of love behind them like two carriage wheels leaving tracks in the dirt. In the beginning there'd been the courtesy of friendship—she'd come home because he asked and he'd come to Scotland because it was far better than sending a stranger. That courtesy had quickly become respect as their conversations deepened, and respect had become protection and sacrifice when they'd reached home. In equal parts, too—he was not the only one sacrificing and protecting in this relationship and he knew it. She could see it when he looked at her. He understood what she was doing and why. He could respect it even if he didn't agree with it.

Beatrice tried one last time. 'I don't want you to regret it, to regret me.'

'Why would you think that?' Preston's grip on her hands was tight.

'Because I'm not worth it.' She might have convinced herself she was worth her own happiness, but she was not worth another man's happiness.

'I must respectfully disagree, Bea. Yes, you are.' Preston moved into her then, kissing her full on the mouth and she was persuaded at last, or perhaps too exhausted to resist, or too logical because just maybe it all made sense after all. They were alike, she and Preston, always looking after those around them, always caring for others. It was only natural they'd want to care for each other. Perhaps it was time to stop making that caring an obstacle to the happiness they could have together.

'Saturday, then. We should do it as soon as possible,' Preston whispered between kisses, 'because I can't wait any longer to have you in my bed again.' It was a romantic thing to say and Bea opted to believe it. It was far better than suggesting it was a ploy to finish Alton's threat.

Chapter Twenty-Three

Saturday couldn't come soon enough for Preston's peace of mind. He said as much to Liam as he lingered over port that evening in the parlour. They'd all gone to the Rushford ball and come home around one o'clock, taking Beatrice back to Penrose House for decency's sake. Everyone had been too tired from the prior evening to make another late night of it. May had gone straight up to bed, perhaps noting that her brother wanted a moment alone with his friend.

'Has there been any news of Alton?' Preston gave the port in his glass a pensive swirl. He couldn't simply believe the man had given up. If Alton had meant to flee his debts, he would have done it long before he invested in chasing down Bea. It was all too easy. He didn't like easy for the simple reason that he didn't trust it.

'Yes. The innkeeper said he paid his bill and left. He must have some tiara money left over.' Liam chuckled. 'There's not much more he can do now except run. He can't make his bills and Madam Rose has given him all the patience she has. Without the promise of a bride and a dowry, Madam Rose won't call off her thugs. Short of throwing himself on his father's mercy and begging for the cash, running is the only option. From what I hear, his father is none too keen to absolve him, so I think he's on his own.'

Preston nodded, giving Liam's words consideration. 'Perhaps it is nothing,' he conceded.

'But?' Liam prompted. 'Why do you think it's something more?'

'He's a desperate man and he just quits? Just walks away after all the effort to pressure Beatrice? Desperation breeds tenacity.' Preston took a swallow of the port. 'I keep thinking about Cabot Roan. He was never more dangerous than when he was cornered.'

'Roan's a rare breed,' Liam suggested. 'I almost hated bringing him in. He was a worthy opponent.'

Preston shot him a hard look. 'Except for his code of ethics, don't forget. Men who deliberately promote war are not heroes.'

Liam conceded with a grin. 'Well, except for his ethics,' he corrected. 'Ethics aside, he was a worthy opponent. He shot me and May. He knifed you. Not everyone can pull that off. Certainly not Alton.'

Preston sighed, no closer to an answer. His instincts told him Alton had a few more tricks to play. 'That's the question, isn't it? What *is* Alton capable of?'

Malvern Alton was capable of great charm when he chose to exert himself. He was exerting that charm now in no small measure on the scullery maid he'd followed from the Penrose town house. He had her market basket looped over his arm and a handsome smile on his face as he said with just the right amount of interest, 'A wedding, you say? Are you sure? I haven't read anything in the papers.'

He tried to keep the panic out of his voice. He'd followed her from the Penrose town house to the market before he approached her for news, not wanting to risk being spotted. He just wished the news had been better. He'd been hoping to hear the engagement was a ruse and she was still free. Instead, he'd learned the wedding had been set for Saturday.

'Oh, no.' The maid was young and pretty enough to think a man of his calibre would be interested in her. 'It's to be quiet.'

'They'll have it at home, then?' he asked, plucking a stray flower from a booth when the vendor wasn't looking. He tucked it into her hair, watching her blush.

'It will be at the Grosvenor Chapel,' she chattered, reaching up a hand to touch the flower before leaning in conspiratorially. 'Mr Worth has connections to have got everything arranged so quickly. I heard Mrs Penrose tell Mrs Worth that she would not have her daughter married anywhere but a church. His wife was quite in agreement, since this is her only son.'

Alton cut her off. He wasn't interested in feminine gossip or fine sentiments. He needed details. A plan was starting to form. 'I suppose it will be in the morning?'

'One o'clock actually,' she supplied happily. 'The wedding breakfast will be afterwards at Worth House. That's funny, isn't it, to call it a breakfast when it will really be lunch.' She rambled a bit, smiling up at him off and on and he smiled back, but his mind was already engaged in plotting.

He parted with the maid shortly after that, the plan coming to fruition in his mind. He couldn't go *to* Beatrice any longer, but she could come to him. He knew just how to do it. There was one person she'd go to the ends of the earth for and even beyond, perhaps even to matrimony. He was counting on it and she would be dressed for it. It would be a pity to have a fine wedding gown go unused.

Putting on the wedding gown would be the last thing she'd do before the ceremony. But between then and now, there was so much that needed accomplishing. Beatrice had a backwards list in her mind the morning of the wedding—the sort of list that counts down from where you have to be by a certain time to where you are right now. She wasn't sure she'd get it all done.

Packing trunks for the wedding trip would be the first task. Her room at the Penrose town house was already showing signs of the effort. Clothes were everywhere: her clothes, Matthew's things, a baby on her hip wanting attention as she tried to direct the maid.

When she'd left Little Westbury, the idea that she would be taking a wedding trip before she returned hadn't crossed her mind. Now, there were lists to make of things she'd need from Maidenstone to be sent on to Shoreham-by-the-Sea for the wedding trip at Seacrest as well as the London trunks to pack. A wedding trip! The thought was as surreal as the idea that she was getting married in four hours. She still couldn't quite grasp the reality. Part of her didn't want to grasp it, didn't want to think about it, only accept it. To examine it too closely meant to examine her happiness, to acknowledge it. She feared if she did that, she'd jinx it. It was too new, too precious. Some day, maybe, she'd be comfortable enough with her happiness to explore it. For now, she just wanted to stay busy and not worry over it.

'Pack the muslins,' Bea instructed the maid. It would be nice by the shore this time of year. Seacrest was an ideal place for the wedding trip, so ideal that Beatrice thought the trip might last quite a while. She could think of a lot of reasons to go; it was quiet and in need of its owner. Matthew would be with them. Preston would be able to take care of the estate as would she. There was plenty for the mistress of the house to take care of.

Bea tickled Matthew's nose. 'It won't be all work, though,' she said to the baby. There would be beaches to explore and a whole summer of adventures out of doors, picnics and strawberries to hunt. And they would do it all together, the three of them. The thought made her smile. She and Preston and Matthew would be a family.

'Is everything all right, ma'am?' the maid enquired.

She must be smiling like a loon.

'*Quite* all right.' Beatrice waved to the mess of the room. 'Just pack it all, I can sort it out later.' Like her happiness. Happiness did horrible things to one's concentration. There was a knock at the door. She was wanted downstairs. Mr Preston Worth was here. Even at the last, with the wedding four hours away, her parents were sticklers for propriety. 'Mr Worth' could meet her in the drawing room like a proper caller, but not in her room. She wondered what he wanted. She'd not anticipated seeing him before this afternoon.

'I thought it was bad luck to see the bride before the wedding,' she teased, coming into the drawing room with Matthew. Preston looked immaculate, as if he hadn't spent the morning trying to wrangle his belongings into travelling trunks.

'We've had our bad luck, nothing but good lies ahead.' He smiled, the gesture crinkling the corners of his eyes as he took the baby from her. 'Good morning, Master Matthew.' He jiggled the baby until Matthew laughed, then pressed a kiss to Bea's cheek. 'Good morning, my bride.'

Every morning would start this way with Matthew in Preston's arms…that smile on Preston's mouth. Every day would end the same way. Preston meant to be a devoted father, a devoted husband. The thought filled her with more contentment than she could imagine, her happiness was working the lid off its box.

'Come sit with me, Bea. I have a gift for you. An early wedding present.' Preston juggled the baby on his lap and pulled a long, flat envelope out of an inside coat pocket. He passed it to her. 'Open it.'

She took the envelope hesitantly, trying to

guess what might be in it. He'd already given her so much, she couldn't imagine what might be left to give. She unfolded the papers, scanning the documents. She had to read them twice. 'You want to adopt Matthew?' The idea overwhelmed her, brought tears to her eyes yet again. It seemed Preston specialised in ways to make her cry.

'I want him to be my son in all ways, Bea. He is already the son of my heart, I think he has been from the first day I held him.' He gave her a wry smile. 'Or should I say the day you thrust him at me in the carriage and me not knowing a thing about how to hold a baby?' He looked down at Matthew bouncing on his leg. 'I know a thing or two more now to know that it's not enough in the eyes of the law to just love him as my own. He needs legal recognition.' Preston gently directed her attention to the other page.

Beatrice took in the second document, a will. His will. She'd rather not think about endings on a day of beginnings. Preston pointed to a paragraph. 'You don't need to read the whole thing, today. Just this part here, the provisions for Matthew. He's to be an equal partner with any other heirs. The estate will go to any male heirs you and I may have, I can't do anything about that. It was part of the inheritance stipulation,' Preston explained, 'but the trust is mine to dispose of as I see fit. It's substantial and, with careful investment, it will continue to grow until Matthew reaches his majority.'

Beatrice looked at the sum and bit her lip. The sum was staggering. Matthew would be a rich young man, which meant everything to society. The adoption was not just a legal gesture, then. There was real teeth to it. Preston had done everything possible to ensure Matthew's legitimacy. 'I don't know what to say.' Truly she didn't. She leaned towards him, capturing his mouth in a slow kiss. Even in the light of day, in a drawing room with a baby wiggling on his lap, she could feel the want rise between them, mutual and strong. It was an amazing sensation. She'd learned so much about the facets of love from this man.

A throat cleared behind her, startling her into jumping back from the kiss. 'Bea, it's time to get dressed,' May scolded. 'I already sent Evie upstairs. As for you, Brother, don't you know it's bad luck to see the bride before the wedding?' She wagged a finger at him.

'We were just practising,' Preston shot back.

'Trying to decide which kiss to use at church today?' May teased.

'Precisely,' Preston said smugly, but he rose from the sofa and gave up Matthew. His eyes lingered on her. 'I will see you in church, Bea, very shortly. I'm going to drop the papers off and then get changed myself.'

By the time Matthew was fed and the wedding gown floated over her head, Beatrice felt as if she was walking on clouds. Evie and May had giggled with her, opening a bottle of smuggled champagne in her bedroom. She'd sipped at the cold bubbly liquid only, wanting all her remaining wits about her for the ceremony. Evie and May had joked they remembered very little of their own weddings, but Bea was determined to do it differently. She wanted to remember everything.

Bea turned in front of the mirror, taking in Evie's handiwork. 'You could start a new trend, Evie. Everyone will want you remaking grandmothers' wedding gowns when they see this.'

The engagement dress had been from one of Preston's relatives, but the wedding dress had come from the Penrose attics, a lovely gown in the *robe d'anglaise* style, with an ivory underskirt peeping from beneath and the bodice embroidered with dark green flowers. There'd been no time to get anything new. Evie had freshened it up with lace and new ribbons, even new bows for the matching shoes.

'Bea, you look splendid. I hardly had to do anything to the gown.' Evie hugged her gently, careful not to crush the dress. 'Shall we go?'

'I want to check on Matthew one more time,' Bea said. He was up in the nursery playing before his nap in order to give them a chance to change clothes. 'Are you sure I shouldn't bring him?' This had been a point of discussion, mostly because Bea kept bringing it up. Everyone else had decided Matthew should stay at home and nap and then be brought over to the Worths' for the wedding breakfast, rested and happy. Weddings were for grown-ups and this one would be a short one.

'Bea, he'll be fine.' May steered her towards the stairs. 'You just fed him and you'll be married long before he needs to eat again.'

'I know, it's just…' She couldn't say what it 'just' was. She'd left him before, at night to attend all the balls with Preston, and for much longer than this afternoon. The Grosvenor Chapel was only a couple of streets away. If the maid needed her, she would be close, Bea rationalised.

The sun was out, a glorious late spring day, that allowed them to travel to the church with the top of the carriage down, drinking in the sunshine and the blue day. Nothing could be more perfect. Except it was. At the chapel with its brick work and soaring steeple, a carpet was spread up the steps for her beneath the white-pillared portico. People milled outside in South Audley Street, hoping to catch a glimpse of the bride. Little girls threw flower petals, and a lone violinist took up a lovely Vivaldi 'Adagio' as she stepped out of the carriage, May and Evie with her.

Could the day be any better? She knew what the inside of the chapel would look like. She'd helped with the hasty decorating. But this, she'd not been prepared for. Another gift from Preston, who understood how important this day was for her, a day she'd given up on ever having. Now, he waited for her inside. The door was held open for her, the violin music giving way to the swell of the oak-cased organ, as she moved towards her future, towards her happiness.

She was just steps away when it all fell apart, trampled to pieces by the sound of clattering hooves on cobblestones overriding the organ, the screams of people scattering in the wake of a reckless rider in a narrow street. She turned from the door in time to see a rider, a boy really, throw himself from the unsaddled horse, yelling horrible words. 'The baby, the baby is gone.'

At first it made no sense. Those words didn't belong amidst this perfect celebration. Surely he didn't mean her baby? She'd just left him, safe and sleeping, having brought him down to her room from the nursery. She'd personally tucked him into the crib beside her bed. May had the boy by the arm, trying to get him to breathe. The poor lad was scared witless. A bystander had the horse by the bridle now, the animal nearly as witless as the messenger.

The boy caught sight of her and tugged free of May. 'Mistress, it's true. The baby is gone. Matthew is gone.' He was sobbing now as he choked out his story. 'We had gone down-stairs for tea after you left. We heard a crash upstairs and ran up to look. The maid went to check on the baby, thinking it odd the noise hadn't woken him.'

Her baby was gone. Bea put a hand to her stomach and staggered, the news rolling over her in a black cloud, the day's perfection de-stroyed beyond reclaiming. 'There's a note, mistress.' A note? She couldn't read a note. She could barely breathe. She was going to fall. She felt herself going down. She wanted to collapse, wanted to wake up and find this was all a dream, perhaps a warning that she wasn't entitled to happiness no matter how tempting the offer of it. Bea made a thousand promises to herself in those flashing seconds. She would give up Preston, she'd give up the lies protecting her, anything if Matthew could be safe in her arms. But she couldn't give in, couldn't collapse. Matthew needed her to be strong. How could she help him if she couldn't help herself?

'Bea!' There were male voices now, pour-ing out of the chapel, the pounding of running footsteps and Preston was there. She wouldn't fall. He wouldn't let her. She felt his arms about her, felt him kneel with her on the carpet like a pietà.

'Matthew's gone.' Her voice broke over the words. If there was any wonder in the world at the moment, it was in the fact that she needn't explain any more to Preston. He knew the rest; who had taken Matthew and why. Preston took the note from her and scanned it once before passing it back. He helped her to stand before she could ask. She was starting to function again, starting to find her strength.

'We'll get him back, Bea.' Preston was focused and grim, the way he must look when he went out for the Crown, the way he'd looked in the taproom the night he'd fought for her. 'Let me talk to the boy.'

Those moments were agony. She couldn't just stand there. Every second her baby was further away. How much of a lead could Alton have? Did it matter? Alton didn't want Matthew. He wanted her. Matthew was just the bait. Alton wanted her to come after him, wanted her to find him. The address of the meeting place on the edge of town was in the note.

Alton knew she'd do anything for her child. This might be the only time she ever gave

Alton what he wanted. Bea looked around wildly, grabbing a boy from the crowd. If the wedding had drawn a crush of onlookers, the panic had drawn even more. 'Find my carriage and bring it back.' Matthew was going to be safe no matter what it cost her.

Preston was beside her, helping her into the carriage, Liam clambering up to take the coachman's place at the ribbons. Preston banged on the rooftop, signalling Liam, his eyes burning as he held Bea's gaze. 'Let's go get our son.'

Chapter Twenty-Four

❧

The bribes had cost him a few pennies he could ill afford, but it had been worth it. Everything had gone off splendidly. Alton was still congratulating himself as he paced the rickety old church on the outskirts of town. He checked his watch. Beatrice should be here any minute.

The building he'd chosen was a far cry from the white and brick elegance of the Grosvenor Chapel, but it was a church with a real vicar and it would do for a wedding and a baptism. He was going to marry Beatrice for the money, but he was going to claim the little brat for revenge, especially since said brat had managed to squall the whole way here and make a smelly nappy that had positively ruined the inside of the carriage. The brat was with the vicar's wife at present. Out of sight, out of mind, like a child should be. A child was never too young to learn that. It was how he'd been raised and he could see now the philosophy had its merits. He'd made it this far in life, after all. Besides, children, babies especially, were needy and annoying little creatures.

There was the jingling noise of a carriage and horses approaching, a unique sound in this part of London. Good. It meant his bride was here. They could get started. He yelled for the vicar's wife, who didn't like him no matter how much money he gave her husband or how many charming smiles he tossed her way. 'Mrs Spalding, bring the brat! His mother's here and will be wanting to see him.'

He pulled out his pistol, taking the baby from the quaking Mrs Spalding in one hand and levelling his gun in the other. A man had to be prepared. What was a wedding without guests anyway? Beatrice might have come alone, she was impetuous that way. It was what he'd prefer, but she also might have brought Worth and Worth might have brought his ever-present henchman, Liam Casek. He cocked the pistol, training it on the carriage door as it opened and a man's foot appeared, followed by his pistol and a drawl Alton was coming to hate.

'Expecting me, were you?'

Damn it. Worth was here.

'I see she sent her lapdog.'

Preston froze, gun arm extended, although no shot was possible with Alton holding the baby. It was a horrific scene that challenged all of his self-control. Matthew was screaming, perhaps sensing that this man was a dangerous stranger, which made the scene all the more disconcerting. Preston prayed Bea stayed in the carriage as he'd asked. He could only imagine what the sound of their son's distress was doing to her. But if she stepped away from the vehicle, she was putting herself into enemy hands.

'Alton!' he called. 'Give me the child and I'll allow you safe passage to leave town.'

Alton sneered. 'You can have him, but first you have to come and get him.' Alton backed up, losing himself in the darkness of the church interior.

'I'm not such a fool as to follow you into a dark building,' Preston called out, hoping to bring the man back out into the light.

Alton reappeared, the gun angling towards the baby. 'I think you will do exactly what I've asked.' He cocked an eyebrow. 'Or have you decided you don't want to play father to another man's child? I wouldn't blame you. Perhaps I'm really doing you a favour.' He gave an evil smile. 'I wouldn't wait too long if I were you. I'm not known from my patience. Do I need to count?' He took a step backwards. 'One, two.' He paused when Preston didn't move. 'Or is it that you think I won't shoot? Perhaps a demonstration is in order.' With lightning reflexes, he moved the gun and fired towards the coachman's seat. Liam ducked, but not without being grazed. An inattentive coachman would have been dead. As it was, the shot took him in the shoulder. Alton tossed away the pistol and drew a knife. 'Don't worry, I'm good with both. Are you coming?'

There was no time to worry about Liam. Once he was inside, Bea could help Liam. Preston had no choice but to follow and hope Liam wasn't hurt too badly to help. He'd been counting on Liam to find a back way inside. He didn't think for a moment Alton had no one in the church. It was to be an ambush and now he would face it alone.

He stepped inside, even knowing the odds were against him. He didn't dare call Alton's bluff this time, not with Matthew on the line. There were five men waiting and he saw them immediately. He fired his pistol at the first man, then swung at the second, using the pistol butt like a club. The third was a big, burly street fighter with meaty fists. Preston would have taken him, though, if he hadn't been jumped from behind by not one, but two men, who held his arms while the brute pummelled away at him. Preston tried kicking, tried using the other two men as leverage to strike the big man in the stomach with his legs, but it was a losing fight. He could hear Matthew crying in the darkness even as consciousness began to slip away. How could he protect Beatrice if he was helpless? How could he reach Matthew? How could he help when he was lost in the dark?

A second pistol sounded from inside the church and Beatrice stifled a scream, her hands trembling as she wrapped Liam's shoulder. The bullet wound was more than a graze although Liam insisted he was fine. She shot

a look at the church door, her decision made.
'That's it. I'm going in.'

'Let me.' Liam struggled to sit up, evidence
that he was *not* fine. 'You don't know what's
happened or how many men were waiting for
him in there.'

'You are in no shape to take on anyone.
You'll be killed. Alton sees you as expendable,' Bea argued furiously, already moving
past Liam to the carriage door before he could
reach for her. 'He won't hurt me. He wants
me. He needs me or he can't get the money.'
She hoped she sounded more confident than
she felt. She was done sitting here. Her child
was in there, the man she loved was in there
and chances were Alton was terrorising them
both. She shouldn't have let Preston go in
alone the first place.

She shut the door against Liam's protests.
'If we don't come back out, go for help.'

'If you don't come out, I'll come in,' Liam
said staunchly.

There was no time to argue.

Bea pushed open the church door, calling
out her presence to avoid being shot. 'Alton!
I'm here.' She could hear Matthew crying.
Still. It had taken more willpower than she

knew she possessed to stay in the carriage the first time she'd heard him.

Malvern was at the front of the church with a vicar, a wizened old man who looked like he might blow away if you breathed on him. 'Ah, my dear, you are here at last.' He spread his arms wide to indicate the dilapidated interior. 'Everything is ready.'

'For what?' Beatrice was hesitant to move down the aisle closer to him, although she could see Matthew off to the side of the altar with an old woman. She couldn't see Preston.

'For our wedding. You look lovely, by the way. Much prettier than I imagined.' She didn't like the sound of that. Alton didn't sound quite like himself. He sounded...well, unhinged. Unhinged meant logic and reasoning wouldn't work.

'Where's Preston?'

'Oh, my dear, those answers will cost you.' Alton smirked. 'Take three steps forward and I'll tell you.' She took a few tentative steps forward.

'Gentlemen, will you bring out Mr Worth?' Alton gestured to the front pew where two men grappled with a third, propped up between them under the armpits, his dark head hanging limply, his face bruised, his shirt bloody.

'Preston!' Bea rushed forward, her body wanting to reach him against the logic of her mind. She knelt beside him, searching him for the source of injuries, searching for signs of life as Alton sent the two men to the back of the church, presumably to guard against any other intruders.

Seeing Preston unconscious was unnerving. She threw a nasty glare at Alton. She was going to kill him for this. 'What have you done to him?'

'It wasn't me so much as it was them.' Alton nodded towards the three men. He waggled a finger at her, stepping closer. 'You were naughty, my dear, and someone had to pay.'

'Like the coachman?' she retorted, thinking of Liam as she stood in front of Preston's limp form out of instinctive protection. 'You shot a man for no reason.'

'For *every* reason.' Alton shrugged as if he hadn't a choice. 'You were told to come alone. That means zero people, not two.' He pulled a face of mock concern. 'I hope no one else is following you. I'd prefer not to shoot any more people on my wedding day.'

'I'm not marrying you. You can't make me.' Matthew must have heard her voice. His crying escalated, his little arms reaching towards the sound. Every maternal instinct in her wanted to run towards him. But that meant darting past Alton, something he wouldn't allow.

Alton grinned wickedly at her indecision. 'I see you're figuring it out. You always were bright. How about I make it easy for you, give you everything you want. It's the only option really, you can choose to marry me or I'll make you marry me. Because I disagree with your assumption that I can't do it.' He twirled a knife in one hand, his eyes wild. She had to stay calm. He wanted her too scared to think. 'This blade here in my hand says I can do it.

'Marry me and I'll give you the baby and when Preston Worth wakes up, I won't have any reason to shoot him. The deed will already be done. You'll be mine.' She'd be beyond Preston's ability to protect her, but Matthew would be safe. Alton laughed. 'It's the ultimate prisoner's dilemma, isn't it?' Matthew was screaming at full force now. 'You should know I have very little patience for crying babies. Marry me and everyone lives. Refuse and I'll start with Worth. I'll slit his throat first. He probably won't feel a thing in his current state. Then, we'll see what you have to say about marriage. If you still resist, there's the baby…' He was out of his mind. She had no doubt about it now. How did one deal with a crazy man? Behind her, she thought she felt Preston stir. She had to buy him time, give him a chance. Together, perhaps they could get out of here.

She stepped forward carefully, her mind whirling at full speed. 'Give me the baby first.' She stood in front of the vicar, her eyes holding Alton's, watching for any flicker of sanity. Maybe she could get the knife away from him. But probably not if she was holding Matthew.

Alton let her have the baby the moment she stepped up to the altar, either because there was a scrap of decency in him or because he'd realised as she had that one could not mount an effective defensive with a squirmy child in one's arms.

'Not exactly Grosvenor Chapel, but it's enough to be legal, my dear,' Alton sneered, keeping a grip on her free arm in case she chose to bolt and propelling her forward to the altar.

'Are you willing?' The trembling vicar turned his attention to her, taking in the struggle she mounted out of a need to at least offer a pro forma protest.

'No!' Beatrice spat. 'This is kidnapping. He stole my son. He's beaten up the man I am supposed to marry,' she argued hurriedly. Perhaps the vicar could be swayed.

'*My* son.' Alton smiled. 'One cannot be accused of kidnapping his own child, certainly not while the child's mother was out playing the whore by marrying another man.' He cocked his head, his gaze lingering on her in triumph. 'What do you think the good courts of Britain would say to that? The child's father offers to marry you, to give the child his name, and you refuse. There's a reason courts prefer children to be with their fathers.'

'You're not his father.' It was an easy lie to mouth. She couldn't imagine a man less fatherly than Malvern Alton, a man who would threaten the life of his own flesh and blood. 'His father died before he was born. Preston Worth is the only father he's known.'

'I cannot perform a coerced marriage,' the

vicar began, giving Beatrice hope. She wondered how Preston was doing, but didn't dare commit the Orphean crime of looking behind her.

'Yes, you can,' Alton growled.

'There will be no witnesses,' the vicar pointed out.

'Your wife will witness it.' Alton was busy with his blade again, targeting the little old woman. 'Unless, you'd rather I slice her?' He shrugged. 'Not that she's got a whole lot of years left. Maybe I'd be doing you a favour. But then, who would hold the baby? Bea, give her the baby. I refuse to have squalling at my wedding.' Alton was entirely unhinged now and she was forced to give up Matthew once more. But this time, the old woman had the good sense to stand on her side, putting Matthew *and* Preston behind her.

The vicar turned pale, rage making his hands tremble even more profusely. 'I was wrong to take money from you.'

Alton laughed. 'But you did. Now, you do your job. You can think of stained-glass windows and a proper cemetery if it helps salve your conscience.' He turned towards her with a look that chilled her. 'As for *your* conscience, the future Mrs Malvern Alton, you can think of me. It's not rape if it's your husband. But you can tell yourself whatever you need to justify it. You were always good at walls.' He winked at the vicar. 'The short version, if you please. You may proceed.'

The vicar's hands shook as he glanced at his wife, yet another potential victim of Alton's knife. His voice trembled but he began. 'Dearly beloved, we are gathered together here in the sight of God, and in the face of this congregation, to join together this Man and this Woman in holy Matrimony; which is an honourable estate…'

The monstrous irony was not lost on Bea; she was supposed to be hearing these words with Preston, supposed to be surrounded by friends and beauty and hope, the occasion a celebration of life. Here in this poky church, with this man, the occasion was none of those things. The joy of the sunlit morning seemed ages ago. She felt a tear spill out of the corner of one eye. She didn't want to cry, didn't want to be reduced to this. But Matthew was safe. She was with him. Preston would be safe. Surely she could bear up as long as that was true. Maybe Preston had been right. Maybe they would have married for love after all. Wasn't sacrifice the purest form of love? Putting others above and before self?

The vicar had barely started. Short version or not, Alton was impatient. They'd just got to the part about secrets of the heart, when Alton took her bodice in both hands and ripped, tearing away Evie's intricate handiwork. She screamed, shocked at the sudden brutality. The vicar stopped, his mouth hanging open at the brazen violence.

'You!' Alton growled at the poor man. 'Keep talking and speed it up!' He dragged her to the floor, ripping fabric, pushing up skirts. 'And you, Beatrice, scream. I want you to scream. Nice and loud for everyone to hear.'

Beatrice spat in his face and steeled her resolve. 'I will not cry out for you!' She fought him, knowing that the busier his hands were with her, the less likely he could harm anyone else. But her resistance was met with the back of Alton's hand across her face. 'I said scream, dammit! By the time Worth wakes up this marriage will be consummated and I want him to see it. I doubt he'd want you, then,' Alton snarled. Somewhere in the background the vicar was mumbling the ceremonial words, nearly done now in his own race to flee the scene.

'Do you think he'd ever be able to come to you without seeing you like this beneath me? Vicar, hurry up!' he yelled, his attention breaking from her for a split second, long enough to give her an opening.

Beatrice took it, bringing her knee up hard into his crotch with a yell. 'Get off me, you oaf!'

Beatrice! The thought woke him, the word joining the pounding in his skull. Oh, Lord, the noise! It was practically deafening. Every ounce of him hurt, but the hurt reminded him where he was, how he'd got there. Why he was there. Alton had Matthew and, from the sounds of it, Alton had Beatrice. Preston cracked open an eye, then both eyes. He was alone. The old woman was near him with Matthew. Matthew was as safe as he could be at the moment. Preston couldn't say the same for Beatrice. The bastard was on her. Anger at his own impotence to rush to her side fuelled him. He needed a weapon. His hand crept slowly to the knife in his boot. It would have to be a throw from a semi-prone position. His sore body would be of no use in a fight and he'd never get to his feet in time.

Beatrice was scrambling now, trying to get away from Alton as he doubled over. Preston readied himself, praying for strength. The church doors in the back burst open with a yell Preston recognised as Liam's and the two remaining henchmen went down. The disruption grabbed Alton's attention. Preston yelled his command, his voice hoarse. 'Bea, get down, move away!' just seconds before he threw. It was a dangerous throw, but he would not get a better chance to save her. The knife took Alton in the shoulder.

Alton screamed, hysterical at the sight of his own blood, and stumbled backwards down the aisle, half-running, half-falling as he clutched at his privates, and his shoulder, in confusion over who had hurt him. 'You bitch, you stabbed me!'

Suddenly Liam was there, neatly capturing Alton from behind and hauling him outside. Preston sagged against the pew, his strength spent. 'Bea, are you all right?' He held out an arm, reaching for her despite the agony the gesture caused his muscles.

'I'm all right.' She was beside him, but she was shaking, proof she wasn't entirely all right. Many things were right in those minutes, though. Matthew in Bea's arms, then them both in his arms. He wanted to touch the baby, wanted to touch Bea, wanted to hold them both close and know they were safe.

'And Matthew? He's all right?'

'He's hungry.'

'Of course he is.' Preston smiled. He drew Beatrice close. 'Thank God.' Those two words encompassed everything he was feeling; thank God his throw had been good. Thank God Bea and the babe were not hurt. Thank God they could look forward to a future together.

He had to give her up, though, for Matthew. He sat beside her in a pew, holding her hand and watching Matthew nurse. He was torn. He didn't want to leave her, yet part of him wanted to be out there with Liam. Liam was wounded—what if Alton got away or worse? What if Alton circled back? Bea would be alone. His place was here. He had to stay.

'Will Liam be all right?' Bea asked quietly, reading his thoughts. 'His shoulder...'

'Liam is always all right,' he assured her,

cutting off the thought neither of them wanted to entertain. The door to the church opened. 'See, I told you.' Preston grinned. He rose and staggered back to meet Liam.

'Well? Did he get away?' Preston asked in low tones.

'No,' Liam said succinctly.

'Is he outside?' Preston probed.

'In a manner of speaking, he is outside. But perhaps not in the way you mean it.' Even for Liam, Liam was being cryptic. His hand tapped the butt of a pistol. Preston understood. Alton wouldn't be bothering them again. He would tell Bea when the time was right. But not right now and maybe not even today. There'd been enough blood.

'Thank you.' His voice was unexpectedly gruff with emotion as he clapped Liam on the back.

'Consider it a wedding gift.'

'Is everything all right?' Bea came up behind him, Matthew content in her arms, her ruined gown tied awkwardly but decently together. Preston's heart swelled. He'd never wanted her as much as he wanted her right now, mess and all. He was tired of waiting.

'Everything is fine.' Did he dare? Horrible

things had happened in this church. It seemed only fitting that something good should purify it. He got down on his knee, reaching for her hand. 'Beatrice Penrose, I promised you a wedding today. I want you to know I'm a man of my word. Will you marry me? Right here. I find I cannot wait a minute longer.'

She made him wait. Perhaps she, too, was considering the rightness of the act in the wake of all that had happened in the last hours. 'Yes. Right now. Not a moment longer.'

In truth, Preston thought as he led his bride forward toward the altar and produced his rather crinkled special licence, weddings didn't take that long to plan after all. One simply needed to do it. Flowers and gowns and violinists and rose petals were just things, symbols at best of what was already in one's heart. Beatrice had proven that today.

She had been willing to sacrifice herself for him today and she'd done it without hesitation. He smiled. 'You love me, Beatrice.'

'I might.' She smiled back. 'Just a little.'

'I guess we have that in common. I might love you, too. Just a little.' He laughed softly as the vicar began again the words of the institution.

Bea adjusted Matthew, who laughed up at him and reached for his finger. Preston gave it to him as he repeated the vows.

'I, Preston James Worth take thee, Beatrice Elizabeth, to be my wedded wife, to have and to hold from this day forward, for better for worse, for richer for poorer, in sickness and in health, to love, cherish, and to obey, till death us do part, according to God's holy ordinance; and thereto I give thee my troth.'

'Now for the ring?' the vicar asked.

Preston panicked. The ring. It was back at Grosvenor Chapel.

'I haven't got it.' After all this, he had no ring. But Beatrice smiled. She pulled at the chain about her neck.

'Your grandfather's ring. I should have given it back to you ages ago.'

Preston grinned, relief sweeping him. 'I think now is the perfect time.' He took the ring and put it on her finger. 'With this ring, I thee wed, Beatrice.' He meant those words with all his heart. Just as he meant the kiss that followed.

'We'll have to do it all again for show,' Beatrice murmured as the vicar pronounced them husband and wife.

'I know. But not tonight.' Tonight he wanted his little family all to himself.

'No,' Beatrice said, taking his hand, her eyes brimming with promise. 'Not tonight. Tonight is just for us.'

Epilogue

When they did it for show, it was not at the Grosvenor Chapel in Mayfair as Bea expected it might be, nor was it a chance for their parents to show off the union to society. It was instead, a double affair, a wedding mixed with a baptism held quietly at the end of the usual Sunday service at Seacrest. They were surrounded by Preston's new tenants, their families and friends who had all made the journey for the occasion, some of them journeying further than others. Jonathon and Claire had come all the way from Vienna.

Beatrice's eyes filled with tears as she looked out over the pews. Evie and Dimitri sat with her parents on one side of the aisle, the Worths and May and Liam on the other, Jonathon and Claire just behind them. She felt so blessed they were with her to share this moment. There were so many times in the last year she'd felt like an outcast, but much of that had been her own doing. She had come full circle, the man standing beside her with their son in his arms was proof of that. Every time she saw Preston with Matthew, her worries disappeared. Preston had faced down the demons of her past with her, slayed quite real dragons for her and for Matthew. Preston proved a man could love a child as much as a woman no matter who the father was and that a man could love a woman no matter her mistakes.

The vicar took the baby, frothy white christening gown and all, a new creation by Evie who had gifted her the gown last night, whispering in a quiet voice that she just might need the practice as there would undoubtedly be more christenings in the future. 'I baptise thee in the name of the Father, the Son, and the Holy Ghost...'

The comfort of the old words washed over her as she exchanged a glance with Preston, his own gaze filled with emotion. His hand reaching out secretly for hers in the folds of her skirt.

Afterwards, there was a picnic on the lawn of the church, a casual affair so everyone could participate. Even the weather co-operated. Children ran among the picnic blankets and adults lounged beneath the early summer sky as Bea and Claire watched their husbands lay out their own picnic blankets beneath an oak near Evie and May. 'I still can't believe you came!' Bea hugged her friend yet again. It had been nearly a year since she'd last seen Claire and she'd missed her.

Claire's hand went to the small bump just beginning to form beneath her skirts. 'Jonathon and I wanted our child to be born in Little Westbury. And raised there, too.'

It took Bea a moment to understand the implication. 'You're going to stay?' This was perhaps the best surprise of all and nearly as unlooked for as Claire's arrival. 'What about Vienna? And Jonathon?' Bea asked cautiously. As excited as she was about her friend's permanent return, she knew how much the diplomatic posting to Vienna meant to Jonathon. He'd only held the post for a little under a year.

Claire smiled softly. 'There are things more important than work, like family and a good community. We want a life here among friends where we don't have to watch every word and wonder at every favour done for us.'

May and Evie approached, arms linked and smiling mischievously. 'Did you tell her yet, Claire?' May's eyes sparkled and Bea sensed another surprise coming.

Claire shook her head. 'Not yet, I was waiting for you. I wanted us all to be together.'

'What?' Bea glanced from friend to friend, all of them beaming with secret knowledge.

Claire took Bea's hand and then Evie's. 'Jonathon is purchasing the old Adair place. He's going to help Dimitri with his museum project.'

'We'll all be neighbours,' May supplied, the shimmer in her gaze mirroring the tears Bea felt rising.

Bea took May's hand and completed the circle. For a moment, she couldn't speak. When she did, her voice was only a whisper. 'Look at us. We are happy. It's all I could have wished for each of us.' And far more than she'd thought possible for herself. When she'd formed the Left Behind Girls Club a year ago, she'd done it to save her friends from lives of mediocrity and regret. She'd never dared to believe she'd have the same chance to rise above the circumstances of her situation.

She squeezed May's and Claire's hands and drew a deep breath. 'There's only one thing left to do. As there is no longer any need for it, I officially disband the Left Behind Girls Club, because *everything* changed when we did.'

* * * * *

If you enjoyed this story, you won't want to miss these other great reads in Bronwyn Scott's
WALLFLOWERS TO WIVES
mini-series

UNBUTTONING THE INNOCENT MISS
AWAKENING THE SHY MISS
CLAIMING HIS DEFIANT MISS

MILLS & BOON®

HISTORICAL

AWAKEN THE ROMANCE OF THE PAST

MILLS & BOON®

EXCLUSIVE EXTRACT

Five years after Viscount Winterton abducts her by mistake, Lady Florentia Hale-Burton discovers her kidnapper is alive—and as dangerously handsome as she remembers!

Read on for a sneak preview of
RUINED BY THE RECKLESS VISCOUNT

'Lord Winterton graced the ball this evening, Florentia, and the Heron girls were all over him, though in truth I did not see him complaining. I think he had danced with each of them by the end of the evening.'

'Winterton is the viscount newly home from the Americas?' Flora had heard of the man, of course. He was the newest and most interesting addition to the ton, a soldier who had made his fortune in the acquisition of timbers from the east coast and transported them back to London town.

'That's the one and he is every bit as beautiful as they all say him to be. It's his eyes I think, a true clear pale green with the darkest of lashes. You would love to paint him, Flora, but that's not my only news. No indeed, my greatest morsel is that the oldest Heron girl, Miss Julia, apparently told Winterton that Mr Frederick Rutherford would be painting all three daughters at their town house in Portland Square across the next few weeks.'

Florentia put down her book. *A true clear and pale green.* The world tilted slightly and went out of focus, so much so that one of her hands twisted around the base of the chair on which she sat in an attempt to keep herself anchored.

'Are you alright, Flora, for you suddenly look awfully pale.' Her sister moved closer as she made an attempt to smile.

'I am tired, I suppose, for London is a busy and frantic city when you have been away from it as long as I have.' Her heart was racing, the clammy sheen of sweat sliding between her breasts. Could it be him? Could her kidnapper have survived? Was he here now in London, living somewhere only a handful of miles from the Warrenden town house?

Don't miss
RUINED BY THE RECKLESS VISCOUNT
by Sophia James

Available July 2017
www.millsandboon.co.uk